FROM
BEYOND

JASPER T. SCOTT
NATHAN HYSTAD

Cover Art by Jake Caleb

https://www.jcalebdesign.com/

Edited by: Scarlett R. Algee

& Christen Hystad

ONE

Lake Como, Italy

T HE HOUSE WAS OBSCURED from view until Atlas crested a steep incline, passing dense layers of tree cover. The sight was breathtaking. He'd seen a lot of beautiful things in his life, but this estate house on the coast of Lago di Como was among the finest.

A security guard in a white tuxedo stopped him at the entrance, giving his car a once-over, like he'd never been this close to a Flaminia before. Gentle twinkle lights reflected off the newly polished hood's white surface.

"It's a sixty-three," Atlas stated with an air of importance. He expected his American accent wasn't unusual at this man's parties, but it was rare enough to surprise the guard.

"Name." The man held a clear Holo, waiting for the introduction. He grinned as if he might have the luxury of rejecting Atlas' entrance.

Atlas didn't bother. He accessed his own personal device and sent the credentials. His holopad was the latest model, a clear palm-sized unit with more processing power than the first Mars colony lander. The security guard's smirk vanished.

"I apologize, sir." He turned and barked a series of orders at a boy lingering near the temporary valet stand.

Atlas maneuvered past him, parked the car in the open, and climbed out. The kid couldn't have been more than sixteen. He tossed the keys.

Atlas whispered to the boy in Italian. "Put it near the exit. Facing forward."

He seemed dumbfounded, but nodded fervently when Atlas sent over two hundred euros from his device. The valet noted the transaction on his watch. "Al momento." *Right away.*

Fifty cars lined the giant driveway leading to the mansion on the lake, each nicer than the previous. Mattia Barone was an affluent man, and he drew kindred spirits like a moth to a flame. Atlas was pretending to be one of those tonight. The car was a loaner, his suit borrowed from an old acquaintance. His fresh haircut was the only thing real about him.

Atlas checked his reflection, straightening his collar. The ivory shirt stayed tucked beneath a snakeskin belt, the jacket crafted from fine Italian wool. It was a little hot for the time of year, but it would do. Atlas didn't plan on being here long.

The house itself was flanked by matching statues. Angels. Why was it always the same things? A colossal fountain lay in the center of the courtyard, and he passed by two elegant women, smoking cigarettes while their rich husbands discussed business in wine country. The pair stopped talking for a moment to study Atlas, and he smiled at them, continuing through the open doors up a quick flight of marble steps.

Music wafted through the room, and he paused to survey the area. A double staircase led to the second floor. Thirty-foot ceilings. Ornate woodwork. Golden accents. Mattia had a specific taste, and it was extremely Old World. It made sense that he was so interested in expensive artifacts.

Atlas went slowly, trying not to look out of place.

What did people do at events like this? They drank expensive wine. He headed to the bar across the room, which provided a barrier to the outside living space. Armed with a sloshing glass full of a robust local red blend, he strode into the fresh air. A five-piece band strummed their stringed instruments, and he caught sight of her.

Isabella Barone, the daughter of the host. He'd done his research, but she was even more striking in person. It was a shame her father was such a dreadful man. Her dark hair hung low, her hazel eyes glazed over as an older man vied for her attention.

Atlas perched himself near the swimming pool, wondering why there were always six or more people in the water at these events. Were they here as guests, or hired to make the party seem enjoyable?

The scent of a cigar carried to his nose, and Atlas spotted his target. Mattia was a large man, his belly a testament to his opulent tastes. He coughed and patted guests on the back as he strode through the living space, sauntering into the yard.

Beyond the rows of cypress trees, Atlas caught a glimpse of the lake. Starlight reflected from the water, reminding Atlas they weren't alone in the universe. He was certain of it.

"I don't believe we've met." Mattia was behind him, speaking in English.

Atlas spun around with an easy grin. "I'm afraid not. My name's Buster Francis." They shook, and he noted the strength in his opponent's grip.

"Buster, I've heard about you. It seems you're quite the collector." The man's cheeks were red, his face clean-shaven in contrast to Atlas's neatly groomed beard.

Atlas laughed like a wealthy socialite. "I've been known to partake in the occasional bidding war."

"Would you care for a cigar?" One materialized in Mattia's fingers, and Atlas had no choice but to agree. He enjoyed the odd smoke, but he was here to do business, and didn't want to delay any longer than necessary.

He puffed while Mattia lit the tip using a golden lighter. "Quite the place you have."

"My wife. She loves Como. I prefer the city, but you know how it goes."

Atlas nodded agreeably, but in truth, he'd never been married. Buster Francis, on the other hand, was married, with two strapping sons. "I sure do. Is there any chance you'd entertain a tour?"

Mattia's brow furrowed, and he waved at someone across the room. "Mr. Francis, are you interested in anything specific?"

Atlas shrugged. "A man of your stature must grow tired of accumulating so many rare items. Surely you'd be willing to share with an admirer such as myself." To his own ear he sounded fake, but Mattia didn't seem to notice or care. His ego had been sated, and that was enough to sell the tour. Atlas had worked tirelessly for this invitation, and was aware Mattia was hoping to pawn off some of his lesser finds to a rich dupe like Buster Francis.

Mattia walked to a woman, whose sparkling silver dress threatened to burst at the seams, and whispered into her ear. She glanced at Atlas, then gave a flirty laugh and returned to her conversation. He thought she was Mattia's third wife. He'd skipped his usual deep-dive research due to the expediency required for tonight's event.

"I hear you pulled up in a Lancia Flaminia," Mattia said, leading Atlas up a set of stairs near the kitchen. Atlas glanced past the railing, finding a dozen serving staff filling shiny chrome trays with hors d'oeuvres.

He'd been watching for Atlas to arrive. That meant he was intrigued, which implied he might share the private showcase he reserved for his wealthiest acquaintances. "It's a bit rustic, but that's what I love about Italian cars. All guts, curves, and power."

"Like our women, no?" Mattia smiled, ashing his cigar on the marble tiles.

They passed a wide hallway, skirted by guest rooms and opulent bathrooms, and stopped at the end of the second story. Mattia Barone pulled a Holo from his jacket pocket, and held it to the invisible lock. Atlas heard the click as it opened, and the door slid into the wall, revealing a study.

Where the rest of the house was light and authentic to the region, this room was anything but. A powerful scent of wood escaped from the black shelving. The floor had a thick carpet, soft enough to swallow your toes. Inside, a fireplace roared and crackled. Above the mantle was the largest tiger's head Atlas had ever seen. Its teeth were bared in a snarl.

"Shot her when I was twenty-three years old." Mattia rubbed his expansive stomach, as if the sight of his kill made him hungry. "First trip. One shot. Back before the regulations changed and"—he smirked—"when this rare breed was still around." Mattia tapped between his own eyes, and Atlas thought he might be able to see the patch work on the animal's stuffed head from the entry point. Atlas hated a lot of things, but there was a special place in hell for men like this. Instead of throttling the man, he grinned amiably as the door sealed behind them.

"This is spectacular." Atlas paced the room, running a finger over the shelving. Books of ancient origin were protected by tinted glass. He figured he could be trapped in here for weeks, and never get through all the astounding collection.

He found an ashtray and set the burning cigar on it. The man was a complete sod, but he still respected the collection too much to be careless.

Another set of stuffed mounts was on the adjacent wall, but Atlas ignored them. His eyes were on the desk. "I heard from a little birdie you recently acquired a new piece."

Mattia actually coughed at this. "Who told you?"

Atlas smiled. "It's my job."

"I usually don't show this, but I like you, Buster." Mattia poured a drink from a bar, filling the glass half full of a brown substance. He handed it to Atlas and repeated the process for himself. "I'm actually in the market to sell. To the proper buyer, that is."

Atlas raised his glass. "To the proper buyer." They clinked cups, and he tested the vintage.

"You're confident, aren't you?" Mattia used the device again, and the desk unlatched. The drawer was six feet long, with a 10mm layer of bulletproof glass covering seven objects. Atlas recognized each and every one of them, but only a single piece mattered. It was smaller than he'd expected, about the size of his palm, but the material was identical. The markings on the upper portion were a perfect match. Three dots in a triangle. Dark blue on the slate gray substance.

The artifact was misshapen, beveled at the edges, and somehow glossy and matte at the same time, depending on which angle it was held at. The blue dots were depressed as though to form indentations for someone's fingertips. Atlas suspected that might actually be their function, but the markings were too modest to accommodate anything more than a child's hand.

He pretended to scan the items with interest, and patted the glass near the far end, seeing if anything was triggered. No alarms sounded, and the Holo didn't chime. "Wasn't this secured by the Smithsonian?"

Mattia downed his drink and shook his head. "No. Let's just say, I wouldn't let it slip by."

Atlas struggled not to stare at the object he desired. He spent the next ten minutes asking about the others, pretending to gauge whether anything was truly for sale. When he got to the artifact with the three circles, he feigned ignorance. "That's unusual. Where's it from?"

Mattia glowered, but recovered quickly. Atlas sensed a possible lead if he played his cards right. "Coast of Croatia. It was brought up in a fishing boat, of all things. Stayed in a local shop for a decade. One of my contacts saw it listed online by the company's new owner."

So simple. Atlas had spent fifteen years searching for fragments of the ship, and this had been sitting under a pile of stinking fish nets right in the open. "What is it?" He almost laughed at his own question. Most were clearly totems or mementos of a long-dead civilization. It was obvious Mattia Barone was obsessed with phallic fertility gods. This didn't fit that bill.

"It's… from Egypt. A piece of the ancient machines flown here from the heavens." Mattia flashed his teeth. "I personally don't believe in that foolishness, but some out there do."

Atlas clenched his teeth to stifle his reaction. "What would you ask for it?"

"Four million."

Atlas froze.

"Euros."

He gave Mattia an appreciative nod. "I hope you find a buyer." Turning from the display case, he walked away, looking at the fireplace. "You have a magnificent study. Thank you for showing it to me."

They exited in silence, and he could tell Mattia was disappointed. But once the booze hit him, and he found another cigar, he returned to his previous enthusiasm. They joined the party, which had become more energetic with time.

"It was a pleasure." He reached for Atlas' hand. "Hopefully we'll have the opportunity to speak later."

Atlas offered him a brisk hug, with no choice but to comply. "Thanks for the hospitality." He felt the man's personal Holo shift from the pocket, while he dropped the decoy in. Mattia was none the wiser.

He waited until someone else had Mattia's attention, which literally took seconds. Atlas returned to the house, grabbed a bow tie off a rack, and draped it over his neck without tying it. He stole a tray of stuffed peppers and crab, grinning at a waitress.

Instead of resuming the party, he headed upstairs. An elderly woman was being escorted by a younger man down the steps, and Atlas clung to the edge of the railing, offering them food. They declined with a huff of Italian, and when they were at ground level, he jogged the rest of the way.

The coast was clear.

Atlas set the tray on a decorative table, which probably cost more than his first car, and hefted the holopad out. It was still unlocked, but he doubted it would be for long. He found the hidden security feature, and tapped it with the device.

"You're American, no?" a husky voice said.

Isabella Barone emerged from the shadows, holding a tube of lipstick. She slowly reapplied, and turned the handle, slapping it into a small clutch.

"That's right. Your father asked for some…" Atlas glanced at the tray ten feet away.

"He's allergic to shellfish." Her English was excellent, and he could smell the expensive perfume on her skin.

"What do you want?" Atlas asked, hoping the electronic unit didn't deactivate before he opened the next lock in the desk.

Isabella leaned closer, shoving him into her father's private study. She scowled at the tiger head as the door shut behind them. "*Lui è così crudele.*"

"Yes, he is cruel." Atlas approached the desk, and opened the hatch. The relic remained intact. Ripe for the picking. He didn't delay, boldly retrieving it with the man's daughter present before him. His time was running out, and her amusement at his actions only made him braver.

"This is mine. It belongs to me now. Understood?" He clutched the cool metal artifact, feeling the dots indent slightly from its side. He slipped it into his jacket pocket, along with the stolen holopad.

"Will it upset him?" Isabella asked, biting her lip.

Atlas nodded as his gaze floated to the camera above the door. He was being recorded, and that was problematic. "I have to go."

"What's so special about it?" Isabella walked across the room, her heels clicking on the hardwood.

"It's not from around here."

"You mean…" She pointed to the ceiling with a skeptical smile.

"Something like that."

"Take me with you," she pleaded. "I can help you escape." Part of him wanted to consider the offer, and he lost his concentration as he gazed into her hazel eyes.

Atlas took a deep breath and smiled again. He reached for her, softly grazing her arm even as he retrieved the pen from his pocket. The needle inserted near her veins, and he doubted she even felt the injection. Isabella whimpered, and he gently lowered her to the floor. "Maybe in another life, bella."

Everyone was gathered downstairs when he emerged, and Mattia Barone was holding court, clinking his champagne flute with a golden spoon.

Atlas ignored the beginning of Mattia's speech as he pushed out of the kitchen's exit, feeling the cooler evening breeze. He was sweating under the wool jacket, and he double checked its oversized pocket to ensure his prize was securely stashed.

His car was parked as he'd instructed, and he snatched the spare set of keys from his pants. The valet gawked as he almost ran the kid over, racing from the property.

Atlas Donovan had done the impossible. He'd uncovered another piece for his collection. Years of dead ends, and here it finally was.

The roads were winding, and he sped down the coast, continually watching his rear-view mirror for signs of pursuit.

Mattia Barone may not have understood what was in his possession, but there were others who did. Powerful people, with unlimited resources.

His real Holo beeped, and he checked it, easing off the gas pedal.

The link from his friend took him to an article. He scanned the headline and nearly drove off the road. *Orbital Development Group Announces Emergency Change to Scheduled Colony Supply Run.*

There was something about the timing of it that made him feel uneasy. Maybe this was an omen.

Atlas had to move quickly.

He used the Holo to read the article as he drove. ORB considered bumping up the mission schedule because of critical damage to one of the greenhouses on Mars, but Atlas couldn't help wondering if there was more to it. Mars was a year away from its close approach with Earth, which made it exceptionally expensive to send the crew of *Beyond III* now, not to mention doing so would make the trek much longer. Coincidence or not, he needed facts. Atlas minimized the article and opened his mail to convey a message to his Russian contact.

Meet me in Rijeka, Croatia.

Atlas hit send, and sped down the road.

TWO

St. Ann, Missouri

D AVID BRYCE SAT ON a park bench with his wife, Katy, their hands laced together on his thigh. After spending the day visiting Tiemeyer Park, they were now watching their kids, Rachel and Mark, running around the playground with the Pattersons' two sons. The children were close to the same ages, in the fourth and fifth grades.

Mark's feet sprayed sand as he skidded around a corner to escape from Brady Patterson. He launched himself at the metal ladder to the monkey bars, but Brady caught his ankle before he could climb out of reach. "Got you! You're it!"

David's lips tugged into a smile. Some games were timeless.

Mark squealed and kicked his friend in the shoulder by accident, still trying to evade the boy. Brady cried out in outrage.

"Oh shoot! Sorry, man! Are you okay?" Mark said, jumping down.

Brady was playing it up, rolling on the ground. "Owwww, I think you dislocated it!"

David rose halfway out of his seat, ready to intervene, but Katy grabbed his wrist.

"They're fine. Look."

Brady jumped up and punched Mark playfully in the arm. "Just kidding!"

"Don't scare me like that!"

The two walked away together, no hard feelings. David let out a breath and settled in his seat, shaking his head. *Boys.*

He glanced at the Pattersons' parents. Mrs. Patterson was on her Holo, so she'd missed the whole thing. And Mr. Patterson was likely taking a nap under his cowboy hat.

David couldn't understand how some people took the day to get out in nature with their families, only to let those precious moments slip by, unnoticed. It was as if they always had something better to do, never stopping to enjoy the moment, to make it last.

Kids grow up too fast. You blink and they'll be married with families of their own.

But maybe that wasn't fair. David's job gave him a unique perspective. Being an astronaut for the Orbital Development Group (ORB) took him from home for months at a time. In special cases, missions could last for more than a year.

He was currently staring down the barrel of just such a beast. Four months from now he'd be launching for Mars to re-supply the colony there. It would take fourteen months for a round trip, and that was actually considered a short turnaround. Mars missions used to take eighteen months or more.

Rachel came running over, breathless and gasping for air.

"You want a juice box?" Katy asked, reaching for the cooler on her side of the bench.

"Yes! Thanks, Mom!" Rachel said, snatching the drink before it even cleared the top of the cooler. She dashed to the playground.

"What about Mark?" Katy called after her, but it fell on deaf ears. Rachel was already with the others, preparing for round two of tag.

David's gaze drifted from the group, admiring the scenery. Leaves rustled in the wind, red and gold, glinting in the sun. Picnics were being assembled on benches under a covered area. A few older boys were throwing a football around on a flat grassy space near the edge of the park. A big black Lab darted between them, barking angrily whenever they caught the ball, as if to say, *I wanna play too!*

And right behind them, striding in from the parking lot, was a group of four men in black suits with dark aviator sunglasses.

David's brow furrowed into a knot. He'd spent enough time working with government agencies and in the military to recognize agents when he saw them. But what were they doing here, in a suburban park in St. Ann, Missouri? And on a Sunday, no less. There could only be one answer. He doubted anyone else had ties to Uncle Sam.

Beside him, Katy stiffened, and her hand tensed in his. She'd seen them too. "Are they here for *you?*" she whispered.

"I don't know... but I think they're headed this way."

The agents strolled past the park, catching stares from parents and children alike. All four of them were armed. David wondered what agency they represented. The FBI? CIA? Homeland Security? *What in blazes is happening?*

David rose slowly from his bench as it became clear he was the men's target.

"Commander Bryce," one of them said, stopping to stand slightly in front of his partners. He had a blue tie, while the others wore gold, gray, and black.

"Yes?" David's eyebrows darted up.

"Please come with us," Blue-tie said.

"What is this about?" Katy demanded, rising to her feet.

"Nothing to worry about, ma'am."

"Too late for that. Is David in some type of trouble?"

"No, ma'am. Don't worry. We'll return him to you as soon as possible."

"When?"

David traded a bemused glance with his wife. He shrugged helplessly. Whatever this was, it had to be important. "Take the kids home. I'll call you as soon as I can, okay?"

Katy held his gaze, clearly troubled.

He leaned in for a kiss. "Love you, sweetheart."

"Love you," she murmured as he withdrew.

David flashed a smile and gave her hand a squeeze before stepping away and nodding to the men. "Can I say goodbye to my kids first?"

"Yes, sir, but don't take long."

David nodded and stalked past them toward the playground. "Rachel, Mark!"

The two came running, acting confused and worried. David dropped to his haunches, rested a hand on each of their shoulders.

"Daddy has to go to work, all right?"

"But we just got here!" Rachel whined.

"You might be able to stay a while. Talk to your mother. I'll see you at home later, okay?"

"Okay..." Rachel replied, her gaze dropping to her feet.

Mark nodded wordlessly, and David tousled his hair as he rose. "Love you both."

He turned to find all four of those men standing right behind him at the wooden border between the sand of the playground and the immaculately manicured park.

"I'm ready," David said, treading onto the grass.

"Follow me, sir," the first man said.

Blue-tie led them across the park, and the other three fell in behind David, escorting him like a dangerous criminal. But his hands weren't cuffed, and these men weren't police.

***

"Where are we going?" David asked as soon as he climbed into the middle row of seats in the rear of the SUV. Blue-tie didn't answer immediately. Instead, he raised his holopad to his ear and waited a few seconds for whoever he was calling to answer.

"Tango Leader, we have Delta Bravo in custody, returning to your position now. ETA five minutes."

A queasy feeling entered David's gut. He glanced at the man sitting in the chair next to his—Gold-tie. That man was staring directly at him, his hand resting casually near his gun. *No, that's not a gun. It's a Taser. His gun is on the other side.*

"What agency are you from?" David demanded.

The question went unanswered. They backed out of the parking lot and sped down the internal park road, going much too fast for a Sunday in a peaceful suburb like St. Ann. The driver swerved to miss a pair of kids in a crosswalk up ahead.

"Hey!" Anxiety began clawing in David's chest like a bird trying to flee its cage. "Will someone tell me what the hell is going on?"

The way they were acting, he was beginning to wonder if they were spies for a foreign government. The Orbital Development Group was an international effort, and a civilian enterprise at that, but governments did intervene on occasion to throw their weight around and lobby for their particular interests.

The silence rattled David. His mind raced to come up with answers to fill in the blanks.

"There's been a development," Blue-tie finally said as he pulled to a jerky stop at the T-junction with Ashby Road. He waited a beat and then gunned it to take the gap between two cars, tires squealing as he pulled onto the main drag. One of the oncoming cars honked at his reckless driving.

"What kind of development?" David asked.

"I'm not at liberty to say, sir."

David waited a second, staring gap-jawed at the back of the driver's seat. "That's it? That's all you can tell me?"

"I'm afraid so."

"Then stop the car. I'm getting out."

But the driver made no move to hit the brakes. If anything, the electric engine only whirred louder.

"Am I under arrest?"

"No, sir."

"Then I have my rights. Who are you working for, and where the hell are you taking me?"

Pretty picket fences and quaint homes with American flags hanging above their front steps blurred by. Old, stately trees turned the sunlight to petals of gold and ruby, flickering over David through the Suburban's moonroof.

"We're with Homeland Security, sir," the driver finally admitted.

"And you're picking me up for a domestic issue?" David's heart pounded in his chest. Was there a terror threat that somehow involved or implicated him?

"Not exactly, sir. Where is your Holo?"

"I turned it off. It's a Sunday. We have a rule, everyone unplugs on Sundays."

"But you have it with you?"

"Yes, it's in my pocket."

"Take it out."

David did as he was told, and held the power button to turn it on. It chimed pleasantly and unlocked as soon as the camera recognized his face. Then came a dozen beeps as it caught up with notifications, messages, and... *twelve* missed calls, which had started early this morning, right after they left for the park.

The calls were evenly spaced about half an hour apart, and were all from the same contact: Sandra Wallace, the coordinator for the Mars re-supply mission. The latest was from an unlisted number somewhere in Washington, according to the area code.

Glancing up from the device, David saw that they were passing under the highway overpass. On the other side, Lambert International Airport sprawled ahead of them.

"We're taking a plane," David said.

"Yes, sir."

All of fifteen minutes later, they drove through a chain-link fence with a sign on it that said *Air National Guard*. Armed soldiers opened the gate, and they passed straight onto the tarmac behind a series of hangars. Waiting in front of one of them was an F/A-18F Super Hornet.

The cockpit was already open, the pilot busy performing his pre-flight checks inside.

"In that?"

"Yes, sir, speed is of the essence," Blue-tie replied as he pulled to a halting stop alongside the fighter jet. "Clear skies, Commander. We'll have people waiting for you when you land."

"Okay..."

One of them opened his door and hopped out, waiting with hands laced in front of him as David followed suit. The agent gestured to the plane and nodded. "Good luck, sir."

"Thank you."

David felt more nervous now than ever. He clearly wasn't in any trouble. Something else was transpiring, and it was serious business. The only reason to put him in a fighter jet to Washington was to save time.

Which left David wondering: what could the powers that be possibly need from him that was so urgent?

He climbed the ladder to the seat behind the cockpit, hearing the fighter's engines already roaring to life. The pilot nodded to him. Her oxygen mask was unclipped and dangling, so he caught a glimpse of the lower half of her face beneath her glossy black visor; she looked young. Maybe late twenties. A sharp whistling sound made him wince as he ducked into the back seat and put on his helmet so he could speak with the pilot.

"Comm check," he said by way of introduction.

"Five by five, Commander. Buckle up and put on your puke catcher."

"My what?"

"Your mask. We'll be flying above ten thousand, and I'd rather bring you down conscious and fully *in compos mentis*."

David knew what she was talking about. Fighter jets, much like rockets, reached high altitudes in seconds, which meant the crew and pilots had to be on oxygen the whole time to avoid altitude sickness.

"Yes, ma'am. What's your name?" David asked as he fumbled with his harness and then clipped on the oxygen mask that was tucked into the back of the pilot's seat.

"Captain Noles. Or Bambi. That's my call sign."

David's mouth lifted in a wry smile. "Sounds degrading."

"Call signs usually are."

The cockpit canopy swung into place, and the engines roared louder, pushing the jet toward a waiting runway. David settled in, and worked to control his breathing and slow his racing heart. This wasn't exactly the lazy Sunday afternoon he'd had in mind.

THREE

Washington DC

D AVID BRYCE COULD HARDLY believe what a whirlwind trip he'd just taken. After a quick flight in the rear seat of an F/A-18 Super Hornet, he'd landed on an air strip right outside the Pentagon. From there an unnamed major from Space Force and two lieutenants had rushed him into a waiting tactical vehicle and driven him straight to the nearest entrance of the Pentagon.

Now, he was through security and racing down the labyrinthine corridors, passing high-ranking officers at every turn. His escorts inside the building were the same officers that had met him on the airfield, all of them armed with next-gen, smart-locked Sig Sauers.

They took an elevator, and then emerged in a sub-level that smelled dank and musty. The walls and floor were bare concrete, the ceilings adorned with exposed pipes and old, buzzing white fluorescent light fixtures.

After walking past countless rooms and yet more bustling groups of soldiers, they came to a particular set of reinforced doors. A pair of enlisted soldiers with X-11 rifles stopped them. One was an Army sergeant. David read his digital name tape—Preston.

"Sir," Sergeant Preston said, saluting smartly.

"I have authorization to bring Commander David Bryce to the Tank," the unnamed major said. Unlike his counterpart, he wasn't wearing a name tape, and he'd made no effort to introduce himself.

"I'll need to check on that, sir," the sergeant said.

"Of course." The major drew a Holo from his pocket and showed the screen to Sergeant Preston. He read the contents, and began nodding to himself. He pulled out a matching device from a pouch on his vest and scanned the major's holopad.

A chime sounded, and the sergeant stepped aside. "Everyone, please look at the scanner." He indicated a black eye above the doors.

David gazed up with the three men in his escort and saw a glowing red dot appear within the dark orb of the camera.

It glowed green with another chime, and the room opened with a whoosh.

They breezed through another dull concrete corridor. Moments later they moved through another security checkpoint to emerge in a slightly better decorated section of the sub-level. This area was carpeted, and the walls were painted.

David faced a pair of brown mahogany doors with a copper plate on them that read: Emergency War Room.

This access was also guarded, but not by soldiers. Two intimidating men in black suits stood with hands crossed in front of them. Secret Service agents.

David's eyes widened as the puzzle pieces clicked together.

The major repeated his orders and displayed the authorization. The agents scanned it again and then opened the room, and David walked in behind the anonymous major. By some unspoken agreement, the two lieutenants stayed outside.

David's heart fluttered in his chest as he entered the room. All eyes turned to him. Eleven of the twelve chairs at the long wooden table were already filled: nine by decorated generals and an admiral. At the head sat President Carver himself. He had thick, wavy black hair, shot through with white at the temples. Intense blue eyes and a ruggedly handsome face had earned him the dubious title of the best-looking president since Kennedy.

"Sit down, Commander Bryce," the president said, gesturing to an empty chair at the foot of the table.

Major what's-his-face saluted smartly, then left the room.

The doors thunked shut, and a smart lock sealed them in with a beep and a glaring red light. David shifted his attention from the exit and saluted the president before replying. "Yes, sir."

David crossed the room to his seat. The generals tracked him, making him feel uneasy. One of the men stood out from the rest. He had a dark, hooded gaze beneath a heavy brow. Thinning salt and pepper hair, cropped short, and a long scar cutting all the way from the right side of his head to his upper lip. He wasn't wearing the stars of a general or the double-breasted jacket of the admiral—just an unmarked black suit and a matching tie.

He could have been with Secret Service, but David had never heard of them sitting in on meetings with the Joint Chiefs of Staff. David took his seat. He leaned forward and folded his hands on the table, fighting the urge to fidget beneath the combined weight of everyone's gazes. Why was he the center of attention?

"Now we can begin," President Carver said. "What we're gathered here to discuss is an extremely sensitive matter that must remain within these walls. We have commandeered your mission to Mars under the guise of providing emergency supplies to repair a greenhouse. You'll be briefed on that before you depart, but no one can ever know the real reason your mission is leaving early. This is still very much an international effort, but outside of your crew, not even the mission controllers at ORB will know the real reason why you're launching prematurely."

"I understand," David said.

"Good. Then let's get down to brass tacks. We've detected an unknown object, approximately fifteen million miles from Earth."

The president touched a holopad sitting in front of him. The lights dimmed, and a shimmering screen appeared—a hologram, floating between a projector in the ceiling and a matching one in the center of the table. The display flickered momentarily before settling on a blurry image of something long and dark.

David's gaze sharpened on the object. It didn't resemble any asteroid he'd ever seen. The edges were too precise, the shape too long and too symmetrical.

"What do you think it is?" President Carver asked.

"I'd guess that it's a spaceship," David replied.

"That was our analysis, too."

"One of ours?" David ventured.

General Davis of Space Force snorted and shook his head. "No, Commander Bryce. None of our rockets are a mile and a half long."

"A mile and a half... that's..."

"Enormous?" President Carver finished. The hologram vanished briefly, and David saw his features set in a grim mask. "This is another angle that the Chinese captured from their space station last week." The projection returned, and the previously cigar-shaped object resolved into a sleek, T-shaped vessel with a curving approximation of wings at the back and a shorter set in the middle.

David's jaw slowly dropped. The resolution of this image was much clearer. Now he could definitely tell that it wasn't an asteroid. This was a spaceship, and it hadn't been built on Earth.

"What..." David trailed off, at a loss for words. "Is it headed for us?"

"Not yet," President Carver said. "As far as we can tell, it's drifting aimlessly, almost as if it's waiting for something."

David's mouth was suddenly so dry that his tongue felt like sandpaper. He swallowed a few times to work some moisture into it. "We're talking about first contact."

"A possibly hostile first contact," General Davis put in. "And we're sending civilians to handle it."

A murmur of discontent spread around the table from the other generals, and President Carver's lips curved up into a dry smile. "Needless to say, my Chiefs of Staff do not exactly agree with the decision to take a passive approach on this. This verdict was not made lightly. I and the leaders of nine other countries, currently aware of the *Interloper*, chose co-opting your mission to Mars as the best, fastest, and safest approach. If the creators of that ship are still alive and actively crewing it, we prefer not to greet them with armed soldiers, or any type of hostility. Do you understand, Commander Bryce?"

David nodded gravely. "Yes, Mr. President."

"Good. Having said that, we'll have contingencies in place if things don't go as planned."

At that, General Davis smirked and folded his hands on the table. David could only imagine what those contingencies might be.

"What is the mission, sir?"

"Your objective is to reach the *Interloper*, to board it, and then to find why it's here, who sent it, and what they want."

"I'll do my best, Mr. President."

"Good. You depart in one week. You will conduct a brief press conference before leaving Washington, in which you will confirm our cover story about transporting supplies for emergency repairs to the colony on Mars. And you will sign this." President Carver nodded to the man in the unmarked suit sitting beside him.

He produced a holopad and a digital pen. The contract at the top read:

TOP SECRET
PROJECT IRIS

David scanned the page, scrolling through paragraph after paragraph of thinly-veiled threats. Then he arrived at a part where divulging details of the mission was classified as treason and a crime against humanity, the punishment for which would be death or life in prison, depending on the severity of the breach.

But there was more—oh, so much more. An entire section of the contract was reserved for culpability, detailing various types of failures that would be blamed on him, personally and legally, if things didn't go according to plan.

"This is a violation of my Fifth Amendment rights," David said, shaking his head. "I can't sign this. It's impossible to guarantee the success of a mission."

"You don't have to guarantee its success," President Carver replied. "You just have to make sure that it doesn't fail because of you."

"That's a lot of weight to put on the shoulders of one man."

"Then you must realize how much faith we have in you. Your record is spotless, both personally and professionally. I can't think of a better person to entrust with the fate of the human race. Please sign, Commander." President Carver smiled. "You're our best option."

"And if I refuse?"

"We'll replace you with someone less qualified. Someone from Space Force. And then we'll have a career warrior going to pick a fight with a species that could almost certainly decimate us in the blink of an eye. Are you sure you want to be responsible for the extermination of your own species?"

"If it played out that way, it wouldn't be my fault."

"And what an empty platitude that will be when we're all dead. Including your children, and your wife. Don't do it for me, Commander. Do it for them and the innocent people who could die if we get this wrong."

"I'm not a diplomat," David said.

"No, you're an emissary, carrying a message to whoever is on that ship. Should you make contact with them, you will relay our wishes."

"And what do you want me to say, sir?"

"That'll depend on how you're received."

David swallowed thickly and stared at the contract. His eyes drifted out of focus on his name at the bottom. The man in the unmarked suit beside him picked up the electronic pen and held it out to him.

Taking the pen from him in a white-knuckled fist, David signed his own death warrant.

FOUR

Three Points Airfield

THE WIND PRESSED LENNON'S cheeks flat as she dropped from fourteen thousand feet. The roar of the small plane's engines disappeared behind her as she fell. She preferred the silence. Lennon always went alone. Never with any other divers.

The sun was high above her, and she closed her eyes for a moment, trying to forget the countless occasions she'd done a similar plunge. They were usually under the protection of the night sky. Weapons strapped to her back. In and out. That's how her missions had always been. Now that she was retired, she practiced every week to remember the rush.

That was partially a lie. It was just part of the bogus story she told people when they asked why someone like her would skydive so often.

Lennon came here to die. Each week it was the same thing, only she was too scared to complete the task. But maybe not today.

She opened her eyes, casting her gaze over the orange and rusty red landscape of southern Arizona. She watched the perfect lines separating people's properties below. Land. Houses. The airfield. All constructs designed by petty humans. The clunky hills beyond were rocky and treacherous. What a wasteland. Dry desert, devoid of life. It was the perfect setting for her ending.

The seconds counted down, and she plummeted, angled to maximize her speed. The ground grew in size, blurred lines focusing. Lennon touched the chute release and held it. She was six thousand feet up. Still time to change her mind.

Lennon watched images flashing before her eyes. She was proud of what she'd done to protect the world, but retirement didn't suit her well. The fact that it was forced on her didn't help. She kept waiting for the message from the top, telling her to dust off her handpiece. But it never came.

Lennon glanced at her wrist-worn altimeter. Five thousand. Four thousand.

She was plunging fast. This was it. The moment she'd been anticipating since she'd first decided to end her own life.

The cord pulled, and the chute jarred her upwards, slowing her descent. Tears fell into her goggles, and she patted her chest, cursing herself for being too weak.

She directed the billowing chute toward the landing zone, where Jack waited in his old dented red pickup truck. This entire region was so far in the past. It was like being dropped in a time machine, back to the 2020s. She preferred that generation. Technology had a way of adding to society's problems, rather than fixing them. Seeing Jack, hearing the rumble of his truck's engine, she was glad today hadn't marked her end. But there was always next week's jump.

She landed gracefully, and her parachute fell behind her with a whoosh.

"Why'd you wait so long?" Jack asked. She saw the binoculars in his hand, and the whiteness of his face. The nest of red freckles stuck out like lightning bugs.

"Got caught up in the moment." She removed her goggles and turned from him, wiping her eyes.

"It's a beautiful morning."

"If you say so," she muttered.

"What?" Jack took her chute, rolled it up, and dumped her gear in the bed of his truck.

"Nothing. Thanks for grabbing me." She climbed in, tossing an empty fast-food bag to the floor.

"Anytime." Jack threw the truck in gear, and drove across the dusty field to the skydiving operation's office.

He knew enough not to ask too many questions, which was a relief. Lennon watched as a nervous couple observed a demo of how the dive was going to work. The guy was probably twenty-five, the girl younger. Even though she was only thirty-five, Lennon felt ancient compared to those civilians about to make their first jump. That's what a decade of black ops did to a person.

She'd always assumed returning to the real world would be simple, until the day the black SUV dropped her off at the Long Island Rail Road station with a battered suitcase and a few thousand bucks. The real world, as it was, terrified her more than any mission. There, she'd understood her role. Out here... it was the Wild West.

"See you next week." She tried to pass Jack a tip with her Holo, but he wouldn't accept it.

"Not necessary. Later, Lennon." He drove off as she went to her car. It was a rusted-out minivan with two hundred and fifty thousand miles on it, but it was hers. Instead of doing the normal routine and heading to the shop, she left the airfield, deciding to go into town. She waved at Bill, the mechanic who was technically her boss, on the way out. Working at a municipal airport gave her just enough money to live, but the existence wasn't her own. It belonged to Lennon Baxter, the US Air Force first lieutenant, along with the dog tags dangling from her rearview mirror.

The true version of herself was buried deep within her body, with over ten million dollars stowed away in a secure location, and a serious body count to her name. She glanced in the mirror, as if expecting to see the scars, but they were hidden as well.

It was her day off, and she drove into town, rolling the windows down, opting to use the van's manual controls instead of the autonomous driver. Traffic was light, and she stopped at the diner, deciding that if she was going to live, she'd have to eat something eventually.

Electronic bells chimed over the door when she entered, and Pauly pointed to an empty seat at the counter. "The usual?" he asked.

"Make it a double."

He glanced at a digital clock projected over the register. "This early?"

"It's never too soon for the good stuff." Lennon smiled at the man, using her persona. The friendly woman. The carefree, pleasant face. Sometimes it hurt as much as waking up.

"Double cheeseburger, coming up." Pauly disappeared to the kitchen after pouring her a thick cup of coffee. She drank a sip of the black brew, and watched the TV in the corner of the deserted diner.

"*The announcement came today, after speculation on the Orbital Development Group schedule notifications,*" the news anchor said. She touched her invisible earpiece, squinting. "*We're being told that the CEO of the conglomerate is moving the timeline for a supply run, which was scheduled to depart in four months, to leave in just one week's time. Rumors state there was an air leak at the secondary greenhouse, which in turn caused loss of water, as well as the ability to feed the current population of two hundred settlers.*"

Lennon figured anyone dumb enough to go to Mars in the first place probably deserved their fate. There was a time in her life when she'd wanted nothing more than to be an astronaut. She'd completed the training, but as she'd graduated, the call from another department came in. There were more important things than traveling to the Moon or Mars.

She took a sip, and the cup nearly slipped through her fingers. They clamped on the handle, and she recovered. Lennon set it down and flexed her hand. It ached. She'd previously broken three fingers, the pointer twice. Luckily it was her left. She shot with the other.

"Order up!" Pauly brought the food himself, letting his waitress watch the news. "She's been staring at that thing all morning. Why is everyone so obsessed with space?"

"No clue." But part of her knew. It was the unknown, a mystery waiting to be unraveled one thread at a time, until the secret was out. But Lennon didn't expect answers soon. She took a bite, now grateful that she'd pulled the chute release. The food was spectacular. Just the right amount of grease and cheese.

A man materialized on screen, a drone mic hovering above his head, and she realized who it was. His face was everywhere. David Bryce, commander of *Beyond III*, and the poster boy for the ORB missions. He and his crew were the only people the CEO trusted to transport him to and from the colony, and for good reason. So far, four ships had failed to land and return to Earth over the last fifteen years since they'd first stepped foot on the red planet.

"*It's not worthy of all the news surrounding it. There's an issue at the colony, and we're being directed to bring supplies. We're glad to be here, ready and capable to assist ORB once again,*" David said.

"What a fake," she mumbled with her mouth full.

Lennon finished the food while the TV resumed a cheesy daytime soap from south of the border, and she left Pauly a semi-decent tip that someone of her position could hardly afford. She didn't care. It paid to be nice to the people who had your back. In her former life, that returned dividends tenfold.

She drove to the outskirts of town and pulled into the trailer park, wondering when she'd stop tormenting herself. Maybe it was time to pack her precious few belongings and head to the city. She could access her money and buy a quaint place in Maine. It had been long enough.

Lennon parked at her trailer, seeing the guy next door tinkering with his bike. Four empty cans littered the ground beside him, and he leered at her.

"Baxter, you wanna gimme a hand with this alternator?" His bike was a piece of junk, some forty-year-old brand she'd never even heard of, made offshore and shipped to the States on an unmarked sea-can. She knew his type, and would rather steer clear. She'd evaded him so far, but he was getting more brazen. It was only a matter of time before she'd have to put him in his place.

"Nah. I'm beat." She turned her back to Ralph, and heard his bootsteps approaching. She tensed, ready to fend him off, but something about her posture must have sent warning signals to the creep.

She unlocked the door and peered out, making sure he didn't follow her. Carol from three trailers down walked onto her porch, wearing a summer dress too late in the season, and Ralph sauntered over. He'd found easier prey. Lennon considered dealing with him sooner rather than later, for the good of the community.

Instead, she went to the bedroom, lifted a floorboard under the mattress, and pulled the sack from beneath the trailer like she did every day. Beside it sat a black container, and she opened it with a thumb print. She touched the 9MM, feeling the cold metal on her palm. She leaned against the bed, clutching the weapon. Lennon missed it. Not the blood, but the thrill. The knowledge that she was doing good, even if she could never tell a soul about her missions. Holding it made her think of Rutger, and she shoved it away, sealing the case.

She focused on the bag, and slowly untangled the knot.

Her hand trembled when she saw the green indicator light blinking on the holopad's clear screen. "What the hell?"

Lennon let it scan her retina, and the screen flashed on.

There was a single message.

You've been reinstated. Welcome back, Dark Three.

Lennon slumped to the floor. She'd spent ten years wanting out, and another five wanting in again. Now she wasn't sure what she desired.

Lennon grimaced and typed a return message. *Where and when?*

FIVE

Rijeka, Croatia

B EING ON THE COAST always reminded Atlas of his childhood. He and his younger brother, Hayden, would run along the shore, feeling the spray of the angry ocean on their faces. They'd gather shells at the beach, eager to run home and show their mother the prizes. Until she wasn't there one day.

Atlas wiped his face, tired after his escape from Italy. All that mattered were the items in his bag. He was confident he hadn't been followed on the train, and the bus into town had been almost empty. The other passenger smelled like he'd gone on a bender, and he'd been unconscious the entire time.

Atlas had made it to Rijeka and was in the clear. For now.

He loved this country. It was one of the less talked about travel destinations, but standing near the port as the sun descended in the west, he thought it might be even more stunning than Como.

His watch buzzed, and he patted it, the time projecting two inches from the device. He was already late for his meeting.

Atlas glanced at his feet, wondering if he was too fancy for the bar. The white boat shoes and the suit jacket were overkill for the area, but he didn't have the luxury of procuring another outfit. He imagined the ticking of the clock, and started toward his destination three blocks ahead.

It must have rained recently, because he had to circumvent pools of water on the slick cobblestone. People were relaxing on patios, drinking wine under dangling orange lights. The mood was uplifting. There had been a dark era when this entire section of Europe was oppressed, filled with constant tension.

Now it was light. Breathable. Atlas inhaled and kept going, not taking the time to admire the shops and bakeries he passed. He turned right at an intersection, and noticed how it seemed bleaker along this route. The shops gave way to apartments, and he slowed when he saw five men standing at a door, cigarettes burning in the dusk air.

They studied him, and he clutched the bag containing the small relics. *Just try it.*

But they didn't. One of them laughed at his friend's joke, and they went in the opposite direction.

Dobar Bar. The name made him chuckle. It literally translated to "Good Bar." He hoped so. His contact had requested this spot, and the moment Atlas entered, he could see why. It was packed. No one would remember their quick meeting, or two random men chatting quietly in the corner.

Everything was dark wood, the lights dim, hanging from old metal fixtures with Edison lamps screwed into the ends. The floor was slightly sticky as he approached the bar, and he recognized Petar sitting solo at a high top. The man was nursing a beer from a green bottle, and Atlas ordered two of them from a slow-moving bartender.

He saw Petar before the man knew he was there. He looked twitchy. Unsettled. That could mean a few things, but Atlas kept it in mind as he strode to greet his contact.

Atlas slid a beer to Petar, and the man glanced up with bleary eyes.

"Petar," he said.

"Atlas," the man returned. "I was surprised by your call."

"I need to know who found something. A fisherman from here." Atlas took a sip after sitting. The new relic remained in the bag, squeezed between his thighs.

"That should be simple. Show me what it was, and I'll find out." Petar drank deeply.

Atlas shook his head. "Should be straightforward for a man of your... skillset." He'd never fully trusted this guy, and now, sitting with him, the feeling remained.

"We've been friends for a long time," Petar said. "Why not show me what you have, and I'll trace it."

"I wouldn't say *friends*." Atlas grinned at him, and received a scowl in return.

"Let's cut the shit, Donovan. I have a buyer."

The tables had turned. "*You* have a buyer? I thought you were working for me."

"Things change. Priorities."

Atlas noticed the fine leather jacket. It was brand new. He saw the latest model of the RX watch was strapped to the guy's wrist. "Maybe next time you're bought off, you should keep it discreet."

Atlas rose, and Petar's hand snaked out, clutching his arm "Don't do it, Atlas. You won't escape this man. He has more money than God."

"Then maybe he can call in some divine intervention when you're lying on the ground with a broken neck." Atlas hissed the words, sticking his nose an inch from Petar's. He felt the grip loosen, and he pulled free, taking his artifact. Who was after him? It might be his only clue to finding the rest of this...prize.

Atlas wanted to beat it out of Petar, but doing it in a crowded bar would just get him arrested. He noted the employee door to the left, and waited until someone pressed through it. He slunk inside, and cut through the kitchen into the alley.

The air blew from his lungs as he was struck in the gut with a blunt object. The bag fell from his hand, clanging to the stone street.

He anticipated the next hit, and grabbed the man's foot, twisting it hard. He heard the crack, and the assailant fell to the ground, writhing in pain. He lunged, decking the man in the face, and he went limp. Atlas grinned, then looked up to find the biggest man he'd ever seen across the alley. He wore all black, and Atlas assumed the baseball cap had to be custom made. His partner was unmoving while Atlas hauled himself to his feet.

"Settle down, big guy," he said, lifting his hands in the air. "We don't have to do this."

The man didn't say a word.

"Seriously. Tell me who sent you, and I'll give you ten thousand Euros." He didn't have much cash on him, but this guy didn't know that. Atlas saw the glint of a gun in the glow of the alley lights.

He jumped as the giant fired at him, narrowly missing. Atlas rolled to his knees and jumped to the side again, crashing into garbage cans. They banged loudly to the street, and Atlas stayed behind them. Another gunshot. This one struck the can he was holding, and he realized there wasn't going to be much of an opening.

He breathed deeply, and acted quickly. Atlas threw the garbage can at his opponent and slid low, tripping the guy. He grunted as his back hit the cobblestones, the can batted away by a thick arm. Atlas didn't hesitate. He jabbed the man's gut with an elbow. It was like striking a brick house.

Again. He kicked out at the hand with the gun, knocking it aside. Now it was even. The thought was fleeting as the giant rose, dusting himself off. Instead of looking angry, he smiled at Atlas, as if he welcomed the chance for a fair fight. Blood dripped from his lip.

"Crap." Atlas dodged the incoming fist, and kicked at the guy's knee. Another time. The same knee. Third attack, and he was hit directly in the face, sending him against a wall. The man hobbled over, still smirking, and Atlas moved right at the last moment. His opponent's knuckles whacked into bricks, and the giant howled in pain.

Atlas dove for the gun, grabbing it as well as his bag. He aimed at the man, his chest heaving. "Who's your boss?"

The door opened to reveal Petar, brandishing a weapon of his own. A Soviet special, by the look of it. "Atlas, you won't win."

"Tell me."

Neither of them spoke. Atlas fired the gun, hitting his larger adversary in the thigh. It was an easy target. The man made a strangled sound, but contained his reaction surprisingly well. He didn't even collapse.

"You're next, Petar." Atlas stepped closer. It was now or never.

Petar let the gun dangle on his index finger. "Okay. Okay."

The giant started to hobble forward, and Petar used the gun, hitting the guy in the back. He fired two more times, and the sound of sirens rang through the alley.

"Get out of here, Atlas. I didn't have a choice. They'll be after me now."

"Who? Tell me!" he shouted over the police sirens.

Petar grabbed a small book from the inside of his jacket, and tossed it to Atlas. "No name, but here's an address. It's all I can do." Petar took one last glance at the enormous man, now dead on the ground, and then to the other guy Atlas had injured. He was cowering in the corner, clutching his wounded ankle. Petar turned to him, then pulled the trigger again. Atlas blinked, stunned at the cold-blooded way Petar dispatched both men, but he didn't have time to worry about it.

Atlas slid the book into his pants and ran through the alley, trying to escape the scene before the authorities arrived to find two dead Russians.

He went to the ocean, threw the gun into the crashing waves, and rushed down the coastline. He could still hear the alarms in the distance, so he stayed out of the light. It was quiet here in the ports, but there was a boat loading cans onto a massive platform. Atlas saw flashing strobes from the main road overhead, and approached the working crews. He found an orange vest, dumped his own suit jacket, and slid it on.

Rain began to fall from a cloudy sky, and Atlas hung back at the end of the loading zone, the beeping sounds of the forklift drowning out the sirens.

He flipped the book open, checking Petar's notes. The pages were mostly empty, save for a few missives in Russian. He stopped scanning when he found an address in China. He wasn't familiar with the terrain, so he used his Holo to mark the coordinates. Remote northern China, near the Mongolian border. It wouldn't be a simple journey, but he'd spent years with nothing to show for it.

Now he had a lead.

Lennon

Three Points, Arizona

She'd hardly slept last night. Lennon poured her second cup of coffee, already feeling her nerves firing on all cylinders. The message had been simple. *Stay put. Wait for extraction.* The same as every other occasion in her life. Only then, she'd been working at US military bases around the world, not a trailer park in Arizona.

The AC unit in her window sputtered and clanked, and she could tell it was going to be a hot September day. She tried to dress normally, and kept checking the clock, but that seemed to slow down time.

Her holotab rang, and she tapped her watch. "Hey, Bill. Sorry, I'm not feeling well. I have to..."

"*Lennon, I appreciate your help, but we aren't busy enough to justify keeping you on staff.*"

She tried to act surprised. "You're letting me go?"

Lennon could picture Bill's face, long and somber while he stroked his wispy white beard. "*You know how it is. There ain't sufficient planes coming here. Why don't you move on up to Tucson? I can put a good word in for you.*"

She smiled, trying to remember the last time anyone had been this kind to her. Even while firing her, Bill was eager to help. "It's okay. I'll be fine. Thanks, Bill."

"*Best of luck, kiddo.*" The call ended, and Lennon heard tires crunching on gravel outside.

Her heart raced as she gathered her things, using her fingers to part the cheap blinds. A black SUV pulled in next to her van. This was it. All the waiting was over.

Lennon paused at the mirror near the door. She smoothed her short brown hair with her fingers, and saw how much she'd aged since leaving the operation. The desert didn't suit her.

Without looking back, she let the screen door slam behind her. A man exited the SUV, and opened the rear passenger door. Prying eyes watched her from porches and windows, but she didn't care. She was done with Three Points Trailer Park once and for all.

Ralph's bike was in front of his trailer. More beer cans littered the property.

"Just a minute." She shoved her bag at the man in the dark suit, and brandished a switchblade from her pocket. Lennon stabbed it into Ralph's back tire, then the front one. She grinned as the air hissed from the balding rubber.

A cool breeze greeted her inside the SUV, and she slid over on the leather, taking the middle seat. "You guys the talkative types?"

The vehicle began to roll forward, neither of them speaking.

"Good," she said, taking the seat behind the driver. Her head rested on the door, and she was out before they hit the highway.

Lennon woke sometime later, feeling more rested than she had in the last five years.

An airplane waited for them, engines running at the private airstrip. She tried to get her bearings. Somewhere south of Phoenix, judging by the landscape. The escorts funneled her onto the ship, tossing her pack up without care.

"You're not coming?" she asked.

They remained silent, returning to the SUV and kicking up dust as they sped off.

She'd seen this type of jet before. It was a Cessna, a luxury private plane, redesigned in the thirties. It was *his* favorite type.

"We meet again," the man said, startling Lennon.

There was no one else in the cabin. The pilot joined them, but only to secure the door, and then he was off, returning to the cockpit.

Her contact was older too. White at the temples, more lines bordering the eyes, but he looked better than he had the last time she'd seen him. A distinctive scar slashed from his hairline to his upper lip, a narrow miss from a switchblade in an alley. Hazards of the job. Lennon didn't know his real name, only that he went by "Dark Leader." It was as ominous as they came, but it fit the type of work he'd required of her.

"Leader," she said, sitting in the white leather seat he indicated. He sat across from her, hands on his knees.

"Dark Three. Would you care for a drink?"

"No. Thank you." This was strange. She nervously fidgeted with her seatbelt. Lennon felt like she'd been out of the game for too long. What kind of task was she being given? Dark Leader had never offered her his full attention.

The plane rocketed down the runway, lifting off into the sky.

"We're facing our most important mission yet." He glanced out the window as he spoke. "You know our organization has fended off countless global threats over the years. You were there for many of them, leading the charge, weren't you?"

She nodded and rubbed her aching fingers. That eased the pain, but nothing could repair the sting of her friends' deaths. That final mission. "Yes, sir. I was."

"You were always the best, and that's why you've been chosen for this specific mission. You'll be acting alone. Can I trust there won't be a problem? That Dark Three will stay focused and... want to be alive?"

Lennon stiffened. He studied her, and for a second, she feared he could read her mind, sense the desire to end things. But he grinned reassuringly. "It won't be for the faint of heart, but the rewards will make up for it, I promise you that."

She managed to find her voice. "What's the job?"

Dark Leader rubbed his bare chin. "You've seen the news?"

"Sure. The troops in Iran are..."

"No. Not that. ORB," he said.

"The Mars mission? What does that have to do with us?"

The plane continued to rise in elevation, and her ears popped. "Everything, Dark Three. Everything."

She had no idea where they were destined, or why she'd been pulled in, but the expression on his face worried her more than anything she'd ever encountered in the field. "Then tell me."

He sat back. "You'll be leaving on the *Beyond III* in one week, under the leadership of Commander David Bryce. You'll listen to him and obey his instructions. Integrate into their big, happy family, and you'll do so with a smile on your face. Understood?"

Her head reeled. Why was she being sent on a rocket, headed for Mars?

"I'm no astronaut," she said.

"But you are," he whispered, passing her a holopad. Her face was on the ID card. "You've taken the preliminary training, remember?"

She had, years ago, when she thought the Air Force was a stepping stone to the burgeoning private space program. It had once been her dream, back when she was young and full of motivation. That was a lifetime before her first mission under this man's guidance. And Rutger. Then it all changed. "I don't see how..."

"They only know you were in the Air Force before transferring to Special Ops, but the details are classified. You're coming to them as a replacement for someone they admire, so you'll have to work tirelessly to blend in."

She thought about Rutger, and scratched where her tattoo was concealed under her sleeve. "Don't worry about me. I can wear a mask for them." She was wearing one right now.

"I know you can, and that's why I chose you over the other operatives," Dark Leader said.

In all the years she'd been following his instructions, not once had he offered any semblance of cordiality to her. This was almost a pat on the back. An acknowledgement of her worth. She hated how good it made her feel.

"And I follow orders," she whispered.

"Yes. Once you join their team, you'll await further instructions." He stared at her, and she sensed a moment of hesitation.

His watch blinked, and he grimaced as he read a private message. "I should have known it wouldn't be that easy. Damned Russians."

"What are they up to?" she pried.

"Never mind." The plane shook in some turbulence.

Lennon knew this man had numerous affiliations, and her mission with ORB was but a fraction of his plan.

He turned from her, pressing an earpiece in before walking to the rear seat.

She overheard the conversation in bits and pieces. Lennon only made out the odd word. *Croatia. Relic. Imperative.*

She closed her eyes, clutching the arms as they continued through the turbulence. This was nothing. She was used to piloting the latest F-15YEX models, but she felt out of her element relinquishing control. Lennon had to acclimate quickly, because her trip on the *Beyond III* wasn't going to be any different.

But despite all her reservations, she concluded there might be something worth living for. At least for now.

The mission always came first.

SIX

St. Ann, Missouri

THE TRIP HOME WAS accompanied by far less urgency and secrecy. A regular commercial flight. Only one man in a black suit escorting him. Another Suburban waiting at the airport to take him home.

Now, he was standing on the front steps of his house barely twelve hours after he'd departed. David placed his thumb against the smart lock. The indicator light turned green, and the door clicked open.

Shadows parted, flickering across the living room as a yellow-orange swath from the streetlights swept in. Silence and the sweet odors of cinnamon and sugar greeted him. Were those Katy's famous sticky buns he smelled? He took a deep breath, inhaling the memories he'd missed. Rachel licking the icing off her skinny fingers. Mark fighting to be the first to get his roll, fresh out of the oven. It felt as if days had passed, but all he'd missed was one Sunday. And he was about to miss so many more.

Being an astronaut in a golden age of space exploration and development was a double-edged sword. He got to be a part of something that mattered. A part of history in the making. But at times like this, he wondered if it was worth it. And now, with Project Iris looming over him, he was more torn than ever. The specter of leading a mission to investigate... what, exactly?

He didn't know. Nobody did. But whatever it was, it wasn't from Earth. The thought of discovering an actual alien vessel, of maybe even meeting the enigmatic beings that had built it... This was exactly the kind of thing he'd always dreamed about as a wide-eyed kid gazing up at the stars in rural Missouri.

As an adult, he'd never actually expected that dream to come true. Failure to handle this mission correctly could spell the end of not only his career, but of his own personal freedom, as well. Failure wasn't an option. He'd make sure of it. He'd signed that document willingly, and in so doing, agreed to be a diplomat for all of humanity.

No, not a diplomat, an emissary. The president himself had made that distinction. David wouldn't be negotiating anything. His mission was strictly recon, and delivering a message. But what message would he convey? He didn't know yet. A small part of him hoped that the craft was empty. A drone ship. Or that the crew was long dead, unaware they'd drifted into range of an inhabited world.

If history was anything to go by, whenever two different civilizations met, it resulted in conflict. And usually, in the utter elimination of the weaker of the two groups.

David crept quietly, and caught sight of his shadow drifting on the scuffed wooden floors. He turned to close the door behind him.

The SUV out on the street hadn't moved. Were those agents planning on waiting outside all night?

Maybe.

The door clicked shut, and the lock automatically turned. The status light went from green to red.

He kicked off his shoes, and went straight to the kitchen that overlooked the formal living room from a pass-through bar counter. Walking by the dining room, he followed the marble island to the sink. Taking a glass from one of the cupboards, he placed it under the tap. The faucet sensed the movement and came on, the water glowing blue in the dark as LEDs illuminated it to indicate the temperature. He drained the glass and then refilled it for later.

A creaky stair heralded his wife's approach.

"David?" she asked.

He saw Katy descending the winding staircase from the second floor. That stairwell flowed into a den that the kitchen opened into. His home wasn't ostentatious, but it certainly tried to be. Katy was hugging her shoulders, cold despite the cozy warmth inside.

"Did I wake you?" David asked.

"No, I was with Rachel. She couldn't sleep. She had a nightmare that your plane crashed."

A light frown creased his lips. "Did you tell her I arrived safely?"

She crossed the living room to meet him at the end of the island. "I did. And then she went to sleep." Katy hesitated, her eyes searching David's. "What did they want?"

He'd already spoken with Katy on the phone, soon after hitting the tarmac in DC, and again just before his return flight on American Airlines 326, and a final time when he'd landed. But at no point along the way had he been free to speak. He had government agents flanking him the entire time, so he'd stuck to the *hellos*, and *I-love-yous*, and *see-you-soons* of empty conversation.

But even now, he couldn't be sure that his home wasn't bugged. And having signed an agreement that guaranteed the mission's confidentiality *or else,* he wouldn't risk giving her more details.

David shrugged and took a sip of water. "Our mission timeline was changed."

Katy cocked a skeptical eyebrow at him. "Those men weren't from ORB."

"Not directly, no." He cleared his throat. "You must have heard about it on the news."

"I watched *you*." Katy cracked a smile. "Mark was so proud. He thinks you're a superhero who's going to save people on Mars."

That incited a smile and snort from David. He drummed his fingers restlessly on the island.

"Is it true?" Katy asked.

David's smile grew quizzical. "Why wouldn't it be?"

"Because you were doing that thing you do when you're lying. You clear your throat too much, like all the words are getting stuck."

"Did I?" Just talking about it made his throat itch. He cleared it again.

Katy took a quick step back, and her brow furrowed incredulously. "You're doing it now! What aren't you telling me?"

"I also do it when I'm nervous," David replied.

"That wasn't an answer."

"They made me sign an NDA."

"Who did?"

"I can't say."

"Where did they take you?"

"I can't say."

"You were on a plane."

"Yes."

"Is the situation on Mars that serious? It's not the greenhouse, is it?"

"No, but that's really all I'm able to reveal, Kate."

She pursed her lips and sucked in a deep breath, and let it out slowly a moment later. "Fine. I understand. Just tell me this: will the mission be more dangerous now?"

David opened his mouth to say something, then stopped with a grimace.

Katy began nodding slowly. "That's what I thought. If you don't come home, I won't be able to forgive you. The kids won't either."

David set his glass aside and crossed over to her, opening his arms for a hug. She pulled away, angry, but he wasn't taking no for an answer. He held her close, her chin rested against his shoulder. "I'll come back," he said, and kissed the top of her head.

He heard her sniffle, and felt tears soaking through his shirt. "When do you leave?"

"Tomorrow morning."

Kate withdrew sharply, her gaze accusing. "That soon?"

"It's not up to me, Katy. But please trust me, this is important. In fact, it might be the most significant thing I ever do."

Her brow furrowed again, and the hardness left her eyes. Back was the fear, and the sadness. "Then we'd better make tonight count." With that, she took his hand and pulled him toward the stairs.

***

Boca Chica, Texas, ORB "Starbase"

It was another whirlwind adventure, this time on a private jet. David spent the flight drifting in and out of sleep and remembering the morning: saying goodbye to Katy, and then to Rachel and Mark. They'd all cried, even him, but Rachel had sobbed the most. She was only nine.

"You'll still call us, right?" she sniffed.

He'd smiled and chucked her chin. *"I'll do my best, kiddo."*

How to explain to a fourth-grader that, yes, he could call, but the communications had to be pre-recorded and routed through ORB's comms center? There'd be no interaction. The ever-growing distance between him and Earth would prevent two-way communication—not to mention security. His messages would have to be vetted, just to make sure he was sticking to his NDA. The last trip to Mars, Rachel had been too young to remember it. He'd missed so much. Her first words. Mark's birthday. A Christmas. Their anniversary...

A knot tightened in David's throat as ORB's self-driving shuttle pulled up to the gate. The transport was empty except for him. The rest of his crew had either arrived earlier, or they were still on their way.

Looking out the rear window of the vehicle, David saw nothing but expanding clouds of dust. He was finally rid of his government escort.

A security guard marched up to David's window and rapped on it with his knuckles.

David lowered it and presented his clear, QR-coded ID card. The man scanned it with his Holo, then took a picture of David holding it.

"Welcome back to Starbase, Commander Bryce," the guard said, emerging from the shuttle.

"Thank you," he replied.

The chain-link gate rattled open, and the electric shuttle whirred on down the dusty road. Texas, dry as a desert. Nothing but brown grass all the way out to the thin blue line of the horizon. David heard seagulls in the distance. The rumbling of trucks, and the faraway shouts of ground crew. Dirt blasted through the opening, making him choke, and he quickly raised the window.

The transport stopped right in front of the training center, between two matching black vans with the ORB logo stamped on the sides: the *O* was the planet Earth with a rocket racing into space, and the thruster trail formed a white line under the other two letters.

David opened his door and hopped out, dragging a duffel bag with him. He was only allowed twenty kilograms for personal belongings. He'd packed his bag full of mementos—Mark's prized baseball, signed by the Cardinals' star pitcher, Gary Fields; Rachel's favorite stuffed animal;

an engraved crystal with one of his and Katy's wedding photos inside and the date they'd gotten married. And then came his e-reader chock full of books he'd intended to read, a bunch of his favorite snacks, and clothes to wear under his uniform or space suit—mostly under-wear, since the laundry room aboard the *Beyond III* could only be used once a month.

"Commander Bryce!" one of the guards outside the training center said, coming to attention as he approached.

David recognized him. Vance was an old Air Force corporal who'd had dreams of becoming an astronaut himself.

"At ease, Corporal."

David's colleague frowned at the fawning display while David flashed his badge in front of the door scanner. Vance hurried to open the door for him before he could.

"Thank you," he grunted, dragging his duffel bag through.

The training center was bright and airy. A massive museum of spaceflight history made up the entryway. A few tourists were present, oohing and awing as the tour guide pointed to the former iterations of ORB's *Beyond* rockets. The first had only been fifty meters tall and nine in diameter. The *Beyond III* was a monster at seventy-five meters high and twelve wide. The crew compartments alone were over a thousand square feet. But then, they had to sustain a crew of six for nearly a year at a time.

Six people that David knew as well as his own family. Cumulatively, they'd spent several years together, and he always missed them between assignments. A smile crossed David's lips as he wove between the scale models of various rockets and landing craft. He was eager to catch up with his crew. Reaching turnstiles before the elevators, and yet another pair of guards, David slid his access ID across a final scanner and walked through.

He recalled the two vans parked outside, and wondered which of them were already here. Hopefully his first officer, Jess Rigel, had made it. The two of them were particularly close; they had a lot of history from the time they'd served together as pilots in the Navy. Katy had been jealous at the start, but she'd cooled down pretty quickly.

David remembered their introduction with a smirk as he waited for the elevator.

"Katy, this is my best friend, Lieutenant Jess Rigel."

The expression on Katy's face had been priceless. Jess was a pretty woman, and back then, he and Katy had just started dating. But Jess's wife (then girlfriend) had spoiled it by returning from the ladies' room sooner than anticipated. Now they were all good friends, but they lived on opposite ends of the country, and it had been more than six months since he and Jess had last seen each other.

The elevator dinged and the doors opened. David stepped through just as a woman he didn't recognize was leaving. He smiled and nodded to her.

Her face morphed into what he could only interpret as a scowl. He wouldn't have given her a second thought, but she was wearing the mission uniform: blue, with the ORB logo stamped on one shoulder and the American flag on the other.

David stopped her in the open doors, putting out the hand not holding his duffel bag in front of her chest.

She glared at it.

"Who are you?" David demanded.

Her gaze rose from his arm, cold blue eyes sparkling with intensity. They widened fractionally, and she seemed to snap out of it. A more genuine smile graced her lips. "It's nice to finally meet you, Commander Bryce."

"You know me?"

"Your face is all over the news."

"Right. And you are?" He read the name tape off her jumpsuit before she answered. "Baxter?"

"Lennon Baxter, yes."

"You're assigned to the *Beyond III*?"

"Yes, sir. Co-pilot and mission specialist."

"Co... what happened to Jess Rigel?"

"Who?" Baxter's head tilted suddenly to one side. A few strands of golden-brown hair fell in front of her face.

"My first officer. The woman who's supposed to be assigned as my co-pilot."

"You'll have to talk to the mission planners about that." Lennon gave another smile, but it vanished faster than it appeared. "I hope you're not too disappointed."

David recovered with a sigh. "It's nothing personal, Miss Baxter. You're not trained for this mission. She is."

"With all due respect, Commander, my understanding is that nobody is ever really prepared for this."

A prickle of suspicion coursed through David's gut. *She knows. Of course, she knows.* He could think of only one reason why Jess might have been yanked off the crew and replaced at the last minute. *Mission specialist, huh? And she just happens to be another American.* Jess was, too, so it wouldn't raise too many eyebrows, but something told him that Baxter was there to guard American interests above the international ones represented by the rest of his crew. "Have you met the others yet?"

"No, sir. I'm about to. They're in the next building, eating lunch. I was on my way to join them. You should come. Maybe an introduction from you would help to soften the blow about Mrs. Rigel."

David started to nod, then stopped himself. He was supposed to report directly to mission control. Besides, he'd already eaten his lunch on the plane.

"You seem like you can fend for yourself. I'll catch you at the briefing at thirteen hundred."

Lennon appeared frustrated, but she covered it well. "See you then, Commander." She nodded to him as she left, and David watched her go with a frown.

This mission was already off to a terrible start.

Lennon

Boca Chica, Texas, ORB "Starbase"

This was going to be more difficult than she'd imagined. It had taken her entire willpower not to shove the commander's duffel down his throat. She hated how perfect his hair was, that classic all-American square jaw. Lennon had reported to countless officers like him in her tenure with the Air Force, and none of them had enjoyed her brazen personality. But that was before Lennon knew how to manipulate them.

"I'll show you fending for myself," she muttered, and exited the building. This place wasn't that different from some of her previous stations, but had clearly been upgraded with financial support from the private sector. It was one thing to be funded by taxpayers, and another to have the backing of the world's largest industries.

The grounds were clean, and she watched a few autonomous road sweepers driving themselves around the concrete, leaving wet circles behind them. Overhead drones surveyed the perimeter fence. Lennon recognized the models. They weren't just there for show. Those units could intercept a Humvee from three hundred feet up. She'd seen it done.

The memory of that hot day in the New African desert brought a smile to her face. Rutger at her side, crouched behind the abandoned building. The town had been deserted, and the only sound around them was the fleeing man and his guards trying to escape in the stolen 4X4.

Rutger controlled the drone with his watch, glancing up into the sun momentarily before confirming the target. The muffled boom of an explosion and a greasy smear of black smoke climbing against the sand dunes marked the kill.

Their extraction came ten minutes later, and the world was a better place.

"Are you lost?" a woman asked, glancing at her uniform. Her eyes widened. She was taller than Lennon by a good two inches, and her hair was a rusty brown color, eyes dark green and soulful.

"I'm supposed to have lunch with the crew of *Beyond III*." Lennon's voice was light, friendly.

"I'm Zasha." She offered her hand, and they shook. Lennon found the gesture archaic. She knew all about Zasha Petrov. How she'd worked as an undercover agent for the Russians before entering Roscosmos. Lennon assumed they had a lot in common, but time would tell.

"Lennon." She tapped her name on the uniform. "Baxter."

"And what brings you to Starbase?" Zasha's accent was noticeable if you listened, but subtle.

Lennon paused while a modified golf cart ushered tourists across the grounds, and continued to the neighboring building. "I'd prefer to tell everyone at once."

"Tell us what?" Zasha held the door open for her, and Lennon walked in, whistling at the sight. They entered a living room with twenty-foot ceilings, the world's biggest flat screen on the wall, and two men sprawled on a cognac leather couch, feet up, playing video games. 3D glasses glowed over their eyes, and Lennon coughed, then cleared her throat. She'd always hated games and found them juvenile, but she wasn't like most people.

The screen turned off, and one of the men yanked off his glasses and hopped to his feet, straight-backed and at attention. The other stared Lennon up and down, and didn't seem amused by her uniform.

"Gentlemen, this is Lennon Baxter," Zasha introduced her. "She's about to inform us why she's wearing a mission outfit."

"She's on the team," the first man said. He had a nice smile. "I'm Liu Teng. Doctor. And this is Carter Robinson, linguist and systems engineer."

Carter stared at her, unblinking, and jutted his hand forward. "Pleasure to meet you, Lennon. Now that's an interesting name. And Baxter. That's Scottish, isn't it? Maybe Northern England. It means..."

"Baker." Lennon let go of his grip. "Perhaps we're related."

Carter's eyebrows rose. "I should hope not." Somehow, with his British accent, the comment didn't come across as invasive.

Lennon set her bag down and kicked it to the side. "Where's Akira?"

"You're familiar with us, then?" Zasha asked.

Lennon nodded. "I've been briefed."

The door opened again, the wind blowing the hair of the newcomer. She was stunning, her eyes bright and shiny. She pulled in a cart with covered plates on it. "Couldn't we have asked one of the staff to do this?" the girl asked.

"Don't be ridiculous. You know the rules. Newbies get the food until they've completed two missions." Carter glanced at Lennon. "I guess you have the honors."

"Not on your life," Lennon said, and he grinned.

She met Akira Mori, the tech expert and flight engineer. "Wait, if you're..."

"It means Jess is not." Liu grabbed his plate and brought it over to the table. It was round, and they all sat. Akira went to the fridge, offering them drinks.

"I'll take a beer," Carter said.

"None for me," Lennon told them. She hadn't eaten yet, and was surprisingly hungry.

Carter cracked his beer and took a sip. "Why isn't Jess around? This is crazy."

Once they were all seated again, everyone stared at Lennon, anticipating an explanation. "Look, I don't know who Jess is. They brought me in and told me they needed a co-pilot for a supply run to Mars."

"Right. The greenhouse." Carter talked with his mouth stuffed full of the burger. "I don't buy it."

"You don't think we're going to Mars?" Akira had a sandwich and a salad, and handed half over to Lennon without asking.

"It's strange," Liu said, poking at his bowl. "My wife spoke with David's wife the other day. Katy was asking if I'd been scooped up by men in black suits as well."

"Seriously?" Carter asked. "Why does David get all the action?"

"Because he's the commander, and you're too busy trying to make dogs to talk to cats," Zasha said with a straight face.

"Hey, that patent would be worth... enough to buy and sell this place a few times over!"

"If you buy *and* sell it, and then buy again, the money goes in a circle. Not so impressive," Zasha quipped.

"Guys. What about the mission?" Lennon felt like she was back home, working with a team already. There was always the young kid, the cocky muscle-bound one, the smart doctor with a quick smile. For a second, she wondered what they saw when they studied their friend's replacement. A cranky woman with a penchant for punching people?

"We're going to learn in..." Carter tapped his watch, and the time projected out an inch from the screen. "Thirty minutes."

Lennon was nervous. She'd been told they weren't traveling to Mars, but didn't want the crew to learn she had more intel than they did. She'd already said too much with Commander Bryce.

She ate the tuna salad, and watched the others interacting. They were like a family. No doubt they hadn't seen one another in a few months, but they slid right back in, talking as if no time had passed.

"So, Akira, did your parents give you their blessing?" Liu asked the young Japanese girl. She looked about eighteen, but Lennon knew from her bio that she was almost twenty-five.

Akira shook her head slowly, and set the corner of her sandwich on the plate. "My father offered me an executive role at Holo."

Lennon hadn't read up on their history beyond the basic bios. Her dad worked for Holo? It was one of the top five largest corporations in the world.

"I'd have snatched that up in a second," Carter said. "Speaking of, can you call him and see if you can get me that position? Imagine what I could do with that kind of R and D funding!"

"No one needs to talk with a seagull, Carter," Zasha told him.

"Come on, you don't want to know..."

The door slammed wide, interrupting them. Two armed soldiers entered, waving them to exit. "The commander is ready." The woman's gun rested at her chest.

"Since when did we require guns to take us to a briefing?" Liu whispered to Zasha.

They both glanced at Lennon. "Hey, I'm just as confused by this as you are."

She turned to leave with the crew, satisfied meeting them went as smoothly as it had. Her pack was still on the floor, and that meant her Holo was inside. She turned back and quickly rummaged through the bag, pocketing the device.

Lennon caught sight of her reflection in a mirror on the wall as she straightened, and she hesitated, feeling suddenly out of place. She was no longer a mechanic at a hole-in-the-wall airfield. Her life had meaning. But the gnawing worry that she would be forced into doing something horrible wouldn't subside.

SEVEN

D AVID STOOD AT THE lectern in a dusty old briefing room on sub-level B, waiting for the crew to arrive. The area was guarded by a sergeant and a corporal from Space Force. Seeing soldiers around ORB's facilities wasn't that unusual, but having their direct attention was. Someone was taking measures to ensure no classified information escaped these walls.

But those security measures might just be the tip of the iceberg. Right before coming here, he'd gone to speak with the mission coordinator, Sandra Wallace, to discuss Jess Rigel's replacement.

"I'm no happier about it than you are, Commander, but I wasn't given with a choice," Wallace said.

"Why was she replaced?" he'd asked.

"She was in an accident. Her EV's cameras malfunctioned, and it drove itself into the rear end of a fire truck."

David blinked in shock. *"She didn't tell me anything about it."*

"It only happened a few days ago. She broke her leg in two places and fractured her ribs. She's still in the hospital recovering from surgery."

"What about her backup?"

"She's pregnant."

"You're joking."

"I wish I were."

"Isn't that a breach of her contract?"

"A breach of contract to get pregnant?"

"I mean, to surprise us with the news."

"She's only three weeks and she just found out herself. Besides, she's only the second-stringer for a mission that launches in six months, so she probably thought it wasn't that urgent to notify mission control. We're actually lucky that Miss Baxter was available, and that she happens to have the required training."

David scowled at the memory of that conversation. *Lucky.* That wasn't David's assessment. A car's cameras happened to malfunction, and then a surprise pregnancy conveniently took out Jess's replacement. Now he was saddled with a complete stranger for a co-pilot on a mission that could actually determine the fate of the entire human race. It didn't seem like a coincidence to him. Whoever Lennon Baxter was, David knew she wasn't here by accident. Someone had *chosen* her for this mission.

The door to the briefing room opened, and a female Space Force lieutenant breezed in, leading a familiar group of men and women sporting blue mission uniforms. She peeled off to the side, allowing them to proceed between the rows of seats before exiting the room herself. David heard the door shut and lock behind them. A few of his crew glanced over at the sound of the bolt sliding into place.

"An armed escort and now we're in lockdown?" Carter quipped from the middle of the group. He always was the talkative one.

David's gaze swept over his crew as they continued down the aisle: Liu Teng from China in the lead, the mission biologist and doctor; followed by Zasha Petrov from Russia, the mission physicist and chemist; then Carter Robinson from the UK, their systems engineer and linguist; the flight engineer, Akira Mori from Japan; and finally, Lennon Baxter, his new co-pilot. She stood out as the one piece that didn't fit in an otherwise perfectly harmonious unit.

David stepped from the podium to greet them in order of their arrival. Liu nodded to him. "Commander."

They briefly hugged. "Doctor. It's good to see you again."

"Likewise, sir." Liu went to take a seat in the front row.

Zasha came next. She smiled and pulled him in for a bear hug and a kiss on the cheek. "It has been too long!"

He withdrew with eyebrows raised. "Or not long enough, depending how you look at it."

"Yes. You will have to fill us in on that."

Zasha sat beside Liu.

Carter came next, and offered his elbow instead of his hand. David smirked as they knocked bones together.

"Hygiene first, Commander."

Zasha arched a dark eyebrow at him. "Whatever any of us have, we'll all be getting it soon."

"Is that a proposition?" Carter asked as he took the seat next to her.

"I'm an engaged woman, Mr. Robinson."

"Engaged, not married," he pointed out.

Zasha snorted and crossed her arms over her chest.

Akira bowed her head, and David returned her customary Japanese greeting.

Then came Lennon Baxter. He tried to stifle his reaction with a smile, but it felt too tight and artificial. "Have a good lunch, Miss Baxter?"

"Yes," she replied.

He gestured to the far end of the row, where the others had left an empty seat. Lennon was forced to walk by them all to the end and sit beside Doctor Teng.

David returned to the podium, but rather than use the touchscreen in the lectern to dim the lights and operate the screen behind him, he moved to the edge of the stage and sat down.

"This is an interesting briefing," Zasha said.

"Are we in trouble, Commander?" Akira asked. Her face didn't even wrinkle as her eyebrows slowly elevated. The blessings of youth.

"No. Not that kind of trouble."

"Would you care to elaborate?" Carter asked.

David's gaze scanned the five faces before him. "What have you heard about the mission's timeline being changed?"

"Only what was on the news," Liu put in. "You, telling everyone about the problems with the agri-dome."

"That's the official story that we're authorized to give to the public."

"Okay..." Carter trailed off, scratching a hand through his prematurely gray hair. "Then what's the real version?"

David sucked in a deep breath, but before he could let it out to begin summarizing everything he'd learned in Washington, the door buzzed and the locking bolt slid away. Everyone twisted around in anticipation, and David found himself frowning as an unfamiliar man and woman stepped in. The woman was Chinese, the man possibly an American. Both were wearing civilian clothes, but the man had a military bearing.

David rose to his feet and came to attention as they descended the aisle. "May I help you with something?"

The door sealed behind them.

"At ease, Commander," the American said as he approached. "Have you briefed your crew yet?"

David slowly shook his head. "I was just about to."

"No need. I'll take it from here," the man said. "Kamar Jackson, Mission Director."

Another replacement? "What happened to Sandra Wallace?" David asked.

"She's still in command, but only until you reach orbit. After that, you'll be communicating directly with me."

David spent a moment studying Kamar. He had dark skin and a shaved head, and looked to be somewhere in his fifties. A no-nonsense expression and the intensity in his eyes only served to confirm his possible military background.

Kamar turned to the others while the Chinese woman went to the lectern and began setting up a presentation on the screens behind the podium. In that exact moment, five different Holos buzzed and dinged with messages, and everyone reached for their pockets.

"Those are your NDAs. Read them, sign them, and we'll begin."

Glowing screens appeared.

"Project Iris?" Carter asked after a moment. The others quickly swiped through reams of text that were probably boilerplate copies of what David had already signed in Washington.

"What is this?" Zasha asked, looking up and shaking her head.

"It is your passport to this mission. If you refuse to sign it, we'll have you replaced."

"Like Jess?" Carter asked.

"She was replaced for personal reasons," Kamar replied.

"Her broken leg, yes," Liu added, stroking his chin.

"I'll give you all a minute to read," Kamar said, and then he raised his holowatch. An old-fashioned clock face projected in the air, and he stared unblinkingly at it. He was literally watching the second hand tick.

Everyone continued scanning their agreements. David noticed that Lennon Baxter was the first to sign. He wondered if that meant something. Had she been briefed in advance like him? He had a lot to learn about his new first officer.

"Fifteen seconds." Kamar frowned. "There's the door, for anyone who needs it."

"You're bluffing," Zasha said.

"Try me. We have at least a dozen replacements for each of you, who'd jump at the chance to join this mission."

"For a year-long slog to Mars and back?" Carter quipped.

"Three seconds…"

David frowned as his crew rushed to sign the documents. None of them could've had the chance to read what they were agreeing to.

"Glad to have you aboard. Now, let's begin. Commander Bryce, you may take a seat."

David gave in with a nod and found a seat across the aisle from Lennon.

The screen behind the podium was already displaying a familiar image: the sleek, T-shaped visual of the unidentified vessel.

"What is that?" Carter asked.

Kamar went to stand beside his Chinese colleague. "This is Professor Chang. She's the astronomer from the Tiangong 3 who captured this anomaly."

Chang cleared her throat and pointed to the image. "This is your mission objective. Twenty-four million kilometers from Earth. Two and a half kilometers long. Code-named the *Interloper*."

Carter jumped to his feet. "Are we being punked?" He glanced at the door, as if checking for a camera crew, then gestured at the screen. "That's a fake. It has to be."

"Sit *down*, Mr. Robinson," Kamar intoned.

"It was only a matter of time," Zasha whispered.

"We've checked the data a hundred different ways. It's no fake."

"Is it coming toward us?" Liu asked quietly.

"No," Kamar said.

"This is first contact," Carter added. His jaw was slack with shock.

"Not yet," Kamar replied. "But it could be. The *Interloper* is in a decaying orbit." The picture zoomed out to display a top-down view of the inner planets and the sun, along with their orbital lines. The *Interloper* was highlighted, and a line appeared to indicate its trajectory. Chang tapped a button on her Holo and the static image came to life, with planets following their orbits and the unknown vessel following its own course in a lazy arc toward the sun. "To the naked eye, it was aimlessly drifting until it was captured by our sun's gravity. The object is currently passing through its close approach with Earth, and it will begin accelerating away from us, the nearer it gets to the sun."

Another icon with an arcing trajectory emerged, this one identified on the screen as the *Beyond III*. "This is your flight path," Chang said. "It will take three months and nine hours to reach your target. Just before you arrive, you'll have to turn around and fire the thrusters in reverse to match velocities."

David noticed that the intercept point was located halfway along the *Interloper's* path with the sun, and it didn't look like it was destined to make several orbits. It was on a direct collision course.

Chang paused the simulation as the *Beyond III* reached the *Interloper*. The remainder of the unidentified ship's route began flashing in red, and a series of numbers popped up beneath the curved line.

"You'll have twelve days to investigate everything you can about the *Interloper* before departing."

Carter's eyes narrowed and he jerked his chin to the professor. "Why twelve days?"

"Fuel," Kamar put in. "It's going to take nearly all of our propellant to catch up to the target."

David frowned at that. "Then how do we return?"

"You're going to slingshot around Mercury."

"Mercury!" Carter exploded. "And I suppose before radiation exposure won't turn us into sterile cancer patients along the way."

"You'll spend most of your time in your quarters and the common areas of your ship, since they offer the most protection," Chang explained. "The radiation will remain within tolerable limits."

"How are we supposed to board the target?" Lennon asked, drawing looks from the rest of the crew.

"Or even dock with it?" David added, to deflect their attention from her. "The *Beyond* rockets were built to reach Mars orbit and drop single-use landers and modules to re-supply the colony. We're not equipped to link up with other vessels, much less ones that we didn't design."

"We've made some alterations to the clamps in the rear airlock," Kamar said. "Explosive bolts will fire diamond-tipped harpoons attached to cables that should anchor you to almost any object. Furthermore, a specially designed docking collar will attempt to make an airtight seal with the *Interloper* while you cut a hole in its hull. Our hope is that by preserving the atmosphere inside the target, we will be able to study the composition of the air on the other end. And if there *is* a live crew, they will surely appreciate us not exposing them to hard vacuum in a clumsy attempt to introduce ourselves."

Carter glanced at David, then Liu. "This is mad," he said. "You don't greet a superior species by cutting a hole in their ship and then boarding them like space pirates."

"He's right," Zasha added. "We could be perceived as hostile."

"We don't believe that to be the case," Kamar replied, shaking his head. "This vessel is almost certainly derelict. It's probable that it suffered irreparable damage and the crew abandoned it, leaving it to drift for untold eons until finally arriving here."

"You can't possibly know that," David said.

Kamar fixed him with a bland stare. "They wouldn't be on a collision course with our sun if a crew had active control of their vessel."

"There could be beings on board who don't have control of the ship."

"It is *possible*," Kamar admitted. "But the sheer distances across interstellar space, and the vessel's velocity, would indicate otherwise. At current speed it would take them more than three hundred years just to reach Alpha Centauri."

"Maybe their species lives for a thousand," Liu pointed out.

"It's all meaningless speculation," Kamar said. "But if you do meet a living crew, it will only add more value to your mission."

"Not if they kill us," Zasha whispered.

"There are too many things that could go wrong," Akira added in a louder voice.

"I agree," Liu added. "This flight plan puts us too close to the sun. The dangers to us and our ship will be multiplied."

Akira nodded. "*Beyond* wasn't built for it. Sensitive controls could overheat and begin malfunctioning. Life support, comms, the electronic guidance, you name it, we'll be risking a systems failure."

"Which is why you and Mr. Robinson will be present to make the necessary repairs if anything goes wrong," Kamar replied. "You're both highly qualified engineers, and you'll have all the necessary spare components at your disposal." He looked to Chang for support.

She set her mouth in a grim line and nodded. "You'll also dock to the aft end of the *Interloper* to use it as a shield for the duration of your rendezvous. This will help to safeguard you and your ship. Once aboard, we assume the sheer size of the alien vessel will protect you as well."

"That will only work *while* we're docked," Akira objected. "What happens on approach or departure? We'll be completely exposed."

"*Beyond III* and its systems have been carefully secured for that very reason," Kamar interjected.

"For a flight to Mars, not to the sun!"

"You mentioned fuel capacity," Zasha stated. "How far will Mercury be from Earth when it's time for our return trip?"

"Just over ninety-six million kilometers," Chang replied. "Which is almost the same distance as the original re-supply mission was supposed to travel to reach Mars in six months' time."

"Convenient," Carter muttered.

"Hardly," Kamar replied. "We've been planning this operation for the past four months."

"Four *months?*" Zasha exploded. "Then why are we only hearing about it now?"

David raised his eyebrows at that. He was wondering the same thing. *They've been sitting on this for four months?* He couldn't even begin to imagine how much work it must have been to keep the discovery of the *Interloper* out of the news. Then again, the clearest images had come from China, not the US, and they were experts at suppressing information.

"You didn't need to know then. Now you do," Kamar explained.

"Any further questions?" Professor Chang added in a high, cracking voice.

Everyone raised their hands at the same moment, all except for David and Lennon. He shot her an inquiring glance, and she shrugged. Apparently, she was content not to ask anything else. Was that because she'd already been privy to the answers?

"Carter." Kamar pointed to him.

"Do we have a plan to communicate if we encounter a living crew?"

"That's where your research comes in," Kamar replied.

"Aha."

"Yet another reason why being told sooner would have been helpful," Zasha muttered, dropping her hand to her lap.

"Doctor Liu," Kamar said. David realized he must be versed in Chinese culture to address him that way. The crew all called him Doctor Teng, or just Liu, a common American mistake. Teng was actually his first name, not his surname, since the Chinese reversed the order of their names.

"What precautions will we be taking to prevent contamination of the alien ship with our microbes, or vice versa?"

Kamar launched into a lengthy explanation about safety protocols, as well as UV lamps and chemical sprays that they'd installed in the aft airlock of the *Beyond III*.

David leaned back in his seat and crossed his arms, listening as his crew fired off a dozen more questions and received a variety of semi-satisfying answers from Kamar and Chang. They'd thought of most everything that could go wrong, but that did nothing to dispel the growing sense of unease in David's gut.

No matter how much new tech they added or how many times they crunched the numbers on trajectories, intercepts, and delta-v, at the end of the day, they were going to intercept an *alien* vessel, and there was simply no way to prepare for what they might find once they reached it.

EIGHT

Eastern Kazakhstan

T HE TRAIN RATTLED AND shook on the tracks. This was Atlas' first experience with this rail, and it would hopefully also be his last. He found it was much simpler to use this mode of transportation than a flight. His Karl Sidorov ID had passed muster with the service counter, and that would keep his trail cool. For a time.

He watched the desolate landscape roll by without really seeing any of the details. Atlas was preoccupied with his adventure. Life hadn't always been so hectic, and there were a lot of days when he longed for that previous existence.

Atlas recalled being a student at Cornell, and how much it had meant to his father when that acceptance letter came. He missed him, but suppressed any further memories. It made him spiral into a bad place, and he wanted to stay focused.

He first saw a piece of the relic when he was ten years old. His dad had returned from Malaysia with it enveloped in an old worn sweatshirt, and handed it to Atlas, as if it was a substitute for a souvenir he forgot to purchase.

Atlas smiled while he stared out the window. He remembered unwrapping the cloth, and seeing the black metal. Feeling the rough, almost Braille-like patterns on the material. He'd asked what it was, and his father had only shrugged. "Probably from the war."

At the time, he'd had no idea what war his father was referring to. His life changed the moment he touched the relic. Because that's what it was. A piece of history, only of our own. He had another piece in his bag, currently stowed beneath his seat, and he was surer than ever that they belonged to an alien ship.

One of the train staff came around and asked him if he'd like another drink. He glanced at the empty glass, and nodded, sliding it to her. Her gaze lingered on him, and his pulse quickened until he realized she was probably just bored. This was a lengthy ride, thirty-six hours from start to finish, and he wished it would hurry up.

Aliens. His fascination had started on that day, when he was only ten years old, and now he was obsessed. He'd only attended college to appease his father, but when he'd died during Atlas' sophomore year, he didn't see the point in keeping up the charade. He'd dropped out, taken his inheritance, and started his own company.

But being the treasure hunter for hire wasn't as lucrative as it had once been, and it didn't help that he was off in search of parts of the lost vessel. The first piece was from Malaysia, and the second found near Croatia. The logistics didn't add up. He required more information to continue. He'd already done his circuits in the Gulf of Thailand, trying to learn when or where the ship had crashed. That had wasted three years of his youth and most of his savings account, and he couldn't afford to do it again.

Atlas smiled at the woman handing him the drink. Vodka on the rocks. Not his preferred choice, but when in Rome. A man with the last name Sidorov asking for a California Red might stand out like a sore thumb. He said thank you, keeping his Russian to a minimum, lest he give his terrible accent away.

He decided to check on the bag under his seat for the fifth time since the journey began, and found the artifacts where he'd left them. Atlas scanned through the train car, but none of the other guests were paying any attention to him.

He grabbed his holotab and brushed the surface clean. Bits of dust clung to the clear screen, and he wiped it, seeing the indicator light. He glanced around and opened the program. It was from his contact at ORB. Sarah was a terrific woman. She'd almost convinced him to settle down, without even asking him to give up his obsession with uncovering life on other planets. In the end, he'd done the proper thing and broken it off. This was better for both of them. Now she was married, and he suspected far happier than waiting for him to come home from yet another excursion.

S – *I saw the plans for the new mission. You're never going to believe it.*

He sat patiently, looking at the screen. After a full minute, he typed a response.

A – *Do tell*

... She was typing.

S – *You know how much trouble I'll be in if I share this with a civvie?*

A – *It's me. I won't tell a soul. Cross my heart.*

S – *Delete this as soon as you get it. The frequencies are unidentifiable.*

Atlas wondered what the hell she was talking about when the image surfaced. It showed the trajectory plan for *Beyond III*, and he grabbed his drink, swallowing it all.

A – *There's no destination.*

S – *It's there. The emittance is constant.*

Atlas finally understood what she was saying. "It's not from Earth. Or a rock." He said it out loud.

A – *Are you telling me this is alien?*

...

He paused while she typed, but the dots vanished after a few moments.

A – *Talk to me.*

Nothing.

He tried again, but received an error in response. "Damn it." Sarah might have been caught sharing information. Perhaps it was an issue with the satellites routing his message from the corner of nowhere Kazakhstan as they neared the western border of China.

The map revealed the path of *Beyond III* from Earth to an empty pocket of space. There wasn't anything near it. Mars was a fair distance from its orbit, moving away from this spot. Why would an alien ship be sitting dormant? If it was truly emitting frequencies, why hadn't the entire world heard about this yet?

He checked the newsfeeds, finding only a few remote passages detailing ORB's expedited mission. This was old news again. There was nothing sexy and riveting about rushing a launch to help with a faulty greenhouse. That didn't sell subscriptions or advertising.

Atlas was wound up, and decided to have a coffee while the sun set. He stayed up, trying to make a contingency plan should this lead end up smoke and mirrors.

By the time the dawn struck again, he'd managed a couple hours of sleep, and his neck ached from the seats. He could have used a private room, but preferred to keep tabs on his surroundings. The train made a single stop before its final destination of Beijing, and that's where Atlas exited. One other man left at the same time, getting off at Bayannur.

For China the city was small, but Atlas knew that was relative. In the States it would have been overpopulated. When the man was greeted by a young woman holding a baby on her chest, he relaxed.

The buyer's address was about an hour's drive north, near a village adjacent to the Mongolian border. Atlas decided to stay a night in the city, and found a nondescript hotel. It was quiet during the lull of the midweek traffic, and he slept soundly until four AM.

In the morning, he wandered the streets as he waited for a few shops to open. He purchased an assortment of local clothing, finding it well made but slightly small for his 6'1" stature. Freshly showered, with provisions in his hand, Atlas flagged down a taxi driver. They haggled a bit, and it was the usual story. Too far out. Not worth the gas. But he finally settled on a price, and they started off.

Atlas had the feeling this was a colossal waste of time, but with the possibility that there might be an alien vessel near Earth, it seemed imperative to follow the lead. He sat in the back of the old car and rolled the window open. It was stuffy, smelling like the old man's body odor. The landscape changed as they exited the city, leaving the bustle of traffic, which was replaced by narrow roads and green hills.

Fields of crops passed along beside them, and the driver slowed to let a cow cross in front of the car. Eventually, the driver took him into a village, and he asked the man where the hotel was, using mostly a translation app and hand waving.

"No hotel."

Great. Atlas slung his pack over his shoulder and thanked the driver, giving him the rest of the promised amount, and almost shouted for him to return when he drove away.

He surveyed the town. It hung low in a valley, and despite the midmorning hour, a mist clung to the rooftops. It looked old, as if the village had defied change for hundreds of years, refusing to be replaced.

The house was a half mile to the north, and that's where Atlas intended to go. Instead he turned into town, using his pent-up energy to stalk down the gravel road.

He would stick out here, a white man with a brown pack on his shoulder, walking around aimlessly.

He needed to find a home base, and then do some investigating. Petar had thought this address would lead him to the man who'd sent goons to gather the artifacts. Could it be so simple? Would Atlas find the answers he'd been seeking in this desolate village? He suddenly felt so far removed from the rest of the world, and took a breath before heading to the only market he could find.

He put on a smile, and used his best Mandarin to ask if any lodging was possible.

As it turned out, the store's proprietor, a grizzled old man named Hu, was willing to rent him a room for what seemed like a hefty sum. Atlas paid him easily, and settled into the basic space: a musty cot with a nightstand and a lamp.

Atlas left his belongings, but slid the pieces of the alien ship into his jacket pocket. He borrowed Hu's truck, for another payment, driving it toward the mysterious address, and stopped one property over. These houses were remote, with open rice fields between them.

He used a scope, finding a car parked outside the home. Someone lived there. He'd need to wait for an opening. The vehicle was fancy, an expensive import, and that spoke volumes in the remote area.

Atlas lingered for an hour, but found no signs of life.

Eventually he returned to town, ready to devise a plan of attack.

NINE

D AVID SAT ON THE foot of his bed in his quarters at the ORB Starbase, wearing a VR band around his forehead. His Holo leaned on a wardrobe in front of him so that the camera could relay his end of the call. The blank screen on the VR band quickly resolved into a familiar scene: the living room in his home in St. Ann filled his entire field of view, making it seem as if he was right there with them.

"Daddy!" Rachel cried, jumping up from the couch and running to the projection of him on her end. Her arms passed through him like a ghost's, swiping empty air. She frowned and peered up at him. "I wish you were really here."

"I know. Me too, sweetie," David said, standing up. He mimed cupping her cheek, and mostly succeeded in keeping his hand from passing through her face.

Kate and Mark walked up to him until the four of them were standing face to face, in a virtual sense. The illusion wasn't perfect, with the holograms projected below the holobands being slightly translucent rather than opaque, but it was as close as they could come to being in the same room together without anyone getting on an airplane.

"So this it is," Kate said. "You're leaving tomorrow?"

David nodded. "At oh nine hundred."

Kate tried a smile, but it crumbled as one corner of her mouth twitched. He reached out for her, and they held hands the best that two ghosts could. If he'd invested in haptics to go along with the VR bands, they could have done better than that intangible last touch, but he hadn't seen the point of spending the money when real-time communication wouldn't even be possible while he was in space.

"You'll still only be gone for fourteen months?" Kate asked.

He nodded. "Give or take a month."

Now that the mission parameters had changed, all bets were off, but Kamar Jackson had assured them that the distance for the return trip wouldn't be much greater than the original flight from Mars. Assuming the way there didn't take more than three months, they would have a nearly identical turnaround, even though they were flying to the *Interloper*, not Mars, and then to Mercury and back. But he couldn't tell his family the truth because of the secretive Project Iris details. He hated lying to them.

Mark scowled and looked away.

"Hey, buddy. It's not that long," David assured him.

"It's more than a year!"

He shifted sideways to stand in front of his son. Rachel burst into tears and retreated to her mother's side.

David winced and focused on Mark. He dropped to his haunches. "Look at me."

Mark's head slowly turned. "What?"

"When I'm back, I'll make up for it. I'll have a whole year off. We just had six months! If I had another job, I'd be working every day instead of staying home with you guys."

"But I'm at school while you're there. We won't have any extra time."

"We will. I'll make sure of it. Maybe we'll get you to call in sick and hit the ballfield. How would they know, right?"

"Miss Abbot will ask for a note from the doctor."

"A little piece of paper? No problem. I can take care of that."

Mark smiled playfully at that.

Kate was giving him a disapproving glare, but he ignored it. She wasn't going to pick a fight with him over bending the rules to spend more time with his kids.

"Come on, buddy, group hug." He guided Mark back to his mother and Rachel, then wrapped his arm around the three of them.

"I'll be home before you know it. I love you all so much."

Rachel was sniffling loudly. David withdrew and looked his wife straight in the eyes. She was crying now, the tears sliding silently down her cheeks.

He leaned in as close as he dared. Her lips moved against his, so close and real, but impossible to touch. Yet he could have sworn that he felt that kiss.

He waved to them. "I'll send you a message every day."

Kate nodded and smiled wincingly.

Rachel broke free of her mother's grip and ran away crying.

"Rachel, come here this instant!" Kate called after her.

David felt his heart shatter into a thousand pieces, but he shook his head and said, "It's okay. Let her be." Rachel disappeared around the corner, and he heard her footsteps echoing on the stairs.

Mark and Kate waved. "Promise you'll come home safe," she said.

"I will. I promise."

They said their last *I-love-you's*, and then the screen vanished, leaving him staring at a blank wall. David turned and walked to his bed, pulled off his boots, and sat with his palms on his knees.

He *would* return, and the mission would be a success. If not for the world, for his family's sake.

Turning his head, he gazed out at the distant, gleaming spire of the *Beyond III*. His room had a clear view of the launch pad. It resembled a skyscraper, standing alone against the dark canvas of a flat, uninhabited landscape, and gleaming in the lights of the bare metal framework of the elevator platform that would carry him and the rest of his crew up to the cockpit tomorrow morning.

Godspeed, he thought.

***

The ORB personnel shuttle pulled to a stop at the safety fence around the launch pad. The gate rattled as it opened, remote-activated by someone at a security station in the launch facility. They drove on through to the platform and the *Beyond III*.

A sense of history in the making thickened the air. No one spoke, not even Carter, and he was almost always running his mouth off about something.

The shuttle stopped at the landing pad, and the doors slid open automatically. David exited first, lugging his duffel bag full of personal effects, followed by Lennon, who was traveling much lighter with nothing but a small backpack. They'd donned their spacesuits already—sleek white and black suits—their helmets on and the visors flipped up.

David took a moment to peer up at the massive rocket, shielding his gaze from the sun with one hand. Clouds of steam were boiling out of the bleeder valves in the sides of the ship. The liquid oxygen and hydrogen in the fuel tanks was warming up, and without those valves to release the pressure, the tanks would explode.

"It doesn't seem possible for an object that big to lift off," Lennon said.

David regarded her with a knowing look. He'd had the same feeling on his debut flight. At seventy-five meters tall, the *Beyond III* was as high as a twenty-three-story building.

Carter whistled as he jumped out. "There she is!"

"Why must the ship be a she?" Zasha replied, arching an eyebrow at him.

"Ships are always female," he said.

"You *do* know what it looks like, don't you?" she countered.

Carter feigned ignorance, blinking stupidly at her. "What are you implying?"

"Kind of like a... never mind."

"I'm going into space with children," Liu muttered, approaching them with his helmet tucked under one arm.

"Enough chatter. Get your heads in the game," David growled.

"Yes, sir," Carter replied.

David waited for Akira to join them, and then led the way across the tarmac to the naked steel framework of the elevator platform.

A dozen fuel trucks went whirring by in a convoy, racing toward the fence, with the personnel shuttle leading the charge. The launch platform was about to be blasted with enough heat to melt glass, so it had to be completely evacuated.

David held the gate of the elevator platform open and then slid it shut behind them.

"Going up," Carter said as he worked the controls.

Halfway to their destination, David's comms crackled to life with Sandra Wallace's voice. "Mission control to Commander Bryce. What's your status?"

"This is Bryce. We're approaching the tower now."

"Good. We're at T-minus thirty to launch."

"Copy that, control."

The ground fell away below. The fuel trucks dwindled to specks, and the gleaming line of water on the horizon grew until it became a shining blue canvas. The elevator reached the top of the tower, and this time Carter opened the gate.

"Ladies first," he said, nodding to Lennon.

She led them down the catwalk to the nearest airlock. David hurried off the elevator platform and, at the edge of the vessel, he placed his hand against a particular panel in the gleaming silver hull. It popped out, and he grabbed hidden handles to crank it around a hundred eighty degrees and unlock the hatch. Heavy bolts slid aside, and then he pulled it open.

Ducking to enter the ship, David went straight to the inner door and triggered it via the control panel. It hissed and then swung wide. He turned and waved to the others before continuing into the ship. The airlock led directly to a circular deck with a hole through the center for access to the storage area below. Their cargo was secured in sealed compartments that could be independently ejected when they arrived at Mars. A narrow access tunnel ran by those cargo compartments to the engineering section and the fuel tanks at the aft end of the ship.

"T-minus twenty-five," Wallace announced, her voice now booming through the vessel's speakers.

David continued around the cargo area until he came to the rungs of a ladder clamped directly to the gunmetal gray walls. The ladder led to an overhead hatch. He slung his duffel onto his shoulders and climbed the rungs, turned the lever, and pushed on the hatch. Clinging awkwardly to the ladder with one hand, he shrugged out of his duffel and shoved it in front of him.

He emerged in the crew compartment, surrounded by twelve doors, only six of which would be used. Those openings led to their sleeping quarters, while the spaces between were fitted with workstations, mission supplies stacked behind cargo webbing, and lab equipment.

David glanced up. The rungs of the ladder continued past three more rings of doors to another hatch. Matching ladders on three other sides gave access to the various compartments. During colony missions, these would be bunkrooms, but since this was technically a supply mission, those areas had been re-configured to carry additional cargo. Now that the objectives had changed, they were being used to carry all manner of equipment that could come in handy aboard an alien vessel. They had everything from breach tools to firearms, which he hoped to God they wouldn't need.

David went straight to his room, behind the door with the glowing number 001 on the digital panel. Inside was a narrow bed beneath a porthole, drawers below the bed, a few storage compartments in the walls, and a small sitting area beside another porthole. That space had a separate entrance, so it could be configured with a collapsible room divider to create another private sleeping area.

"T-minus twenty minutes," the speakers boomed.

Opening his closet, David hurriedly stuffed his duffel bag in and strapped it below a rack of ten spare flight uniforms. He turned and exited his cabin to see everyone busy packing their things into their quarters. Liu was already done and shutting the door to his compartment so he could strap in for launch.

David crossed the deck to the main access ladder. Lennon made her way up ahead of him to the common space.

He followed her, spotting a door to one of the ship's two bathrooms to his left, and a food storage compartment to his right. He crawled through the hatch after Lennon and into the communal area. This level was devoted to a combination of recreation and mess areas, exercise equipment, quiet spots for reading or listening to music, and two green rooms to grow fresh vegetables and fruit, as well as more compartments for food containers. The crew could easily gather here to pass their free time. A few workstations were also crammed in between meal prep areas to augment the ones on the deck below.

David followed Lennon's lead towards the bridge. She opened the final hatch, and they both crawled through into a cramped space with just two seats, one for him and one for Lennon. They were at the top of the cavity, making it necessary to climb *up* into them.

"T-minus fifteen minutes," Wallace intoned.

Lennon took her seat and lay down. She secured herself in, and her hands began flying across the controls and touch screens arrayed around the co-pilot's seat. David went next, strapping in and then booting up his station. Displays glowed to life all around him. The three primary ones showed a clear view of bright blue sky and scattered clouds. It was a direct feed from the cameras in the nose of the ship.

"Comm check," David said, activating the comms with one hand, and simultaneously checking on the rest of the crew via internal camera feeds on his left display. Liu, Carter, Zasha, and Akira were all strapped into their beds and busy working on the screens above their heads.

"Reading you loud and clear, Commander," Wallace replied.

Carter flipped a bird at the camera. "I know you're watching, you pervert," he said over the intercom.

David smiled and shook his head. "We are all positioned and ready for launch, control."

"Copy that. We're at T-minus twelve."

"Lennon?" David asked. "Systems check."

"Air quality nominal. Carbon scrubbers functioning. Fuel supply lines are clear..."

"Fuel weight?"

"One point two one two million kilograms, pressure values nominal, vents open, all filters and shut-offs nominal, hatches and cargo secured."

"Copy that," David said, reaching for his primary display. He flicked over to the ship's engineering panel to check the systems for himself. Scrolling down the list, only one item was flagged by the internal diagnostics.

"What is it?" Lennon asked, her brow furrowing with concern. Her visor was up, so he could still see her face.

Rather than answer her, he activated his comms. "Uh, mission control, I'm reading a problem with the emergency shut-off valve in bay twelve of the stage four booster."

"Stand by, Commander. We're looking into it."

"Standing by."

A moment later, Wallace returned. "Flight says it's non-critical. Probably a faulty sensor. Mission and countdown are still a go. Swing arm is retracting."

"Copy that, control."

Lennon waggled her eyebrows at him, and he pointed to the diagnostic report on the faulty shut-off valve.

Lennon nodded mutely. "I don't know how I missed that."

"The primary systems logger doesn't identify tertiary emergency systems. You have to open the full diagnostics."

David switched the screen back to the forward cameras and pulled up the mission clock. It was ticking down to five minutes.

"T-minus five," Wallace said a moment later.

"Copy." David closed his eyes and worked to regulate his breathing, slow and steady... the smiling faces of Kate and kids flashed through his mind's eye, calming him.

David blinked his lids open and focused on the launch prep.

"Stage four pressurized," Lennon announced. "Closing the vents for three."

David nodded.

"Third stage pressurized," Lennon added a few seconds later.

"T-minus one minute," Wallace put in.

"Stage two pressurized," Lennon said. "Closing the vents for the primary…"

"Thirty seconds and counting," Wallace added.

"What's the hold up?" Carter asked. "It's not like this is rocket science or something."

"Shut up, Carter," Zasha replied.

"T-minute ten seconds. Begin ignition sequence!"

"Ignition sequence started," David added as he flicked the switches to ignite the engines. A building roar came rumbling through the ship, and everything began to shake and rattle around them.

"Five, four, three…"

The roar reached a crescendo, and then a gut-sucking surge of acceleration pinned him to the back of his seat.

"And liftoff! At forty-two minutes past the hour," mission control cried.

"Roger. Clock set," David said, and punched the button to reset the countdown. It began counting up to mark the time elapsed past launch.

He glanced at Lennon as the mighty rocket rattled and tore into the sky. Her visor was secure, so he couldn't see her face. "She's going to shake herself to bits," Lennon said.

"She can take it."

Comms blared with mission control and flight, relaying velocity, altitude, pitch, and the execution of the different stages of the rocket. He conducted the pitch and roll maneuver to set their heading.

And before he knew it, the bright blue veil of sky faded to black and a bright swatch of stars appeared.

Lennon sucked in a sharp breath.

"Your first time in space?"

She slowly opened her mouth to speak, but no words came out. She tried again. "I can't…"

"I was speechless too," he said.

David reached over and keyed up the view from the aft cameras in the stabilizer fins. Earth appeared, vanishing far below. The bright blue of the oceans was draped in white swirls of cloud, with a few scraps of brown and green for land.

"It looks so…"

"Beautiful?"

Lennon just nodded.

TEN

Beyond III, Earth's Orbit

L ENNON HAD HEARD OF the term "overview effect," where an astronaut experiences a cognitive shift when finally viewing their planet from space. Her attention was glued to the big picture, seeing the various aspects of the world in an altered sense: the spherical shape, the distorted haze of our atmosphere, and the masses of land surrounded by vast blue oceans.

She began to interpret specific details. Clouds. The greater United States, sandwiched between Canada and Central America. Suddenly borders made no sense to her. This world wasn't intended for strife and constant clashing. And just like that, she snapped out of it as an alarm sounded from the dash.

"Baxter, are you picking up on this?" Bryce's voice was calm, but there was something hidden beneath the words.

She checked the readouts. "It's fine. The booster's have been deployed, but we've encountered some ice buildup."

Beyond III moved with Earth's orbit, preparing for the thrusters to be ignited, and Lennon felt the lightness around her. She lifted into the strapping, aware of the lack of gravity. She wanted to unstrap and dash through the ship, floating in the vertical corridors, but she quashed the childish impulse.

"Carter, are you on this?" David Bryce asked, using the comms.

"Roger that, Commander. The ice has been removed. Melted. I have a system." Carter sounded like he was having fun.

"Baxter, proceed with the final ignition sequence," Bryce said.

Lennon watched the planet for another moment, enjoying the view, before following the order. "How many times have you been to Mars?"

"A few," he said.

"You don't like me much, do you?"

Bryce stared forward as his visor reflected the planet below. "I liked Jess. I don't know you."

Lennon silently said her goodbyes to Earth, having the distinct feeling she wasn't returning. They had to reach the *Interloper* and board and investigate the ship, using it as a shield from the radiation until they could slingshot around Mercury for the return to Earth. It was a fool's errand. She'd always considered herself to be bright, but maybe she wasn't. It had only taken a single conversation for her to fall in line with Dark Leader.

And when he eventually contacted her with her real mission, she knew she would carry out whatever he asked.

Lennon glanced at Bryce again, and started the countdown. "Ignition in ten..."

Atlas

Northern China

The old square tube television showed the image of *Beyond III* racing from Earth before cutting to a Chinese newscaster. They were featuring a story on Liu Teng, the crew's Chinese doctor. Atlas turned his focus onto his dinner. The bamboo was chewy, the dish overdone with salty fish sauce to hide the mediocrity of the food. The town had limited options, so he ate what he could find.

The restaurant was crammed into the back of a market, with thin walls and a tarp near the entrance that flapped in the wind. Atlas felt uneasy in the space, but if he wanted to track more portions of the relic, this was his only hope. A man and woman sat in silence near the kitchen, both of them sipping tea from small cups. Atlas guessed they were married. From his experience, all couples ended up like this. Nothing to talk about, nowhere to go. They just... existed.

Atlas' Holo buzzed in his jacket, and he pulled it free, finding that his cameras had been tripped. The luxury sedan cruised down the gravel road, away from the house he'd been observing. He dropped a bill on the table and dashed from the room, jumping into Hu's truck. Atlas was grateful to have borrowed the vehicle from the man providing him a place to sleep, but it stank and ran on gasoline. The engine sputtered as the key turned in the ancient ignition, but it worked. A minute later, Atlas was driving toward the empty house, taking the long way so he didn't cross paths with his target.

He slowed as he neared the home in question, his Holo chiming again as he set off one of his own cameras. Atlas turned, parking at the shoulder of the road another half a mile down on a farmer's dirt path. He checked behind him, ensuring the truck was concealed in the trees.

Atlas wasn't a stranger to clandestine missions, but rarely did he break into people's houses. In the case of

Mattia at Lake Como, he'd been invited. That was different enough in his mind. Plus, these men weren't hon-
ourable people. Whoever owned this house had hired
Petar and those goons to kill him for the artifact he'd
stolen from Mattia.

The house was unassuming, but far nicer than the rest
of the local structures. It was well maintained, two stories, with an upper balcony circling the entire front of the
home. The roof was curled at the corners in a traditional
design.

Atlas moved as fast as he could, and glanced up, seeing
the cameras here. It wouldn't matter. He'd be in and
out. The door was locked, but the second window was
unlatched. With a shove of the screen, he was inside.

Could another segment of the relic be attainable? His
entire body thrummed with nervous energy at the possibility. The main room was sparsely decorated, and it
only took Atlas a few minutes to search through the
drawers. Nothing of interest. He guessed the place had
been cleared out in a hurry. The kitchen was empty, just
a couple of take-out containers on the wooden counter-
tops.

Atlas rushed upstairs, checking the bedrooms. In the
main one, he found an office, probably converted from
a closet. The desk had no laptop or computer, but there
was a cord dangling from the edge, suggesting someone
had used a laptop recently. It wasn't dusty, meaning the
buyer was utilizing this place for business.

Atlas examined the desk and discovered a stack of old
printed photos. He thumbed through them, checking out
the window every few seconds. The perimeter remained
dark.

The pictures were random, family shots from decades
ago, but he paused on one. It showed a man presumably
with his son, holding up a large fish from the end of a

pole. It was the tattoo that caught his attention. Three dots in a triangle. It was the marking from the artifact.

Atlas set the photo aside and went through the rest, hesitating on another. It was the same man, fresh-faced, wearing a white tank top and camo pants. He flipped it over, seeing the year scrawled in Chinese numbers.

– 1964

Another showed the guy with two other buddies in the jungle, their sleeves rolled up. They each had the tattoo on their forearms. Atlas checked the date, seeing it had been taken four years later.

He pocketed all three of the photos, and noticed another on the bottom of the drawer. It was newer, maybe twenty years ago. The image was of Petar's buyer, a much younger version of the man he'd seen driving away in the car from this very house, but what surprised him was the company he kept.

Atlas didn't know a ton about the military, but standing beside the buyer was a three-star general of the US Marine Corps. His target was in uniform: a US Marine captain. He snatched this one too, folding it, and shoved it next to the others.

There was nothing else of interest. The home wasn't fancy, and it barely looked lived in. Atlas assumed the original owner was the father, and he'd likely died, leaving it to the son, who'd held onto it all these years. But the tattoo was the most fascinating part. This buyer would be drawn to the artifact because of the connection to his father, as Atlas was. Their fathers had both served in Asia, only for different wars.

One thing was clear. They'd found something in Vietnam between the years of 1964 and 1968. It was up to Atlas to find out what.

He went to the hallway, and heard glass breaking. Atlas froze, listening for signs of pursuit, but only heard tires spinning and rocks shooting against the house's front porch. He sniffed, catching the rotten-egg smell of natural gas.

"Oh no," Atlas muttered, running to the nearest room. He saw taillights flash red as the car turned a few hundred yards away, and he attempted to pry the window open. The scent of burning reached the room, and a smoke alarm sounded from the main floor. He had only seconds before the gas from the stove reached a high enough concentration to explode.

The window was stuck. He looked around, grabbing an end table, and chucked it through the glass. Atlas jumped outside, and felt the tug of the jagged shards on his pants as they sliced his thigh. He didn't waste any time on the injury and slid down the black shingles, flipping his body to catch the gutter. It snapped free, and he plummeted the single story to the bushes below.

An explosion boomed, and flames burst out of the windows and onto the porch. Atlas fled as quickly as he could, sprinting from the home. He understood what came next. These guys wouldn't want him to escape alive. The cut on his leg hurt, but he pressed on, not willing to pause for a moment.

Instead of going to the road, he went behind the property as the ground shook violently. Another explosion threw Atlas to the dirt. He covered his head with his arms as shrapnel rained down. A minute later, he was climbing over a wooden fence, his feet covered in mud as he stumbled to the truck.

Atlas froze, half sitting in the driver's seat as he watched the building burn. They'd be looking for him. He tried to even out his breathing as he started the ignition, and drove the same route back to town, grateful for the cover of night. The village was quiet, and he kept the lights off.

Even so, he was going to stand out. Atlas drove to the far edge of town, climbing from the truck with a slight limp. He was glad he'd hidden the artifacts with the restaurant owner, instead of Hu.

The old man, Wei, sat on a rocking chair in front of his shack, humming a tune. Atlas sized up the place, ensuring they were alone.

He spoke to the man in his own language, slowly and without confidence. "Where are my things?"

"Where you left them," Wei replied.

Atlas went inside, opening a laundry basket lid, and pulled out his pack. "Thank you," he said, slipping the man a hefty sum. Wei's eyes went wide, and he hopped to his feet, patting Atlas on the back.

He momentarily considered ditching the truck, since it was identifiable, but decided it was his best means of escape. Four men stood with Hu, his lantern sending long shadows across the alley. Atlas' windows were rolled down, and he heard bits of their conversation. He did his best to translate.

"Where is he?"

"Not here."

"Where's his room?"

"In the back."

One man stayed with Hu, and Atlas saw the M7 in the Chinese guy's hands.

The others returned, shaking their heads, and Atlas cringed as the bullets rang out. Hu, his host, flailed his arms and fell to the street. Atlas saw the imported car and stayed in the truck, hidden in the dark alleyway, as the buyer got out and walked from the vehicle to the dead body. He spoke quickly, and Atlas couldn't make out his words. The others jumped into a white van and ripped after him.

Atlas remained where he was, not willing to move until he was sure they were gone. He stared at Hu while the neighbor lady ran to him, crouching near her friend. What could be so important about the relic in his pack? Or the piece he'd been given by his father? Atlas needed to figure it out before more people were sacrificed.

He threw the truck in gear, turned around, and descended the muddy side roads toward Bayannur, hoping not to encounter the armed men along the way. Atlas had a clue. A time period in Vietnam where young foreign soldiers had seen something they couldn't explain, and a Marine general that was inexplicably tied up with it. How did it all connect?

Atlas left the truck's lights off, letting the moon guide his passage. His gaze lingered through the cracked windshield and into the night sky. What was really going on in space, and why had *Beyond III* been launched early? He intended to find out.

He pressed the gas harder, knowing just the place to go. If there was one person who might help him lie low while he planned his next steps, it was Lawrence.

Atlas grabbed his Holo, almost sending a message to his old buddy, but stopped himself. A three-star general could be tracking his communications. He tossed the device onto the passenger seat, and kept driving.

ELEVEN

Beyond III

AFTER THE MAIN THRUSTERS ignited, David climbed from the bridge with Lennon to meet the others. The rest of the crew was already sitting in jump seats around the edges of the communal deck.

"Our course is set," David announced, jumping the last two rungs with an echoing *boom*. He reached up and twisted his helmet off, tucking it under his arm. "Acceleration is a steady one point five *G*s."

"Is that what that sinking feeling is in the pit of my stomach?" Carter asked. "I thought it was butterflies."

"Do we *need* to accelerate that quickly?" Liu asked, his face pinching with concern. "Prolonged exposure to excess *G*s will have certain effects on our bodily functions."

Carter arched an eyebrow at that. "Such as?"

"Constipation, for one."

"No worries, doc. I'll eat a few prunes."

"Please, don't," Zasha said.

"It's only for the next six hours while we accelerate to cruising speed," David assured them.

Carter made a show of leaning back in his seat and folding his arms behind his head. "Piece of cake."

David nodded.

Footsteps ringing lightly behind him signaled Lennon's approach. He turned to her as she removed her helmet.

Akira's quiet voice brought his attention the opposite direction. "I heard about the emergency shut-off valve in the stage four booster. Did you manage to fix it?"

David shook his head. "No."

"But we're using the fuel in the stage four booster," Akira added. "If something goes wrong, and that valve doesn't do its job, we'll be dead before we even realize what happened."

"It's one valve out of twelve. What are the odds that we have a problem in that fuel tank?" Carter asked.

David nodded. "Mission control determined it wasn't a serious enough issue to stop the launch, but now might be a good time to look into it from our end. Akira?"

She unstrapped from her jump seat. "I'll take a peek."

David watched as she crossed to the hatch in the deck and descended the ladder.

"What's our ETA?" Zasha asked.

"Three months, nine hours, and counting," Lennon supplied.

"Well, that's anticlimactic," Carter said, as though he was unfamiliar with the mission timeline. He slapped his knees and unbuckled, standing up from his jump seat. Arching his back languorously, he asked, "Who's hungry?"

Liu raised his eyebrows. "I could eat."

"Me, too," Lennon said.

Zasha shrugged. "May as well, since we have gravity to keep everything in its place."

David followed Carter to the meal prep area and opened a drawer labeled "breakfast," finding neat rows of vacuum-packed meals and snacks in transparent packets.

"What do we have here," Carter said. "Scrambled eggs and bacon."

"One for me," Liu said.

"Same," Lennon added.

David withdrew three of those meals, and proceeded to heat and add water to rehydrate the eggs. A few minutes later they had their meal trays strapped to their laps, utensils clasped into the foam holders on the edge, and juice packs open with straws sticking out.

Zasha chose yogurt and granola with a side of chopped fruit. Carter went with the scrambled eggs, but he added a packet of baked beans to his.

"You are determined to compromise our atmosphere," Zasha said, eyeing his beans.

"What about Akira?" Liu asked around a mouthful of scrambled eggs.

"She'll have to eat when she's done looking into the malfunction," David said.

Lennon watched them closely while they ate.

"Is something wrong, Miss Baxter?" Liu asked.

"No, not at all. It's been a whirlwind since I was assigned to this mission. I haven't really had a chance to get to know any of you yet."

"What do you want to find out? I'm an open book," Carter said.

Lennon appeared to hesitate. "Maybe I should go first."

David smiled. "It's a good idea. We'll each take turns and share a bit about ourselves."

Lennon nodded. "Okay. I'm single, thirty-two years old. I was working as an aircraft mechanic until I was assigned to this mission. I trained to be a helicopter pilot in the Air Force, and then I ended up directing drone strikes on targets from the safety of a bunker for the next eight years."

"Whoa, what was *that* like?" Carter asked.

Lennon shrugged. "About what you'd expect. A bit like playing a video game. Pull the trigger, see the burst of light, and chalk up another successful mission. It was clean, detached... bloodless. Hard to even feel guilty or bad about the kills. We didn't know the targets, who they were, or why they were being killed. They were just kill boxes on a screen."

"Is that why you were assigned to this mission? Because of your military connections?" David asked.

Lennon appeared to hesitate, then shrugged. "Maybe. I'm not sure. They didn't tell me why, or even give me much of a choice."

"About the same as the rest of us," Carter said while scraping beans from his tray.

"I'll go next," Liu said. "I am thirty-nine—"

Carter smirked. "You old fossil, you."

Zasha glared at him.

Liu went on, "I have a PhD in microbiology from Peking University. After that, I attained a scholarship for medical school in NYU, where I became a surgeon. I did my residence in Mount Sinai, then worked for seven years at New York Presbyterian."

"So how did you get to be an astronaut?" Lennon asked.

"Someone at ORB read my microbiology thesis. It was about convergent evolution. My team and I created an entirely synthetic multi-cellular organism, only to discover that it began to evolve similar characteristics to life already seen on Earth. The goal was to determine what extraterrestrial life might look like by creating it in a lab. In the end, we were forced to conclude that alien life could parallel what we have on Earth—at least, on a microscopic scale. Beyond that, we can only speculate."

"That's very interesting, Liu," Lennon said.

"He's all work and no play." Carter balled up a napkin, tossing it across the table.

Liu threw the garbage back. "I'll take that as a compliment."

"I didn't say it wasn't," Carter replied.

"Why don't you go next, Carter?" Zasha said. "I'm sure it will be a brief introduction."

"Don't count on it. I could go on for days about myself."

Zasha made a face.

"So much to tell..." Carter added with a grin.

"Let's stick to the bare bones," David said.

"Spoilsport. Fine. I'm thirty-one. Single. Have a kid, though. Robin. She's ten. The job keeps me away, but we see each other now and again. She took after me. Funny, smart, a real looker... charming, intuitive, a budding linguist like her—"

"We get it," Zasha interrupted.

"What? I'm bragging about my progeny, not myself."

"Actually, you're doing both," Zasha replied.

"All right, thank you, Carter," David added.

"I wasn't done yet. I'm the mission linguist and systems engineer. That means I'm fluent in both human and computer languages. My claim to fame was a machine that allowed dolphins to communicate with us, and vice versa. We used an underwater speaker and artificial calls to assign sounds to things that dolphins could relate to. They began to mimic the sounds we'd invented, and pretty soon we'd expanded their vocabulary to the point that we could actually have rudimentary conversations."

"And that was what made ORB ask you to become an astronaut?" Lennon asked.

"No, I asked them. But it didn't hurt to have *speaks Dolphin* on my resume."

Zasha went next. "I'm thirty-seven and engaged to be married. I was an astronaut for Roscosmos for six years before joining ORB. I've been up to the International Space Station twice, landed on the moon once, and I was with SVR RF for seven years before all of that, making things go boom. My daughter is twelve, and she lives with my mother in Saint Petersburg. Like Carter, my work keeps me away, but I do my best to visit as often as I can."

"That must be very difficult, being away from your daughter," Lennon said.

"It is, but my job allows me to provide for Nike the life I never had. She won't want for anything. She'll have a good future because of my work with ORB."

"You mentioned you were engaged?" Lennon asked.

"Yes, to my *lyubimyy.*"

"Your what?" Lennon asked.

"*Lub-eem-we,*" Carter supplied. "It means *my fa-vorite*—something like *darling* or *sweetheart* to us."

"Yes," Zasha confirmed.

"Linguist, huh?" Lennon asked.

"Told ya," Carter said. "I'm a wonder."

"What about you?" Lennon asked, looking straight at David.

"I'm thirty-eight. I have two kids, Mark and Rachel, ten and nine respectively. I'm still married to my high school sweetheart, and we live in St. Ann, Missouri. Before joining ORB I was a commander with Space Force..." David trailed off with a shrug. "There's not much else to tell."

"Ever the shrinking violet," Carter said. "He's too modest. Commander Bryce has more hours in space than the rest of us combined. He once saved his entire crew by taking a space walk, and then nearly made atmospheric entry in a spacesuit. He's also one of the only people here who's spent any real time on Mars."

"And hated every minute of it," David said.

"In short, the man has a messiah complex," Carter finished.

Lennon smiled. "Sounds like a good attribute for the mission commander to have."

"Yes," Zasha replied.

The hatch to the lower decks groaned as it opened, and Akira emerged, looking sweaty and irritated.

"Did you fix the valve?" David asked.

"Yes. I lubricated the mechanism and sealed it up. We should be fine."

"Nice work," Carter said.

"What's for breakfast?" Akira asked, glancing around at everyone's empty trays.

"Carter, would you bring her some food, please?" David prompted.

"Coming right up," he replied.

Akira sat on the deck between Lennon and David. She glanced back and forth between David and Liu. "What did I miss?"

"We were telling Lennon about ourselves so she could get to know us better," Liu said. "Maybe you'd like to share something?"

"Oh, okay, sure." Akira swept sweat-matted black hair away from her forehead. "I am from Tokyo, but I was born in Miami. I am twenty-five years old. I graduated high school at fourteen, and I obtained my master's in engineering at nineteen. I worked for four years as a flight engineer before joining ORB just last year. I'm single, but I was recently engaged. I might be on my honeymoon now if I hadn't found out that my fiancé was cheating on me with one of my friends. So here I am, no commitments, no ties. Akira Mori, the astronaut."

Lennon's expression scrunched up in sympathy. "I'm sorry about your fiancé."

"Don't be. He was an asshole."

"Clearly," Lennon replied.

Carter came over with a tray full of rehydrated eggs and pancakes for Akira. "Dig in," he said, handing her the meal.

"Thank you." Akira took the food and plopped into a seat.

Carter sat cross-legged on the floor and spent a moment glancing around at the others. "So who thinks the ETs plan to kill us all?" He raised his hand.

"This is a great topic," Zasha muttered, scraping yogurt from her tray.

Lennon frowned, and Liu appeared uncertain.

David shook his head. "I don't believe that's why they're here at all."

"All right, let's hear your theory, then," Carter said.

"Think about it: they're not approaching Earth; they're just drifting along. So that ship might not even have anyone on board. At least, not anyone alive. But even if they came with the intent of destroying us, shouldn't they be changing course? Why the sun?"

"Easier to navigate with the stars," Liu pointed out. "It's hard to see Earth from another solar system, but the sun will be visible for many light years."

"Fair enough," David said. "But now that they're here, and they can clearly see which of the planets seem habitable, they still haven't changed course."

"Well, that certainly fits with the derelict theory," Carter said.

"Maybe they're sleeping," Akira suggested while cutting off a wedge from her pancakes.

"You mean some type of stasis?" Carter asked.

"More like cryogenics," Akira replied. "It's theoretically possible. You don't age in cryo, so an alien crew could have been coasting in that ship for thousands of years and still be alive."

"An intriguing theory." Liu stroked his chin. "We don't have the technology for it, but they might. Or their biology is more compatible with the freezing and thawing processes."

Carter's eyes sprang wider. "Or maybe they're robots and don't require freezing."

"Then why haven't they activated?" Zasha asked.

"No power," Carter suggested. "Their reactor could be damaged. Their batteries ran out, and now they're waiting for us to come along and recharge them."

"Could be, but it's doubtful," Lennon said.

David forced a smile. "Whatever the case, I think we're going to be pleasantly surprised by first contact. There are endless movies and books about aliens determined to annihilate us, but it's just not probable. Any society that advances far enough to reach other star systems must have evolved past petty conflict. In fact, the more aggressive species would wipe themselves out before ever reaching the depths of space."

"Like humans," Carter said, bobbing his head. "Commander has a point."

"We're still here," Liu said.

"Give us time. We haven't gone interstellar yet. You ever watch that old show about Mars and Earth going to war? That's us in a few hundred years."

Akira snorted. "Science fiction is not reality."

"No, but a lot of it comes to pass, doesn't it?" Carter said. "And history tells the same story. We colonized the New World, and pretty soon we were at war with it."

"Maybe this mission will change things," David said.

Carter's brow furrowed. "How so?"

"Finding out that we're not alone, and that someone else out there is more advanced than us—it might be enough to disrupt our tribal mentality. Force us to start thinking of the human race as one rather than as a stratified group of different cultures and ethnicities."

"Yeah, keep dreaming, Commander. The only way that happens is they try to eradicate us and we suddenly have bigger fish to fry."

"Let's hope that doesn't happen," Lennon said.

A sharp buzzing sound roared through the compartment, drawing everyone's eyes up to the ceiling. Then came a familiar voice: "This is Kamar Jackson to *Beyond III*. Report mission status, over."

"I'd better get that," David said. He passed his tray to Carter, who made a face. Zasha piled on with hers, followed by Liu, and then Akira.

"You've been nominated for dish duty," Zasha said.

"So it's like that, is it?" Carter asked.

Lennon handed her tray over with an apologetic smile. "Sorry."

"Nah, you're not, but it's all right. I'll summon you when it's time to clean the lavatories."

"Speaking of, where..." Lennon twisted around curiously.

David pointed to a hatch across from them as he pushed off the deck. "Right there." He held out a hand to help her up.

"Thanks," Lennon said, angling for the indicated compartment.

Lennon

Beyond III

Lennon sealed the latrine doors and stayed with her back pressed to the plastic barrier. She breathed deeply, stifling a cry from her lips.

It was so hard to act normal. All those stories about education, fiancés, and children. Lennon wiped her bleary eyes and let out a deep breath. She couldn't do this. It had been a huge mistake joining the crew, but it wasn't like she had a choice now.

The rocket was already underway at an insane speed, racing to make contact with an alien ship, and here she was, having an anxiety attack. Some of what she'd told the crew was true. She *had* sat in those trailers, issuing drone strikes from the protected comfort of a secret base, but not for long. That had only lasted a year.

Everything had changed the moment Rutger walked through the doors, all smiles and pleasantries. Before she knew it, she was in the middle of Kandahar, with a heavy Sig Sauer strapped to her thigh, and enough explosives to take down three city blocks.

She closed her eyes, feeling the heat from the sun on her face, the sand that never seemed to leave her clothing. When she opened them, the fear and panic receded.

"You're fine, Baxter. This is *Beyond III.* Not hell. You've already endured that, and survived," she whispered to herself.

Carter banged on the door from the other side. "Pep talk?"

"Shit," she muttered.

"Oh, sorry to interrupt. I'll give you a little privacy, then." She heard Carter leaving.

Lennon unstrapped, forcing herself to pee. She couldn't hide in the bathroom every time she had an anxious thought. She'd made the conscious choice to live, and there was a reason she'd pulled that ripcord every week on the airfield as she plummeted from the sky. This was it.

All her trauma, the killing, the orders from Dark Leader. It had led her to this moment. Lennon let the last of the tears dry out, vowing to be stronger. For herself. For the crew, who'd taken her under their wings. After a tumultuous start with Bryce, she actually thought there might be a place for her on the team.

Lennon allowed herself a few moments to freshen up before returning to the communal deck. Just Carter remained, crushing used food containers from their lunch and dumping them into a waste compartment. He whistled an old rock song, and she went to help him with the stack of dirty food trays.

He raised an eyebrow as she took one from the stack and began wiping it with a damp, sudsy cloth. "Only this once."

Carter switched to humming, and they worked in silence.

Lennon recalled the pictures of the *Interloper*, and their earlier conversation. Bryce was optimistic, but she wasn't as naïve as him. Whoever had sent this ship was looking for a fight. And Lennon was pretty sure she was Dark Leader's weapon.

"All done," Carter said. "Want to check out my laboratory?"

"I'd love to," she told him.

There would be lots of time to kill on this trip. Over three months. She was determined to know every inch of *Beyond III* before they made contact with their new friends.

TWELVE

Tokyo, Japan

ATLAS WAS USED TO cities, but this one was much more than an expanding metropolis. Everywhere he looked there were bright lights, automated cars, trains, and people. He watched the night skyline from the balcony, sipping his cocktail slowly. The Skytree jutted up into the air, standing guard over Tokyo a mile away, and the sight grounded him. He was on the right track, but sensed someone was on his trail. A chance to reset in Japan was just what he needed.

The waitress returned, her skirt slit halfway up her thigh. It reminded Atlas of his own gash, and he was glad the wound had healed nicely in the last week. It still pinched when he shifted in his seat towards her.

"Another?" she asked him in English.

He drained the rest of the glass and slid it across the table. "Sure. Thank you."

She smiled, and meandered to the next patron. The pair of businessmen behind him was speaking in hushed tones, their expressions dire. Both wore suits, but their ties were loose, and they'd each consumed a handful of beers since Atlas had arrived.

He checked his holopad and saw a message. "Finally," he muttered, opening it.

I ran the photo through the system. No record of that general anywhere. The facial recognition operates at 99.8% efficiency, meaning that even if he was posing as a Marine, we should come up with a match.

Atlas drummed his fingers, thinking how to respond. *What about the other guy?*

Barry Wan, Captain, US Marine Corps (RET)

Atlas asked for an address.

Listed as Nashville, Tennessee.

I doubt that very much, he thought. At what level could a person *vanish from the system?*

The general? I've never heard of it being done, but I could see a man in his position being cleared. I tried to cross-doc Wan's time with the Marine general's, but this man wasn't listed anywhere. He's a ghost.

A ghost. Atlas covered the Holo when the waitress returned with his glass, and he accepted the drink, taking a quick sip.

Thanks for the help. He sent the message, knowing how risky it was for his contact to leak this information.

Anytime. What is this about?

Atlas pictured Bill, face scrunched in concern. The man had been a good friend before Atlas dropped out of school, in a time when his own father was alive, and he still spoke with his brother.

It's better if I don't tell you.

Roger that, Bill typed. *And as always, we never spoke.*

Understood. Atlas signed off, hoping Bill didn't meet any repercussions for his reconnaissance.

The time shot from his holowatch at the press of the screen, and Atlas peered around the dimly lit bar. Where was Lawrence?

He heard movement behind him, and jumped from the seat, knocking the stool aside.

"Whoa, settle down, Donovan," Lawrence said, lifting his hands defensively. "I wanted to surprise you."

He felt embarrassed, but just picked up the stool. "Sorry about that. Haven't slept much." He almost tried to shake hands with his friend, but pulled him into a hug instead. They broke apart, and Lawrence assessed him at arm's length.

"You look..."

"Tired," Atlas muttered.

"Different."

Atlas ran a hand through his recently groomed hair, feeling like a stranger in his own skin. Instead of his usual beard, he was clean-shaven, and he absently rubbed an old scar on his chin. "I thought it was time for a change." The moment he'd settled in Tokyo, he'd found an out of the way barber, opting for a trim and shave. He'd dyed it lighter, hoping the alterations were enough to confuse anyone searching for him.

"And you look the same," Atlas told him. "Any tips?"

"Diet and exercise," Lawrence said, waving down the waitress. "What are you drinking?"

"Old fashioned."

Lawrence lifted two fingers, and the woman nodded from across the room. "Why, after all these years, am I getting a visit from Atlas Donovan?"

Atlas cringed at the sound of his own name. "I need a new ID."

Lawrence raised an eyebrow. His mother was from Wisconsin, but his father ran a big tech firm in Tokyo. They'd attended the same private school early on, when Atlas had dreams of a normal career, filled with days at an office and a 401k. "You realize I don't actually do that kind of thing anymore, right?"

"Sure. You're a lawyer."

"Precisely."

"But you'd probably know someone that makes passports?" Atlas paused when the drinks came, and Lawrence checked the food menu on his Holo, as if not taking their conversation seriously. "Come on, you must have a contact..."

"Same Atlas, different decade. Look, man, we go way back, but I can't get mixed up in your scheme," Lawrence said.

Atlas wondered if he could trust this man with his dilemma. "It's no scheme."

"I'm getting the steak." Lawrence was diverting.

"Isn't it kind of late for dinner?" It was nearing midnight.

"Not when I got out of the office an hour ago. It's called work ethic," he barbed.

"Sure. But unless your name is on the building, you're making someone else money," Atlas reminded him.

"You have a lot of opinions for an unemployed guy." Lawrence took a drink.

"Can you help me?"

His friend sealed his lips, staring Atlas in the eyes before nodding. "I have a guy. But he's not cheap."

"I'll pay," Atlas said.

"Then I'll set it up. Can you tell me what's going on?"

"You remember that relic my father gave me?"

Lawrence's demeanor shifted momentarily, but enough for Atlas to notice a change in the man. "Not that stupid piece of metal."

"Yes. I found another."

"Damn it, Atlas. You're still chasing after that? It's nothing."

"It's important." He pointed to the sky. "There's a clue waiting for me. We're not alone."

Lawrence looked around, as if someone might have overheard his dinner companion. "Can you keep it down?"

"You know the ORB mission?"

"The Mars supply run? What does that have to do with anything?"

"I think it's all related. They visited us during the Vietnam War. I have proof." Atlas knew he sounded insane, but it also felt good to share the details with a friend.

"What, like, ET? You really believe this?"

"I do."

"Fine. You assume aliens landed on Earth, and now... what?"

"It was a recon ship. And I think it crashed."

"And the Mars group?"

"They're going to meet the mothership." Atlas finished his drink with a swig.

"And what are you planning on doing about it?"

"If there's evidence on Earth, I need to locate it. This might be the difference between life and death," Atlas whispered.

"For whom?"

"Everyone." Atlas watched his friend clutch his glass harder before downing the rest.

"Can I get you another drink?" the server asked, making Lawrence jump.

"Please. And a steak, medium."

"Make that two," Atlas added, suddenly hungry despite their choice of conversation.

She walked away, and to his credit Lawrence didn't even comment on her skirt.

"Where you staying?"

Atlas gestured toward the Skytree. "Hotel a couple blocks from here."

"Nonsense. You'll take my guest room." Lawrence peered out at the city.

"Wouldn't want to put you out."

"Nah. It'll be nice to have the company," Lawrence said.

"Then I accept." Atlas fully expected to lie low for a couple weeks while researching his final destination, and he preferred to do it from the comfort of a condo, not a public hotel.

"I love it here, Atlas. Have you even settled down?"

"I have a small place in New York. It's not much."

"New York? You never liked that city," Lawrence said.

"Things change."

"That's the truth. Are you serious, Atlas? You think aliens might be coming?"

Atlas shrugged noncommittally. "My gut tells me I need to finish what I started. Find the source of the artifacts."

"Fine." He barked a laugh as the pair of suits beside them had another round of beers delivered. "Why do I always let you convince me to join your stupid ideas?"

Atlas chuckled and rubbed his freshly shaved cheeks. "Remember the time we broke into the library?"

"Even then, you were searching for something intangible. And I went because I thought the aide there was cute. Too bad I left flowers on the wrong desk. I shouldn't have signed the note," Lawrence joked. "But at least Mrs. Young waved my late fees."

As the clock struck two in the morning, the pair stumbled into Lawrence's condo. It was meticulously kept, in one of the finest buildings Atlas had ever seen. Ultramodern, with a doorman and a shiny, white-tiled lobby.

"Nice place," he said. "I take it back. Maybe you can make bank working for other people."

"It's been a lot of effort, but here we are." Lawrence waved his hand, like he was showing a prize on a game show. "Where are the rest of your things?"

Atlas hefted his pack. "This is it."

"You always could travel light." Lawrence entered the living space.

Atlas was instantly drawn to the spectacular view. The lights from the city were brilliant from this vantage point. The furniture was boxy, and seemingly unused. Lawrence showed him to his room. It had its own attached bath and king-sized bed. After weeks on the road in low-rent motels and sleeping in the truck, this was a welcome change.

"I better hit the pillow. Big day tomorrow." Lawrence stayed in the doorway. "Be careful, Atlas."

He took a moment, untying his shoes. "I'll try."

"I mean it, man. You have that look in your eyes again."

"Don't worry about me. I've made it this far." He struggled with the second shoe, and it went skittering across the floor.

"Where you off to next?"

"Vietnam. But I'll need that passport first," Atlas said.

"Why?"

"You'll find out soon enough, Larry." Atlas used to call him that, but after freshman year, his friend had preferred to sound more grown up.

"No one's called me that in years." He laughed from the hallway. "Have a good sleep."

"Goodnight." Atlas closed the door, connected to Lawrence's private network, and checked if he'd received any hits on the location of Barry Wan's father. Nothing. He'd keep searching. Sooner or later he'd find a clue.

Atlas showered his trip off and climbed into the most comfortable bed he'd ever occupied.

He fell asleep with alien markings in the form of three dots circling in his mind.

THIRTEEN

Beyond III

D AVID TOOK A BITE of his protein bar while watching the displays on the bridge. A crumb tumbled away from the wrapper, drifting and spinning in the micro-gravity. He snatched it up, popping it in his mouth, and returned his attention to the task at hand.

The central monitor displayed a fuzzy magnification of the *Interloper.* The alien craft was roughly T-shaped, black and sleek, possibly smooth on the surface. He could imagine it reflecting the stars around it like a mirror. The optics in the *Beyond III* weren't good enough to obtain a clear close-up of the hull from this distance, so it was impossible to confirm if it had any viewports or airlocks. Even after more than a month of traveling, they still had a long way to go to reach the vessel.

It had started out twenty-four million kilometers from Earth with a velocity of over forty-eight thousand kilometers per hour, which meant that to catch up with it, the *Beyond III* had to reach a speed well in excess of that. They'd done so soon after leaving Earth, and the *Beyond III* had been cruising ever since. Even so, heading off the *Interloper* would mean a total flight time of more than three months, and that was just one way. Upon reaching it, they'd have twelve days to study the alien craft, and then they'd make a short hop to Mercury to avoid the *Interloper*'s eventual collision with the sun.

But planning an intercept course wasn't the hardest part of the mission. The waiting was. So far they'd had nothing but interminable stretches of boredom, filled with empty routine.

Carter was working on his device to communicate with the aliens, should actual living ones be encountered aboard the *Interloper*. Lennon took turns with David crewing the bridge and keeping an eye on their progress. Zasha was putting her training with the Russian secret service to use, planning tactical scenarios and contingencies in case they encountered hostile forces. Liu kept busy developing protocols to protect the crew and their ship from any alien pathogens they might encounter. And Akira spent her time obsessively checking and rechecking the ship's systems to make sure everything was functioning as it should be. So far so good on all fronts. But the wait... that was wearing on everyone.

David supposed that their impatience was understandable. The *Interloper* might possibly be the biggest discovery in the history of the world. Taking three months to get there and learn its secrets was enough to drive anyone stir crazy.

A chime sounded from the ship's computer, drawing David out of his thoughts. He sat up straight, scanning for the source of the noise. He quickly found it.

The ship's guidance system registered a change in velocity from the target. David leaned forward, frowning at the display. His eyes burned as he stared at the number on the screen: V_2: *48,542 kph.* Moments ago the target's had been clocked at 48,634 kph.

A few seconds passed with no change. David blinked. Maybe it was a glitch in the computer.

But then it fell to 48,484 kph. And below that, the target's acceleration appeared where previously it had been designated as *N/A*. The value for A_2 was reading as -125 m/s^2. Not only was the *Interloper* slowing, but it was doing so at a rate that would turn a human being into a pancake.

"Baxter!" David called.

No reply. He twisted around to face the sealed hatch behind him. Of course she wouldn't hear him through that. He keyed the ship's intercom instead. "This is David Bryce, requesting Lennon Baxter to the bridge. We have a new development."

"On my way," she replied.

Within seconds, the hatch swung open. Lennon sailed up beside him and caught her momentum on the co-pilot's seat. Flipping over it, she landed gracefully and strapped in. "What's the development?"

David gestured to the guidance screen. Analytic data of both *Beyond III* and the *Interloper* showed two different arcs for their trajectories: green for theirs, yellow for the target's. Where before those trajectories had been set to reach an intercept point within a little under two months, now the individual lines diverged completely.

"It's moving?" Lennon asked in a faint whisper.

David nodded.

"But... it was supposed to be derelict."

"Supposed to be. That was an assumption made by Kamar Jackson and the rest of the mission planners."

"So something *is* alive on board," Lennon marveled. She looked to him, her eyes wide and sparkling with wonder.

David hesitated. "Possibly. Or it's been soaking up the sun's rays all this time, recharging, and now it finally has enough power to adjust its course."

"Even if that's true, it doesn't have any bearing on whether the ship is crewed or not."

"No," David admitted.

"So how does this affect the mission?"

David studied the screen again.

"We're going to miss," Lennon realized.

"By more than a million kilometers," David agreed. "We have to modify our own flight path as a result."

Lennon blinked once, slowly, absorbing the information. "Can we? Fuel was already a problem, but now..."

David grimaced. "I know. See what you can come up with."

"We'll have to ensure we have enough fuel for the return trip. I'll find Akira," Lennon decided, unbuckling from her seat and drifting to the open hatch behind them.

David nodded. "Good idea. Let the others know, too. They might have some ideas. Liu also has a strong background in math."

"I'm on it." Lennon caught herself on the edge of her chair to regard David with a frown. "You're not coming?"

He shook his head. "I have to call this in. Maybe mission control can offer something on their end."

Lennon nodded hesitantly and exited through the hatch. David heard it close. He sat with the silence for a long moment, staring at the numbers on the guidance panel. The *Interloper* continued to decelerate at the same rate. It had gone from a deserted object with a set, predictable velocity, to a moving target. In order to intercept them, they would have to flip around and burn what precious fuel was left in the fourth and final stage of the *Beyond III's* booster rocket. They'd been saving it for the return trip. But now...

David swallowed thickly. An image of his family jumped to his mind's eye. He saw his wife, Katy, with their kids, Mark and Rachel, standing on either side. The three of them were smiling for a photo as they posed in front of the giant geodesic sphere at the Epcot Center in Disney World. They'd taken that vacation just a few months before David had been recruited for this mission. A lump rose into David's throat as he realized that he might not be around for the next vacation his family took.

He squeezed his eyes tight to push the image away. Giving in to despair wasn't going to help anyone. His crew might discover something. Or mission control would find a solution.

David blew out a slow breath, letting the tension ease from his shoulders as he did so. He put on his headset and keyed the comms panel to send an encrypted message to Earth.

David

Beyond III

"Akira, why don't you tell everyone about the changes to our flight plan?" David said.

Akira straightened her posture with a grimace, despite the nearly two G's of acceleration crushing them into their jump seats. Everyone was strapped in around the circumference of the crew deck.

After more than a day of number crunching and careful monitoring of the *Interloper,* both mission control on Earth and Akira had agreed on the best means to reach the alien vessel. Their course changes were already well underway, so relaying the news to the rest of the crew was just a formality. This wasn't a democracy. David had received his orders and followed them to the letter. Now all that was left was to understand and accept the consequences.

"We're adjusting heading now, burning hard to decelerate at a pace that will allow us to reach the *Interloper* in forty-two days. That puts us more than two weeks ahead of schedule. The *Interloper's* velocity has stabilized, and they're once again drifting, but no longer aiming for the sun."

"Then where are they going?" Carter asked.

"Nowhere that we can fathom—unless they deviate again, which we can't rule out."

Zasha nodded in agreement, her brow pinching with concern.

"What will this mean for the mission, besides our early arrival?" Liu asked.

Akira hesitated. "We're burning through a significant fraction of our fuel reserves to make the necessary adjustments, and it'll no longer be possible to slingshot around Mercury for the return to Earth. In fact, we won't be able to do a return trip of any kind."

Eyes widened and faces paled. David glanced over at Lennon to check her reaction. She already knew what Akira had recommended, but upon hearing it again now, he saw a muscle jerk in her cheek. She'd taken the news remarkably well when she and Akira had independently reached the same troubling conclusion as mission control. David wondered what that said about Lennon. Did she not have anything to live for?

For his part, David was struggling to hold himself together. He had to stay strong for the crew, but inside he was crumbling. He couldn't imagine how he would deliver the news to his family, but he probably wouldn't even be allowed to contact them. What line would they be fed by ORB? Some type of critical mission failure? A fuel supply problem caused the *Beyond* to explode en route to Mars? Whatever their loved ones were ultimately told, it wouldn't be anything close to the truth.

Carter drew himself up with an angry sneer. "So the mission goes on, but we're suddenly expendable?"

David sucked in an uneasy breath, his ribs aching from the G's they were pulling. "Mission control is working around the clock to help us. They've committed to sending another rocket with enough fuel for the return trip, should that be necessary."

"The *Interloper* is still coasting, correct?" Liu asked.

Everyone looked to him. "Yes," Akira said, nodding for him to continue.

"Then by the time a second rocket can be sent, we will be much farther from Earth."

Carter's expression darkened. "Our mission is almost three months, one way. It'll take a few months at least for ORB to organize a second trip. Then another four or five to reach us. That's seven months from now, best-case scenario. If you tack on the trek home and the added distance, it could be over a year."

David set his jaw. "Our original re-supply to Mars would have been more than that for a round trip."

Zasha muttered something in Russian. "You're all assuming that ORB can even organize refueling in only a few months. The *Beyond III* is their sole operational interplanetary rocket. They'll have to dust off the *Beyond II* for this."

David acknowledged that with a dip of his chin. "At least they have another vehicle that's capable of making it."

"And what happens if the *Interloper* changes course again?" Liu asked. "It could speed up next time, maybe even after we've already boarded it, thereby carrying us far beyond the reach of any refueling mission."

Uneasy silence answered that concern.

David cleared his throat. "In the absence of hard data, jumping to negative conclusions is unproductive. Let's try to stay positive."

Liu arched an eyebrow. "I can do that, but you have to answer the question. What happens in the worst-case scenario?"

"We'll address those outcomes only *if* they arise. Besides, the mission director put forth an interesting theory as to why the *Interloper* redirected, and I agree with him."

"What's his theory?" Zasha prompted before he could go on.

"Jackson believes that the vessel may have slowed down in reaction to our approach."

"For what purpose?" Zasha countered.

A light of understanding was already dawning in Liu's eyes.

"For the purpose that it already accomplished," David said. "To meet with us sooner." His gaze skipped around the circumference of the deck, checking the reactions from his crew.

"Then it *is* a manned spacecraft," Carter said, nodding to himself. A smile formed at one corner of his mouth, as if the possibility of meeting real live aliens somehow made up for the fact that they no longer had a definitive plan for getting home.

"It may very well be," David replied, allowing a grin of his own. Liu nodded, looking uneasy.

"So it won't all be for nothing," Akira said.

"Yeah, we get to be the first to meet our new overlords," Carter quipped. "Quite the honor."

David frowned. Maybe he'd misread Carter's smile. Zasha and Lennon also seemed troubled. The crew was evenly divided in their opinions about how first contact would go. David, Akira, and Liu shared the conviction that an advanced alien race wouldn't come all this way to start a war or enslave humanity. But Lennon, Carter, and Zasha believed two different cultures mixing would inevitably result in conflict, even if that wasn't the original goal.

Maybe they were right, but David felt that cooler heads would prevail. And if they did meet the creators of the *Interloper,* they would establish a common ground with them, and their meeting would usher in an age of enlightenment and peace the likes of which the world had never before seen.

"You might be surprised," David said. Carter's eyebrows lifted slowly. "Perhaps we can even convince our new friends to escort us to Earth themselves."

"Perhaps," Carter said, his head bobbing agreeably. "It's not so much trouble to take on hitchhikers when you're moving in the same direction."

"If they're destined for Earth, then why haven't they turned around already?" Akira countered.

Carter shrugged.

Liu ventured, "I think they want to meet us first and see what they're getting themselves into."

David smiled at that. "Whatever the case, we'll find out soon. But stay optimistic. This isn't the end of the line. I promise you that."

"Shouldn't make promises you can't keep," Lennon said.

David glanced at her, holding her gaze momentarily before saying, "I never do, Miss Baxter."

FOURTEEN

Tokyo, Japan

O NE MONTH. OVER FOUR weeks in Tokyo, and he still didn't have anything to go by. He was convinced that within Vietnam's borders lay the lynchpin to his success.

There had to be a link, but the records for the Chinese service were locked down harder than a vault. He wasn't getting anywhere trying to barrage through a closed tunnel. He needed a new angle.

He was a couple of days from taking the flight, using his new identity to travel from Japan to Vietnam. It looked good, and he'd already tested the details by booking and canceling a trip to Indonesia. With the passport, he was certain no one would know he'd gone to Ho Chi Minh. There was a chance this general suspected Atlas had died in the explosion, but he didn't think it would be so simple.

Or maybe they'd moved on from him. For all Atlas knew, this missing general was involved, and already had the crashed alien vessel in his custody. But Atlas wouldn't stop until he found out for certain.

He rose from the library chair, stretching his aching spine.

"Excuse me," a woman's voice said. British accent.

He glanced at her, and couldn't help but smile.

"Are you an expat?"

"No. Just visiting," he said, motioning to the chair across the table.

"I don't want to bother you. American?" she asked.

"Born and bred."

"And now?"

"New York," he said, cringing at his quick response. According to his passport, he was Brian Delaney, from Pittsburgh.

"One of my favorite cities," she replied.

"What brings you to Tokyo?" Atlas noticed she hadn't sat yet, but she did the moment he landed in his own chair again.

She slid her seat farther from the table, crossing her legs. Atlas surveyed her. Short dark hair, thick eyebrows, a touch of rouge on her cheeks. Her eyes were blue, and he wondered if they were really that color, or if contacts were an accessory. Her outfit was entirely black. "I came for business. I'm from *Move UK,* doing a piece about the rise of expatriates selling their homes and heading for Tokyo."

"I'm Brian," Atlas said, finally remembering his manners.

"Bethany." She offered a hand, and he shook it gently.

"A reporter. That's not something you hear everyday. And for *Move.*"

"You've heard of us?" she asked.

"It's on nearly every flight's Holo display," Atlas told her.

"Then you travel a lot?" She glanced at his hands, which were folded on the table. He assumed she might be searching for a ring. He made sure to give her the full view of his bare fingers.

"Seems I'm on the road more than home."

"For work?"

Atlas had an entire persona created for Brian, should he encounter anyone with questions. "Import broker. I'm an intermediary between a few substantial electronic manufacturers here and in other Asian markets, primarily. I also have a business on the side."

This seemed to pique her interest. "What kind of business?"

"I got bored running over spreadsheets and negotiating for an extra half percent on deals, so I have a rare gemstone acquisition firm. But I prefer to be discreet." He didn't know why he added this part. It wasn't in his original character description, but there was something special about Bethany that drove him to impress her. He couldn't be truthful and admit he was almost broke, living in a bachelor pad in Brooklyn.

"Now you have my interest," she said.

"I thought that might do the trick." Atlas checked the time. "You hungry?" He closed his Holo, and saw she was carrying a bag big enough to house an old desktop computer in it.

"I could eat." She glanced at his Holopad. "Why are you at the library?"

"I..." *Think, Atlas, think.* "Working on my Japanese."

"You're not fluent?" Bethany asked in perfect Japanese.

"I understand the basics." He slowed his speech down, carefully accenting the words.

"That's pretty good. Come on. I saw an Italian restaurant a few blocks from here. I've had more sushi than I thought possible."

"Can I take your bag?" Atlas asked, and she passed it to him.

"Handsome, and a gentleman." She slid her arm into his, and he glanced at her profile as they approached the elevator.

This was the last thing he needed to be doing. Lawrence was likely at his wit's end, with Atlas taking up his spare bedroom. He was being gracious, but part of the reason Atlas hadn't left was fear. After considering the severity of his trip to Italy, the near-death experience in Croatia then again in China, he realized this wasn't a game. And no matter how hard Atlas wanted to play, he wasn't as well-equipped as his opponent.

"Sir, when will you return for the results?" a young man asked him in Japanese as they entered the elevator.

Bethany watched for his response.

"Sorry, what did you...?" Atlas feigned ignorance, and Bethany relayed the man's message.

"Can you tell him I'll be back later this week?"

Bethany spoke in his language, and Atlas pretended not to listen. "He'll return in a few days. What is he researching?"

"Vietnam meteor showers," the boy said, and Atlas silently berated him. He'd slipped the kid a thousand yen to keep his mouth shut.

The elevator doors closed. "He said 'no problem'."

Atlas' instincts were to be wary of the woman, but he doubted she had anything to do with his endeavors. He'd been careful to cover all his tracks. She was probably just curious, and he doubted the boy's reply would incite any great reaction.

The sun was setting as they walked the few blocks to the restaurant, and as promised, it was authentic Italian. The moment he stepped foot in the door, after holding it open for Bethany, his stomach growled.

The place was packed, but luckily there was a spot near the kitchen unattended. It was off in a corner, but close to the serving staff's pathway, making it the center of activity. Bethany didn't seem to mind, and neither did Atlas. It was nice being out for dinner with someone other than Lawrence for once.

"How long have you been in Tokyo?" she asked.

"A couple of weeks," he said. Anything more might raise suspicion. "You?"

"A few days. I should be heading home soon, but the editor is giving me carte blanche. The government is thrilled at the exposure."

"I'm sure. Everyone loves an influx of out-of-country dollars flowing into the economy," Atlas said.

"Then they must love doing business with you." Bethany ran a finger over the wine list. "I hope you like expensive Barbaresco."

"I have a feeling I do," Atlas told her.

"Because it's on *Move*."

"Nonsense, I asked you to dinner."

She leaned in and whispered, "I'm not the kind of woman to expect things from a man."

He smiled, sinking comfortably into his seat. "Then I'd love to try the wine."

Across the room, near a bar, Atlas saw a report on the ORB mission to Mars. He squinted, trying to read the scrolling lettering.

"You follow that stuff?" she asked.

"A bit. More of a passing interest. It pays to be curious in life."

"I agree."

The server took the order and delivered the wine, slowly uncorking. He poured a splash, and Atlas waited while Bethany tasted it. "Even better than I remember. I wrote an article about them a couple years ago. They sent me home with a case. It costs more than a month's rent."

Atlas raised his glass. "To new friends."

"New friends."

He was fully aware that a distraction like Bethany wasn't going to get him answers any sooner, but looking at her, it was difficult to care.

Lennon

Beyond III

A week after their changed trajectory, the crew was in better spirits. Lennon glanced at Carter, who rarely seemed fazed by anything. He roamed through the ship, climbing rungs with a tool kit slung over his shoulder. Akira was on the bridge, nestled behind the front pair of matching pilot's seats.

"Are we good?" Lennon asked. They would be, but Akira was doing her due diligence. Running numbers was her forte, and if she discovered anything off about their route, it was better to find out sooner rather than later. Not that they could afford the fuel to burn in another direction.

Akira peered up with glossy eyes. "Nothing to report."

Lennon glanced at the camera feeds, finding thousands of stars. "Why did you join ORB? I bet you could have been anywhere. Including Holo." She took the seat next to Akira, watching the series of complicated mathematical equations running through their program.

"My father is traditional, but that's how it is in Japan. I know he loves me, and is only looking out for me, but it can be overbearing. Especially after spending a couple of years at MIT for my master's. I got to see families having dinner together. Holidays. I stayed on campus one Christmas, and went to my friend Wendy's house. It was so quaint, with decorations and kids singing along with her grandma on the piano. It seemed so... alien." Akira glanced at the guidance panel, toward the location of the *Interloper*.

Lennon's hair raised at the sound of the word. Was that what they were about to encounter? They were halfway to the mysterious ship, and with any luck they'd actually make it there alive. Getting home was going to be the issue, but Lennon didn't have faith in that endeavor. Not like the others. Unless they were just putting on a show.

Lennon had never seen people with so much blind faith in their leader. She blinked, gazing at her left hand, and rubbed it as the ache set in. No. That wasn't true. Rutger had demanded the same loyalty, only he did it with actions, not words. And when he died, the entire Dark team went to hell. Thrown out with the week's garbage.

But here she was, back in the hot seat under Dark Leader. Flying through space at unfathomable speeds, trying to intercept an obviously alien vessel.

Lennon realized she'd been quiet, and cleared her throat. "Sorry. I was thinking about my own family." That was a lie. She hated to give them more than a cursory thought.

"What are they like?" Akira asked, typing a refresh command on her program.

"No father. Mom called him a donor dad." Lennon laughed, even though it wasn't funny. "She's gone." Another fib. Her mother was alive, she assumed. But they hadn't spoken in twenty years, so she was as good as dead.

"I'm sorry."

"Don't be. She's happier dead than alive." Lennon pictured the stream of deadbeats parading into their trailer for most of her life, and was glad she'd run away at sixteen. "You didn't say why you chose ORB." She wanted to change the subject from her history, and checked the time, her pulse quickening.

"It was a means to explore the unknown. Mars. What a concept. It's far from being perfect over there, but that feeling of setting down on the rocky landscape, seeing the domed structures and feeling the gentle shove of another world's wind against your visor. It's history in the making. And so is this." Akira nodded to the guidance screen, which firmly showed the arcs of both ships' trajectories coinciding.

Lennon cringed to herself. She'd never had romantic notions of traveling to Mars, or any other world, where death surrounded you at every turn. They weren't made to be in space, or even to walk through the Atacama Desert. If so many had to die to pave the path for people to survive on Mars, should they even bother?

"What about you?"

"Sorry?" Lennon asked.

"*Beyond.* Why did you accept?"

Lennon licked her lips. "I didn't have a choice."

"There's always a choice."

"I suppose," she said, not believing herself. "But they called, and I answered."

"Well, we're lucky you're here. Between us, Jess was a bit of a pill. Too much like the commander. You can't have two alphas. It divides people." Akira smiled at her.

"Thanks. I'm pleased to do my part." Lennon left her to it, and bounded to the crew quarters. Her bunk was at the far end from the access ladder, beside Zasha's. She entered after making sure the others were still engaged.

The message had come the day prior, encrypted on her private Holo. A time to meet Dark Leader, which she was nearly late for.

She double checked her hatch was sealed, and tapped the Holo on. They weren't supposed to be able to retrieve their messages, not without first routing them through the ship's comms and mission control, but Lennon suspected Dark Leader wasn't playing by those rules. Because of their distance, each note would take a few minutes to reach its destination, making it all the more nerve-wracking.

"*Dark Three. Are you well?*"

She was thrown off by the question. Why waste time with pleasantries?

"Yes, sir. The issues with the Interloper are resolved." She sent the reply.

"Don't get spooked by the trajectory change. It's likely a defense mechanism built into the sensors. They detect a threat, and automatically move."

"You're adamant this is indeed an extraterrestrial vessel?"

"Yes. Because we've found signs of them prior to the Interloper's *arrival."* As if in answer to the unasked question in her mind, two more words appeared. *"On Earth."*

She could only stare, trying to process the news. "This isn't the first time?" she whispered out loud.

The minutes dragged on, and she listened for signs of anyone approaching her bunk door.

"I've already said too much. There's a reason I'm breaking protocol, and it's not for a chat. The explosives are on your ship. Along with the weapons."

She considered how to respond. *"Weapons?"*

"Did you think we'd send a weapons specialist on a mission without any armaments? Cargo hold. Beneath panels seventeen and fourteen." The communications vanished from her screen a few minutes after they were sent.

It was the first time she'd ever heard Dark Leader use the word *we* in regards to a hierarchy, and it put her off. She'd assumed he was the boss, but was he in fact working for someone else?

Lennon made a mental note. *"What do you want me to do?"* She hit send, tapping her chin.

"There are enough explosives to destroy a tenth of the Interloper. *Choose the spot wisely. From the mission photos, we suspect their engineering is in the rear third of the craft. That would be the ideal location to place them."*

Lennon shook her head slowly, not because she was denying his command, but out of disbelief.

She swallowed a lump in her throat. *"Is there a scenario where we don't destroy them?"*

"I trust your discretion, but remember what that entails. Don't get attached to this crew. You're part of something bigger than a Mars delivery team. This is the fate of the planet, Dark Three, not a contest. All those missions will be for nothing if that ship holds what I suspect."

"And what is that?" she tentatively asked.

"Stop questioning me, soldier. Do your job, and when it's over, we'll honor your name."

He didn't expect her to return home either. *"Of course."* She waited for a final response, but nothing came after five minutes, so she closed the program and tossed the Holo onto her bunk.

"Dammit," she whispered.

It was up to her to protect the world again, only this time it wasn't from a terrorist threat or a nuclear arms deal. This was extraterrestrial. Who knew what kind of horrible events would transpire if this *Interloper* arrived at Earth? But he'd said it was at her discretion. She doubted that was the case. He wanted her to destroy the alien craft before they had a chance to find out why it had really come.

Earth would be none the wiser. *Beyond III* would be reported lost on their trip to resupply Mars, and life would go on.

The commander's wife would get a payout, and Akira's father would start an investigation. But even the owner of Holo would come up blank, because men like Dark Leader knew how to bury bodies, and they'd do anything to keep it that way. Not all of Lennon's previous missions had been overseas. She rubbed her temples and exited her quarters.

"Lennon, you interested in a game of chess?" Liu asked, glancing up as she passed him at his research station.

"Maybe in a bit," she said.

Lennon needed to see what she was working with. It gnawed at her. If there were enough explosives on

Beyond to destroy their target, then it was a danger to the entire crew sitting in the cargo hold.

Lennon moved lower, traversing the three levels to the ship's storage. Crates of all kinds were below, some carrying extra parts, others food and water, tools, and EVA equipment. She drifted between stacks of freeze-dried meals and containers of distilled water until she found the panel labeled *fourteen*. With a glance to the entrance, she pried up the three-foot-wide board. The cases were black, unmarked. She saw a keypad on one, and tested her private code. It had been the same since she'd started with team Dark. 3918.

It worked.

Lennon gasped at the sight of the miniature explosives. They were round, cased in clear shells with blue liquid within. Lennon quickly went to the next panel, and found half a dozen various detonation triggers, ranging from the newest iteration of the BX597 to a model she'd never seen. She'd never even touched one of the digital display versions, and picked it up, feeling the trigger button on the screen. The Holo chip sprang to life, sensing her credentials, and it modified the display to her personal settings. Impressive.

She heard someone approaching. "Shit," she muttered, trying to close the cases in time. She replaced the panel.

David's voice carried into the hold. "Is that you, Lennon?"

"Just a second," she said, clicking the first section closed.

"What are you doing down here?"

"Nothing." She went to the nearest crate, opening the top, and rummaged inside.

David appeared. "Do you mind if we..."

She grabbed the contents, holding her palm out to him with a smile. "Protein bars. I've been craving something sweet. Chocolate or peanut butter?"

He studied her, his eyes still. "Peanut butter. Obviously."

She passed it to him, and watched as he unwrapped the bar. When he turned his back, she finally relaxed, her breath tight in her chest. If the commander realized what was hidden, Lennon had no doubt they would tie her up and throw her in a storage compartment. If she was lucky.

"I'm more of a chocolate person," she said, keeping her voice even. Sweat beaded on her skin, and she hoped he didn't notice as they exited together.

"What do you say we go over our arrival plan again?" he asked.

"Okay."

Lennon followed David Bryce up the rungs, and took a final glance toward the cargo hold, knowing she'd be returning for the explosives one day soon.

FIFTEEN

R AIN FELL IN A gentle mist, and Atlas found he didn't even mind. He was close to obtaining the information he required, and that pushed all other worries aside.

The library doors greeted him, and he jogged up the steps, getting into the elevator. When they opened, he dripped all over the floor on his way into the research facility. He waved at the kid he'd been working with.

"Do you have it?" Atlas asked.

Haru nodded, smiling wide. "Yes. Follow me."

They went into a cramped office, every surface covered with papers. Three monitors sat on the desk, each filled with images of newspaper clippings, and Haru spoke so quickly, Atlas struggled to keep up with the translation.

"Slow down," he urged the kid.

"I found what you were looking for." He jabbed a finger at the central display, and Atlas took a seat, the swivel chair creaking.

"Da Nang," he whispered. "Can I make this in English?"

"Yes." Haru leaned over, tapping a few keys. The file opened on the left display, translated from Vietnamese.

"A meteor sighting," he said. "Why haven't I seen this before?"

"Most of the salvaged papers were blemished, and this particular press went under after they burned to the ground in sixty-eight," Haru told him. "I only discovered it by sheer luck. It wasn't on any of the databases, but I noticed that a local historian there, Duc Le, kept a blog with details. The entries stopped after a few postings."

"Do you have his address?" Atlas asked.

Haru sent a message from his Holo. Atlas pulled his own free, seeing a location as well as a copy of the article. "What is so interesting about this?" Haru leaned closer, as if he was part of something mysterious and eventful.

"Nothing. Just a hobby of mine." Atlas tossed a thousand yen on the desk, thanking the kid again, and he was off, rushing from the library. He'd heard a few offhand remarks about meteors during the war, but most were actual misidentified ballistic assaults. This might be the same thing, but by sixty-eight, the locals knew better, and could tell the difference between various explosive devices.

Atlas had one dilemma.

As the elevator took him to the library lobby, he checked his Holo. Bethany Williams was waiting for him.

"Dammit," he muttered, emerging into the rain. He was already ten minutes late.

The restaurant was only a short distance away, so he decided to walk rather than hail a car.

Atlas called Lawrence while jogging, trying to stay beneath the building's awnings as the precipitation intensified.

"Atlas, what's up?"

"Hey, I'm heading for dinner. We'd mentioned doing something later, but..."

"Don't worry about it, bud. I have to work late. Feel free to bring her home if you're getting tired of that fancy hotel," Lawrence said with a laugh.

"I'll be gone soon."

"You said that two months ago."

Atlas smiled. "True, but this time for real. I have what I need."

"*Okay, then we're going out tomorrow. Before you leave and don't call again for another decade.*"

"Deal," Atlas said. "And Lawrence..."

He heard someone speaking in the background at his friend's work. "*Yes?*"

"Thanks for everything." The call ended, and Atlas hurried to the restaurant, annoyed that he was soaked. He stood in the entrance, shaking his jacket off, and stomped his shoes a couple times. Using the window's reflection, he tried to fix his hair, but it didn't work.

Atlas spotted Bethany inside, swirling a glass of red wine and absently staring at the table. She was a sight. It had been years since he'd allowed himself to get caught up like this. Whatever he felt, he was confident she reciprocated it. Why else would she still be in Tokyo after this long? For a piece on expatriates? He didn't think so.

"Sorry I'm late," he said, sitting across from her.

She grinned as he took the seat, eyeing him up and down. "You could have used a ride."

"I was close."

"At the library again?" she asked.

"Yes."

"Did you find anything?"

"Think so."

She took a sip, and the server came, pouring him a glass.

"I have to leave," she said, making eye contact.

"Right now?"

"Tomorrow. I've been assigned to Germany."

"Okay."

Bethany stared at him. "Is that it, Brian?"

"What do you want me to say?" He hated that she used his alias. Every time they were together, he fought the urge to come clean. But this would be easier. A fresh break.

"That you're going to miss me. That maybe you would consider working remotely in Germany. You should see the hotel I'm staying at. It's practically out of a fairy tale." Bethany's face was full of possibilities.

"I can't."

"Fine." Bethany snapped her gaze to the menu. "But maybe we can enjoy one last night?"

Atlas recalled what Lawrence said. He would be at the office for hours. "We can go to my place."

"Finally."

"What's good?" he asked, scouring the fine dining options. Bethany sure had expensive tastes.

"How about we skip the meal and get right to dessert?" she purred.

Atlas smirked, downing his wine. "Sounds good to me."

He waved a hand at the server and paid the bill.

A half hour later, they entered Lawrence's place, barely making it to the bedroom before her olive dress slid onto the hardwood.

***

Atlas woke, feeling hazy. His head spun, and he instantly knew something was wrong.

He heard water running in the bathroom. "Bethany?"

He got up, his bare feet cold on the floor. Everything ached, and he stared at the bottle of wine beside the bed. Barely opened. A single glass sat on the nightstand. He'd been drugged.

"Bethany!" He stumbled from the room, realizing he was in his underwear.

She had his bag open, the contents strewn over the kitchen countertop.

"What the hell are you doing?" Atlas demanded.

Bethany paused, and lifted a hand. The gun aimed in his direction. "Don't move an inch."

"This is insane. Who are you?"

"I could ask you the same question, *Brian*," she muttered. "I have to admit, this was one of the more enjoyable missions I've been on, but they all end the same tragic way."

"How did you know to find me?" Atlas asked.

"He knows everything, Atlas Donovan."

Atlas smacked his dry lips. "He? He who? What did you use on me?"

"Doesn't matter. But it obviously wasn't enough." The gun was still pointed at his chest from twenty feet. She handled the gun like a pro, and he doubted she'd miss from this range. "Where is it?"

"What?"

Bethany held the Holo up. "Perfect."

Atlas considered his options. Let her take the Holo and hope she didn't kill him, or fight for his life. He was still groggy, but his vision was getting clearer. Judging by her expression, he wasn't leaving here alive.

"Don't even think about it, Donovan."

"I thought we made a connection. It doesn't have to play out like this, Bethany," he pleaded.

"That's where we differ. This is exactly what has to happen. Failure is not an option. They're coming," she said.

"Who is...?"

Her Holo chimed, and Bethany seemed furious at the interruption. "What?"

"Is it in your possession?" The voice was low.

"No. I have the Holo. It'll lead me..."

"Dark Nine, do not leave that condo without it," he ordered.

Dark Nine? Who the hell was this?

"He wouldn't be stupid enough to have the artifacts with him," she said, looking Atlas in the eyes. "Or are you? All this time, I could have just broken in here. I've been trailing you, trying to determine what bank you were storing them in. But you were foolish enough to hold on to them, even after China."

Atlas didn't move.

"*Don't miss this opportunity, soldier.*" The call ended.

"Who do you work for? Is it the general?"

Her eye twitched.

"We can team up. This is important," he said. What was he even trying to accomplish? If there truly was an alien ship on Earth, why should he be the one in charge of finding it? Wouldn't this general, with his vast resources, be the better option? Unless his motives were corrupt. But were Atlas's anything but selfish?

"Show me." She placed his Holo into her pack and waved the gun at him.

Atlas went into the bedroom and lifted the mattress. The bag with the relic from Lake Como was inside, along with the section from his father. He saw something as she reached for the prize. The make-up on her arm was smudged, revealing a distinctive tattoo with three dots in a triangular configuration.

"You in there, Atlas?" Lawrence's voice carried from the front entrance.

Bethany turned toward the sound, and Atlas took his chance, rushing in and tackling her to the floor. He still had the lingering effects from the drugs, and his arms felt heavy. She easily shoved him off, and he slid onto his back.

"Atlas?" Lawrence called.

"Get out of here!" he shouted in warning, but it was too late. The gun fired, and Lawrence, his oldest friend, stood in the doorway, blood soaking his collared shirt.

Atlas saw red. He sprung toward Bethany, knocking her across the bed. They bounced, and tumbled into the bathroom. The back of her head hit the shower base, and a spreading pool of red appeared. The gun fell from limp fingers to the tiles, and Atlas sat up, blinking in shock.

"No, no, no..." He stared at her, then at Lawrence. Both were sprawled out, unmoving. He checked for a pulse at Bethany's neck. Nothing. Running out of the bathroom, he repeated the exercise with Lawrence... with the same result. He was in a condo with two dead bodies.

Instead of waiting for sirens to ring down the street, he threw on his pants, socks, and a button-up shirt. A minute later, he rushed to the exit, his heart pounding and his hands sweaty as he clung to the pack with his alien relics inside.

Before he left, he returned to the bedroom, and snatched Bethany's Holo up with his.

The first thing he did was disable the GPS locator on both and run into the hall, panting from adrenaline more than the exertion.

It was time to visit Vietnam.

He closed the door and held his breath. No one seemed to have noticed the gunshot.

Atlas took the stairs despite the wobbly feeling of shock flooding his legs. He tried not to picture Lawrence sprawled out on the floor.

By the time he arrived at the airport, the sun was beginning to rise, marking the start of a new day. But Atlas felt like darkness was surrounding him.

"Da Nang," he told the airline clerk, who eyed him suspiciously. His outfit was random, his shirt wrinkled. Atlas assumed he resembled someone leaving a late-night party. He did his best to smile at the woman as he paid for the tickets.

He went through security, making up a story about the items in his carry-on, and sat near the terminal, hoping no one intercepted him before boarding.

Atlas had a location, the two alien remnants, and a head full of regrets. His hand wouldn't stop shaking as he closed his eyes, trying to figure out who was after him.

SIXTEEN

Beyond III

"Everyone strap into your jump seats!" David called over the *Beyond*'s intercom. "We're five hundred and seven kilometers from the target and about to execute our final approach. ETA is one hour and fourteen minutes." He flicked a display over to a live feed from an internal camera on the crew deck. Peering down from above, he saw the four members of the crew secured around the circumference of the deck.

"Strapped in and ready, Captain!" Carter called. He looked up and saluted the camera, as if he somehow knew that David would be watching.

"Ready," Zasha added.

"Sitting tight, Commander," Akira put in, hooking her thumbs under the belt running across her shoulders.

"I am ready," Liu said in a grim voice, staring straight ahead.

"Beginning our final approach now." David flicked the display to the external camera. He gently seized the joystick for manual flight on the right side of his chair, and the various thrust control sliders on the left.

Glancing at his co-pilot, he nodded at Lennon. "You good?"

She blew out a breath and smiled tightly. "No."

David barked a laugh. "Honest. Nice call, Baxter."

He focused his gaze on the guidance screen and a real-time magnified image of the *Interloper*. Now they were close enough to get a detailed view of the alien vessel, and it was as shocking and awe-inspiring as the first time he'd seen it several weeks ago.

It was one thing seeing the dark, T-shaped vessel in a blurry, pixelated magnification from Earth, or an even fuzzier view captured from the *Beyond*'s own telescopic cameras. But this was a sharp 32k image with every little curve and facet laid bare. The vessel's hull was black and mirror-smooth, a flattened ovoid with two curving wing-like projections at the rear. He couldn't see so much as a single visible porthole or seam where an airlock or door might be located.

The hull was, however, covered in spiky, hooked projections, swept back from the nose. The purpose of those hooks he could only guess at, but it reminded him somewhat of the carapace of a giant beetle. The design certainly appeared organic—insectile, even. None of these details had been visible previously, and David was almost glad for it. He wondered what the aliens who built it might look like. Was this a clue?

They were about to find out.

The nav system beeped out a warning that they were drifting off course, pulling David out of his thoughts. He made a minor adjustment, firing the starboard maneuvering jets to bring them back into line. "Approach is good," David said. "How are things on your end?" he asked with a quick glance at Lennon.

"All systems nominal," she said. He could tell she was concerned about the ship. Her brow was furrowed, and her lips parted like she wanted to say more.

"Good."

"No reaction from the *Interloper?*" Lennon asked.

"Not yet, but we'll see what happens when we try to dock and cut a hole."

"Yeah." Lennon grimaced. "That will be interesting."

Another warning beep from the nav had David making a small correction to starboard.

Lennon frowned. "Can't you set the autopilot to take us in?"

"I've found it's better to be hands-on for docking maneuvers, especially when the target could start turning at any given moment. I need to be able to react if that happens."

"If they were planning to go evasive, don't you think that by now they should have done that already?"

David shook his head. "I don't—"

The screech of an alert tore through the bridge, and a series of flashing lights lit up on the engineering panel.

"Baxter! What's happening?"

Her hands flew over the panel. A diagnostic report began scrolling down one of her screens, peppered with red lines of warnings.

"Multiple system failures!" Lennon cried. "Thermal sensors in the maneuvering jets are showing the hull temperatures several thousand degrees hotter than expected. Something is melting through our hull!"

David released the thruster controls and examined several different external views to check the indicated areas. The exhaust ports for the maneuvering jets were blackened, and glittering globules of the stainless-steel hull plating were dribbling off into space. "That's impossible," David said. "The melting point of the hull is..."

"Over fourteen hundred degrees Celsius," Baxter supplied.

"Exactly," David said. "And why only there? Why not some other part of..." He trailed off suddenly.

"What is it?" Lennon asked.

He grabbed the controls and tried rolling the rocket, watching on the external cameras as stars pinwheeled around the exhaust ports. After a few seconds, the hull alloy stopped dissolving.

"This isn't good," he muttered.

"What is it?" Lennon asked as he stared fixedly at the camera, waiting to see what would happen next.

After a few seconds, the hull plates grew piping hot again. Another shriek sounded from the engineering panel.

"Our fuel temperature is increasing!" Lennon shouted. "If this keeps up, the ship is going to explode."

"Vent the fuel into space."

"What?" Lennon gaped at him. "But we need that fuel for the return trip!"

Mission control had ultimately found a way to save them from the crisis that had evolved two months ago when the *Interloper* began slowing down. They were to remain on board for seven days, investigating the alien vessel before pushing off and burning for Mars. The *Interloper*'s new trajectory would allow them to reach it with their remaining fuel; then, once there, they'd sit in orbit until a new supply mission to come and rescue them. But if they vented their fuel now, even that plan would be impossible.

"You heard me!" David snarled while rolling the ship again. "Shut all the valves from the tanks and vent them!"

Lennon blinked once before snapping out of it. Her hands flew across the controls, following his orders.

"What are you doing?" she asked, sparing a momentary glance from her station.

"I'm offering them a moving target."

"Them?"

"Whoever is shooting at us from the *Interloper.*"

"Shooting?" Lennon paused to glare at the screen with a visual of the alien vessel. "I don't see anything!"

"That's because you can't see lasers in space. There's no air or dust to refract the light. Is our fuel vented yet?"

"Almost... damn it!"

"What's wrong?" David asked.

"That valve in tank six is giving me an error. It won't close."

"Isn't that the same one Akira fixed at the beginning of the mission?"

Lennon nodded. "If we don't close it, we can't release the fuel."

"It won't take another hour of this," David said. "Sooner or later, they're going to heat the fuel to the point of combustion, and then we'll be done." He keyed the intercom. "Attention all hands, we're under attack!"

"Under a-*what?*" Carter asked.

"Akira, the shut-off valve for tank six is malfunctioning. I need you to cycle it manually."

"Copy, sir."

"Hold on just a minute! Why are we venting our fuel?" Carter asked.

"Because if we don't, it's going to combust and destroy us along with it," David said.

A heavy silence answered that statement.

"What can we do?" Zasha asked.

"Help Akira with whatever she requires."

"What about the mission? Will we still be able to dock to the *Interloper?*" Carter asked.

"I'll program the last leg of our course into the autopilot. We'll have to reduce our velocity and drift from here to the target, but assuming it doesn't move again, we should get close enough to fire the docking harpoons."

"And if we don't?" Liu asked.

"We will," David insisted. "Now go. Get that valve closed. We don't have much time."

"Copy that," Akira said. David flicked an auxiliary screen over to the feed from the crew deck to see Akira clambering down the rungs to the engineering sections below.

Zasha shot out of her seat and pushed off the wall to float toward the ladder. With the ship rolling around its axis, her target kept swinging into and out of reach. She managed to arrest her momentum with a handrail beside the entrance of one of the crew quarters, and from there, launched herself.

The others remained seated, but Liu was sitting on the edge of his seat, seemingly eager to help.

"Stay there!" Zasha said to them as she began her descent. "I'll assist Akira."

David turned his attention to his maneuvers and began programming the autopilot. Their approach was far too fast to dock with the *Interloper.* The primary thrusters at the rear of the rocket were already flipped around and facing the alien vessel, approaching tail first so they could slow down before docking. So far, the *Interloper* hadn't opened fire on the much larger exhaust ports at the back, a fact that he found strange. Why only target the maneuvering jets?

"What is it?" Lennon asked.

She must have noticed his hesitation. "They haven't hit our primary thrusters."

"So? Isn't that a good thing?"

"Yes, but why?" he countered.

"Maybe they're trying to cripple us."

"Or they haven't seen those thrusters ignite yet," he mused. "We might have been too far away the last time we used them. We've been cruising toward them on a set course for the past two months straight. Now that we're within spitting distance, they saw me making subtle corrections with the jets, and they opened fire."

"To them the jets appeared hostile?" Lennon suggested.

"Maybe. Whatever the reason, if I ignite the main thrusters now, there's a chance that they might attack there, and the fuel tanks are a lot closer to the primary propulsion system than they are to the attitude jets."

"So we won't be able to slow?" Lennon asked, her voice pitching up an octave.

David shook his head. "Not in the traditional way."

"What's that supposed to mean?"

He glanced from his screens and held her gaze grimly. "We're currently on a collision course with the *Interloper*. Our relative velocity to theirs is four hundred and eleven kilometers per hour. And that's how fast we'll be going when we make impact."

"We won't survive that!" Lennon shouted.

"Not true. This entire ship is a massive crumple zone. The storage area alone—"

"Will get pushed up through the crew deck, crushing us against the nose!"

"Not if we empty it first."

"In one hour?"

"It'll work," David insisted. "Besides, we'll bounce off long before the entire ship crumples up the way you're thinking."

"And then what?" Lennon demanded. "The docking airlock is at the back. It'll take the brunt of the crash. We won't even be able to fire the harpoons after the collision mangles them."

"We'll shoot them right before we hit. Then, when we rebound, we'll stay moored to the *Interloper*."

"We'll depressurize," Lennon added.

"Quite likely. But it won't be a problem if we're already wearing our pressure suits."

"So we have one hour to empty storage, suit up, and prepare for impact."

David nodded grimly. "It's the best we can do."

"With nothing but our suits' air to breathe, there's no chance ORB will have enough time to reach us for a rescue."

A cold weight settled in David's gut. "No," he agreed. "But perhaps the air on board the *Interloper* will be breathable."

"That's bullshit, and you know it."

"At this point, Baxter, all we know is that if we light up our main thrusters to slow down, we could blow up a few seconds later."

"We have to report this to Earth. These aliens, whoever they are, have declared war."

"We can't assume that."

"They attacked an unarmed vessel!" Lennon roared.

"Maybe they thought we fired the first shot. Or these are automated defenses designed to keep anything from reaching a certain proximity. Remember, we're on a collision course. As far as they can tell, we're a space rock hurtling toward them."

"They'd have to be very stupid to think that. And their target was extremely specific."

"True, but my reasoning stands. Whatever passes for automated defenses aboard the *Interloper* could be fairly rudimentary. Have you ever bumped into a car while climbing into yours and accidentally set off the alarm? We could be dealing with something like that."

"You're saying a trigger-happy alien AI has sentenced us to death."

David shrugged and nodded. "It's possible."

"Fantastic."

A crackle from the speakers in the cockpit drew their attention away from each other. Akira's voice came through. "The valve is shut," she said, sounding out of breath. "Heading back now."

"Copy that," David said.

"What's that sound?" Lennon asked.

"What sound?" he replied.

"Her breathing."

"She's in a pressure suit. The manual controls for the fuel system are behind the rear airlock in a depressurized section of the ship."

Another squawk from a siren drew David's gaze to the systems panel over on Lennon's side of the bridge. The fuel temperature was climbing again. They were running out of time. "Baxter, dump the fuel."

"Copy th–what the hell?" Lennon frowned and shook her head.

"What is it?" David asked.

"The valve is open again."

David hit the comms. "Akira, we're still reading that valve as open. Can you confirm?"

"Yes, sir. I'll need a minute..." Moments later, Akira's voice returned. "It keeps jumping open. There must be something wrong with the sensor. I'll have to hold it shut while you vent the fuel."

"Understood. Initiating fuel dump now." David nodded to Lennon. "Do it."

She blew out a sigh and hit the switches to start the process. One of the auxiliary screens flashed a shrinking progress bar to indicate their diminishing fuel supply.

Meanwhile, the droning wail from the temperature sensors was somehow growing louder and more emphatic. "Bryce, we don't have that long!" Lennon yelled.

"We'll make it!" he said, increasing the rate of the rocket's roll to hopefully distribute the heat from the *Interloper*'s lasers more rapidly.

"Almost there, Akira," David said, eyeing the narrow bar of remaining fuel.

"Copy." A sharp *plink* sounded, followed by a sharp hissing noise.

Lennon paled. "What was that?"

"I don't know." He tried the comms again, even as he brought up a view from the nearest camera to get eyes on Akira. "Everything all right?"

There was no reply.

On the camera, he saw Akira floating there, motionless between two fuel tanks. "Akira?" he tried again. Still nothing.

Then he saw the shimmering crimson ribbon snaking around her in a lazy circle. It looked like a party streamer, but the truth was far less trivial. Something had hit Akira's suit, puncturing it and injuring her in the process.

"Zasha! Come in!"

"I'm here, Commander. What do you need?"

"Get out there. Akira's hurt, and she's not responding."

"Copy!"

"Liu, I need you standing by in the airlock to administer emergency aid."

"Already on my way, Commander."

"Good. Let me know when you have her."

David stared helplessly at the screen, itching to do more.

"Fuel dump complete," Lennon said quietly.

David nodded slowly and watched the camera feed. Zasha drifted into view, bouncing off the fuel tanks to reach Akira faster. She caught her momentum on the rungs of a ladder, speeding her along.

"Oh God, no," Zasha whispered over the comms. "Commander, she's..."

"She's what?" he demanded.

"Dead."

"Get her inside!" David snapped. "Liu might still be able to revive her."

"Okay. I'm on it."

David sat with his breath frozen in his chest as Zasha climbed back up with Akira in tow. He switched camera feeds when they reached the airlock, and the young Japanese woman's face came into view. "Oh no," David said.

"Zasha was right," Lennon said. "She's definitely gone."

The shattered visor of her helmet was sprayed with blood, and a gaping black hole glared where her right eye should have been.

There was nothing Liu could do for her.

"She saved our lives," Carter said.

"Yes. She did," David replied.

The airlock opened, and Zasha pulled her through. Within seconds, Liu pronounced her dead. "She died instantly. She wouldn't have felt a thing."

"What do we do now?" Zasha asked, staring at the crimson smears of blood on her gloves and suit.

"Leave her there," David said.

"Copy that," Zasha replied.

"We should give her proper service," Liu said.

"There's no time. We need to dump as much of the cargo as we can before we hit the *Interloper*."

"We can spare a minute to send her off and say a few words," Liu countered.

"All right. Send her out."

The outer door slid open, and Liu and Zasha both gave Akira a good push. She careened down between the fuel tanks on a relatively straight trajectory for the small, star-studded circle of space at the end.

"See you on the other side," Lennon whispered.

"Thank you for your sacrifice," Liu added.

David managed a few words of his own. "We won't forget you, Akira Mori."

"Godspeed," Carter put in.

Zasha added something in Russian, and then silence reigned.

David cycled camera feeds again as Akira sailed past the primary thrusters. She rapidly dwindled to a tiny white speck, winking brightly at them as she tumbled. Just another star, lost among the rest in the vast ocean of space.

No, not lost, David thought. Akira had died saving the mission and her crew. Few people ever found themselves in life as profoundly as Akira had in death.

And she would be remembered as the hero she was.

SEVENTEEN

Da Nang, Vietnam

D A NANG WAS FAR different than it used to be when Barry Wan's father had fought alongside the North Vietnamese forces. Now it was a beautiful metropolis, but after spending two months in Tokyo, it seemed like a small town.

Atlas emerged from his hotel on the waterfront, taking a moment to stare at the East Vietnam Sea. The object he was searching for might be out there somewhere within the dark depths. What would he even do if he located it?

Instead of rushing, Atlas found a breakfast spot, and was pleased they offered American cuisine on the menu. He filled up on bacon, eggs, and hash browns, washing it down with too many cups of a thin dark roast coffee.

He did his best not to think about Lawrence, but that was an impossible feat. When he scanned for news articles on the killings, they mentioned a probable lover's quarrel. If the reporters or police dug deeper, the truth might come out.

He'd visited Da Nang before, in his early years, knowing his father had stepped in this very city during his tenure in Asia. But the leads had run dry, until eventually he'd returned home with nothing to show for the trip.

Now he had a name to go on. Atlas glanced at his Holo, seeing the address listed for Duc Le. It was in the remote region, just west of the city. He'd managed to sleep an entire day away, delaying his trek into the jungle. His body had refused to operate after landing and settling into his hotel. Atlas already had a car rental, so it wasn't a complete waste.

If Duc had been around since the 1960's, that would put him far into his golden years. And that was if Haru's data was correct, and he wasn't deceased.

Atlas surveyed the bridges behind him. The city was built around a divided river, making it necessary to have crossings throughout. Each structure was magnificent, a unique spectacle drawing tourists and onlookers. Today they were quiet.

Instead of delaying any longer, Atlas decided to leave. He checked his Holo after entering his mid-sized sedan, to find no messages from either his contact at ORB or the military. He hoped the two connections were okay. Atlas assumed they'd been placed under strict non-comm orders, but he couldn't shake the feeling they might have been caught sending a civilian confidential information. And Bill was investigating the mysterious General. If that raised any red flags, the man might be gone. He wouldn't have thought that possible, but after the string of dead bodies piling up behind Atlas, he realized the severity of the situation.

Atlas started the car, and the electric engine ran silent. What was he doing?

"Go home, Atlas. You're in over your head. So what if there are more artifacts?" he whispered to himself. Instead of heeding his own advice, he threw it into reverse and vacated the parking lot. The car's autonomous braking system slammed on as two bikes darted by. One of them seemed startled, but continued racing forward, the driver not even fazed by the near accident.

Atlas saw two futures ahead of him as he began to drive down the road, more cautiously this time. The first had him returning to the States to focus on the curation business he'd unenthusiastically begun almost a decade ago. He worked for refined people, sourcing collector's items and various trinkets. It made a decent living. The more he thought about it, the better that option sounded.

Or he could continue on this path, seeking another piece of an alien craft. He glanced at the pack on the passenger seat. There was a chance these were man-made. The costly tests had proven otherwise, but he might have been swindled. Rare elements, never seen in combination before. That's what the woman had alleged, and when she'd begun to ask specific questions, he'd bailed, grateful he'd used an alias and paid her cash under the table.

No. He was confident he was on the proper track. But even so, where did it leave him? If he located a third piece, what then? He'd have more of the general's agents trying to kill him. Atlas recalled the woman he'd dated. She'd fooled him so easily. *Dark Nine.* What did that mean? And the tattoo. Three dots.

How did it at all connect to the mission to Mars? Atlas hated dealing with half-truths, but had no alternative other than to press on. He considered the evidence as he headed to the outskirts of Da Nang, but lacked significant details. His father had brought the first artifact from Malaysia; the second was from the coast of Croatia. Why were they scattered so far apart? And what was here in Vietnam? Had the ship burst apart in the atmosphere like a meteor, spreading across the globe as it rained down?

The car's GPS told Atlas he was an hour from the destination as he finally exited from the city, finding fewer cars on the road the farther he drove. Several bicyclists kicked up rocks on the curb, then turned right, leaving him isolated for a handful of miles. The jungle grew thicker with each passing stretch of pavement, and the roads more broken. Soon there were no lines on the concrete, and eventually it turned to gravel.

He slowed as he approached a village, and noticed the locals pausing to peer at his rental car. The ground was wet, as if a morning deluge had hit the region. He avoided a pool of water, trying not to splash a group of men walking in the ditch.

The elevation was increasing, and his ears clogged with the pressure change as he climbed higher into the hills. It was humid. He tried the AC, and nothing happened. Atlas lowered the window, but that didn't help much, not with the high humidity.

"Where are you?" He checked the GPS, seeing Duc Le's address straight ahead. Instead of finding a home, there was a dirt road, almost as wide as the car he was in. He wasn't willing to risk the rental, so Atlas shoulder-checked and pulled over. He grabbed his pack and locked the doors.

Outside, a cluster of black flies mobbed him as he hurried up the path, anticipating the man's house was close. Twice he slipped on the steep incline, but managed to catch himself before falling. By the time the ground leveled off, he was out of breath and covered in sweat, his ankles caked with mud. *This had better be worth it.*

The home was barely a shack, with a straw-covered roof and a bamboo porch. He smelled a fire from around back and went that way, keeping his gaze on the front door in case someone emerged.

"Hello?" he called. First in English, then Vietnamese. *"Xin chao."*

The man was skinny, with a patchy grey beard and wary eyes. "Who are you?"

Atlas could speak a handful of words, but used his Holo to confirm the question. "I'm Atlas."

"American?" the old guy inquired.

Atlas nodded.

"What do you want?" he asked in English.

"Are you Duc Le?"

"Who are you?"

"Name's Atlas Donovan." He extended his hand, but the guy kept his distance.

"Go away."

"I need to ask you about the article you posted a few years ago. The Meteor."

He stopped poking his fire. "What of it?"

"I was wondering if you'd tell me where the crash happened. Were you there?"

Duc Le smiled, his eyes crinkling at the sides. "Do I look like I'm in my nineties?"

Atlas laughed. "I didn't mean to offend you. I just thought..."

"My father told me. Always talked about the night it fell. I was curious, so I did some research. I was a professor in Da Nang for a couple of decades. Taught local history. The war wasn't the only thing of importance in our country." Duc slapped a mosquito on his arm.

"Why are you out here?" Atlas asked.

"The city was too bright. I prefer solitude. Since my wife passed."

"I'm sorry." Atlas sat on a wooden bench, dropping his pack between his feet.

Duc grunted. "Such is life."

"Can you tell me the location?" Atlas stared at him, but the man remained quiet.

"Why?"

Atlas considered his response. "You're a historian. I think you might appreciate this."

He opened the bag, and brought the first piece out. Atlas carefully unwrapped it, and hesitantly handed it to Duc. They were in the middle of nowhere, and he was sure they'd have discretion. Very few people had laid eyes on this item, and for good reason.

Duc touched the surface of the ship segment, running a finger over the triangle of dots. His eyes closed and he chuckled, the sound growing to a growl. "I can't believe it."

"Will you help me?"

"Where did this come from?" Duc asked.

Atlas could have lied, but what was the point? This man was his only lead to the location of the crashed ship in the sea. "Malaysia."

"Incredible. Is it related to the meteor?"

"I don't think it was a meteor at all."

Duc flipped the artifact over, and returned it. He examined his fingertips, as if they might have been burned. "Any proof?"

"Not really. But I have this. Found in Croatia." He opened the second piece, the one the general had been desperate to retrieve.

Duc recoiled at the sight. He shook his head. "You should leave."

"Why? What do you know?"

Duc peered into the jungle beyond his hut. "I prefer to be alone. I don't want any trouble."

"There won't be any. Just give me the coordinates. That's all I'm asking."

Duc Le met Atlas' gaze, his mouth open. "Okay. But you didn't get this from me."

"No problem."

Duc licked his lips. "You'll never return. I don't exist."

"Deal."

Duc stood, his knees creaking as he hobbled into his home. Atlas wrapped the two prizes and returned them into his bag, zipping it tight.

"Here." Duc handed him a piece of paper. Atlas glanced at it, seeing a pair of numbers that he recognized as GPS coordinates.

"I'll find it there?"

"Unless somebody else already has," Duc told him.

"Thank you," Atlas said, but the man had already returned to the fire, dropping another piece of wood on the coals. An unknown animal hung from a stick above the flickering flames.

He jogged down the decline, sliding in the muck, and hopped into the car. He opened the proper app on his Holo and keyed in the digits. The location was about fifty miles off the coast, nearly straight east.

Atlas turned around, rushing to the city. This time he drove faster, a clock ticking in his mind to the beats of his heart. For the first moment in years, he sensed his search was coming to an end.

He entered Da Nang with a renewed sense of optimism, and wound his way over the bridges, past his hotel, and straight to the docks.

There had to be someone willing to take him to the site and rent him diving equipment. Atlas parked the car, his hands shaking. He scanned the docks, searching for signs of anyone following him. He didn't have a clue what to look for. When he thought the coast was clear, he climbed from the car, and drew in a lungful of the ocean air.

He was close.

EIGHTEEN

Beyond III

"IMPACT IN T-MINUS FIVE minutes," David announced through the comms. "Relative velocity holding steady at four hundred and eleven klicks per hour. All hands, safety check."

"Strapped in and ready," Zasha declared.

"Likewise," Carter added.

"Standing by," Liu said.

David studied them via the camera feed on his auxiliary display. Each wore a pressure suit and was secured directly to the communal deck with cargo webbing and other improvised restraints. The jump seats weren't ideal in this case, because while sitting, the force of the impact would compress their spines to the point that the vertebrae could fracture. Liu had informed them that the best way to tolerate the extreme forces of the collision was to lie down.

David and Lennon would be fine in the bridge since their seats were facing the nose, which put their backs on the same plane as their corresponding deck. Because they were going to collide tail-first, it placed them as far as possible from the impact.

"T-minus two minutes," Lennon stated. "Any changes?"

David glanced at the nav display and shook his head. After dumping their fuel, an encouraging prospect had occurred to him. If the *Interloper* was reacting to their approach by trying to disable them, wouldn't they also have collision avoidance systems? Their ship had already proved that it could maneuver, when it had cut its velocity and shaved two weeks off this encounter. But with precious little time remaining before impact, the *Interloper* was as enigmatic as ever. If it could speed up to avoid the collision, it had clearly chosen not to do so.

"Maybe their computer already scanned us and ran the numbers, and they realized we can't even dent their hull," Lennon suggested.

"It's feasible," David said. Whatever the case, they were ready. They'd emptied the bottom twelve feet of the cargo bay. That, plus the empty fuel tanks and the thrusters themselves, would create a good forty feet of crumple zone. By all estimates, that should be enough for them to survive the impact, but the damage to the living compartments would be severe, and depressurization was a very real probability. Hence the pressure suits they were wearing.

"T-minus one minute!" Lennon called.

David tensed and reached for the docking harpoon controls. He flipped up the safety cover and watched unblinkingly as the range to the *Interloper* ticked down steadily.

6840 meters... 6612... 6156...

The harpoon cables had a maximum range of fifty meters, which meant that he had to fire them less than a second before impact. Human reaction time was about a quarter of a second, and he needed to hit the button a half-second before impact, but if he went too soon, they'd fail to reach the *Interloper's* hull. *Beyond III* would bounce off and drift into space. If he shot them too late, the results wouldn't be any better. They'd become snagged on the debris of the buckling thruster assembly.

"Ten seconds," Lennon said. "Nine... eight... seven..."

David's vision narrowed to a hazy tunnel. He became hyper-aware of his surroundings: the range to target scrolling on the nav, the raised edges of the square button under his fingertips, the steady hammering of his heart against his sternum.

"Three, two, one!"

The range dropped from triple digits to double, and he pushed the button. Harpoons streaked past the rear airlock camera with silver cables reeling out in their wake.

Then came the monstrous, shrieking roar of the impact. David slammed so violently into his seat that he couldn't see, and his breath froze in his aching chest.

And it was over. He blinked his eyes clear, listening for something past the ringing in his ears. He still couldn't breathe. The wind had been knocked out of him.

Whiplash jerked them against their restraints, but their helmets and suits wouldn't allow their necks to bend that far, so rather than suffer debilitating injury, David's neck and forehead dug into the suit's padding.

Moments later, the second impact came. They yanked against the cables and harpoons, proving that they had deployed properly. David took comfort in that, and continued struggling to inhale past his burning ribs.

A few seconds later, he managed a burst of air, and heard Lennon gasp as she did the same. He reached for the screen displaying the rear airlock feed—now showing the ruined aft end of the ship—and flicked it to another aft-facing camera. The *Beyond III* was crumpled like a tin can, but more than half of the twelve harpoon cables were holding steady, slack growing in the cables as they drifted toward the *Interloper*. Without any air to slow them, they'd continue bouncing until all of the energy from the collision had been fully spent.

"Ouch," Lennon muttered, pressing on her breastbone through her suit.

"Crew check!" David croaked into the comms.

"Here," Carter said.

"Alive and well," Zasha added.

"Only minor injuries," Liu said.

He noticed Carter fumbling with his restraints, as if to release himself. "Everyone stay put," David said. "It's not over yet. ETA to the next collision, twelve seconds."

"The *next* collision?" Carter groaned. "How many more?"

"Several dozen," Lennon said, "but each one will be slower and weaker than the last."

"Bloody hell," Carter muttered.

David glanced at his co-pilot. "Baxter, damage report."

"The aft end is ruined. The cargo bay depressurized, but the crew decks are maintaining atmosphere—for the moment."

David blew out a painful wheeze. They couldn't have hoped for a better outcome.

The next collision lasted for an instant before they began drifting again, rapidly taking up the slack in the harpoon cables.

"That was pretty mild," Baxter said. "We can probably remove our restraints after the next one."

"Agreed," David replied. He still couldn't believe that they'd all survived. If it had been a car crash at the speed they'd hit, they would have died instantly. But their advantage was the massive crumple zone they'd had to buffer them.

Everyone waited until they hit the end of the cables and jerked forward. David checked the external camera again to make sure the harpoons were intact. He saw that another had broken free and was writhing around restlessly, like a living entity. He counted seven of the original twelve in position, and with the force pulling on those cables diminishing with each bounce, he suspected the remaining ones would hold indefinitely.

David cleared his throat before reaching for the comms panel. "Time to send an update," he said.

Lennon grimaced behind her helmet. "They can't do anything for us at this point."

"Maybe, maybe not, but they need to know that we've reached the target. The mission isn't complete."

Lennon nodded.

David selected the nearest commsat in line of sight. This one had a Chinese name, which meant they were facing the eastern hemisphere, but it didn't matter which government received their message first; it would be relayed around the globe to every other major power, as well as to the intended recipients at Mission Control.

Prior to the collision, they hadn't had time to contact home. Now, David shared both the news that they'd successfully intercepted the *Interloper* and the fact that they'd been forced to dump all of their fuel in the process.

Any chance of a return trip had dwindled to nothing. They were outbound from Earth at better than thirty thousand kilometers per hour, and that figure was set to increase steadily as the *Interloper* continued sunward. A rescue dispatched from Earth, even if launched immediately, would likely never catch up with them, and the crew knew it. They were resigned to their fate.

Except for David himself. He still held out hope. At this point, it was a vague dream that they might locate whatever passed for manual control systems aboard the *Interloper.* Then they could manage to turn around and head for Earth—or more likely, decelerate enough to make a rescue mission possible.

David sent his update as a voice recording and a word-for-word transcript of the same. He kept it brief, sticking to the facts and leaving emotion out of it. He did, however, ask for permission to record and send final messages to their loved ones back home, should it come to that.

"Now what?" Lennon asked, releasing her restraints.

"We unpack the breach equipment and focus on what we came to do," David said.

NINETEEN

Beyond III / The Interloper

L ENNON PEERED AT THE *Interloper* through the hatch window. Lights blinked on the vessel, indicating it was
indeed powered on. The glowing green ambiance sent
shivers down her spine.

The rest of the team was preparing the breach gear,
and she barely heard their chatter. It was mostly Carter's
nervous banter. The man had a penchant for bad jokes,
but Lennon was focused on something else. The explosives were secured beneath the storage panels, and
she struggled to think of a reasonable explanation for
bringing them.

Lennon glanced at the crew. Dark Leader would suggest she kill them all and finish the job, but she wasn't a
murderer. Not without reason. She clenched her aching
hand, and bit her tongue. Anything to distract her racing
mind.

Instead, she altered her plan. She'd help get them on
board the *Interloper*, inspect the vessel, and return to
Beyond for the explosives. Lennon was a professional,
and she'd been in similar circumstances. She just had to
be patient. It's what she did, or what she used to do. It
was becoming familiar again. The anxious energy faded away, replaced with self-assured certainty she would

succeed. Lennon had completed every mission, and her track record had only a single blemish.

She pictured Rutger's face as the door slammed shut, the gunfire that followed. One day later, she'd been dropped off on the eastern seaboard.

"Lennon, you okay?" Zasha asked.

"Sure. Just thinking." Their ship was in stasis, and the harpoon tethers were pulled taut as they lingered a short distance from the alien hull. The green light blinked twice and faded. Was someone observing them? When she glanced at Zasha, she noted the pain in the woman's eyes. "I'm sorry about Akira."

"It wasn't your fault." Zasha hefted a metal case and set it on the airlock's floor. Without gravity or acceleration it floated up, drifting an inch from the surface.

"Still..."

"We knew what we signed up for," Liu said.

"It should have been me out there," Carter added.

"Stop it!" David ordered. He was clinging to a handrail near the breaching kit, and a plastic tool floated near his face. "We're in this together. Whatever we find, her loss will not be for nothing."

Carter seemed ready to argue, but Zasha elbowed him in the chest, and he relented.

"Where are the guns?" Lennon asked.

"You heard the orders. We're to appear peaceful," Zasha responded. Lennon appreciated the use of the word *appear*. There was clearly a subtle meaning behind it.

"To hell with that," Lennon muttered. "They fired first. In wartime, that's cause for retaliation."

"This isn't a war," Liu countered.

"Then what is it?" Lennon urged him. "Because it looked to me like they melted our hull, and killed Akira."

"Technically..." Another elbow shut Carter up again.

Lennon noticed how David stayed silent during the discussion. So he wasn't a dictator. Either he was trying to let the crew come to an agreement, or he was distracted after realizing he was never going to see his family again. Luckily for Lennon, she didn't have something weighing her down. She had no children or a spouse.

"We're going in armed," Lennon said.

"Weren't you in the Air Force? Flying around in one of those cool jets?" Carter asked. "What do you know about guns?"

"Yes. But I'm trained…" Lennon decided not to say any more. Zasha was the team's weapons specialist, though Lennon was willing to bet Zasha didn't understand half as much about the subject as herself.

"I have to agree with Lennon." Zasha's words transmitted through her suit's speaker.

"Seriously?" Carter shouted. "If we walk on there with a big boom stick, those aliens are going to blow our heads off!"

"Enough," David finally said. "Give your vote."

"No to the guns," Carter huffed.

"We can't seem hostile," Liu added. "Commander, you suggested the assault could have been an automated response, like their change of trajectory due to an inbound object. If that's the case, whoever may be aboard has done nothing wrong. The computer system was just doing its job."

"Good point," Carter said.

"Be that as it may, we have to be pragmatic. I vote we bring the handguns," David said, changing the rules.

Lennon wished to complain that their firearms might not be as effective as the high-powered rifles ORB sent with them, but she refrained. A win was a win. And she was as deadly with one gun as the next.

"Then it's settled. Let me retrieve them," Lennon said, wondering how to bring the explosives closer to the ship's exit.

"No. It's my responsibility." Zasha pushed off the bulkhead, drifting out to the cargo area. Lennon silently groaned.

"Okay. Here's the next problem." David turned to face the hatch. "*Interloper* is over a hundred feet away. We were supposed to latch on, use the breach kit, and place the hatch."

Lennon watched the lights flashing in a steady stream from the black hull. "I have an idea."

"Go for it," David ordered.

"I'll make the jump. Propel myself to the hull and secure a spare harpoon tether to this airlock." She nodded to the coil of cable that they'd already fitted with clamps. This way it could be used like an extra-long EVA tether.

"Wait, you intend to shoot out of here and try to hit that?" Carter laughed. "That's crazy. If you miss, you could slip off the tether and float into oblivion."

Lennon shrugged. "You have a better idea?"

"We could do a spacewalk to the nearest harpoon. Climb over there." David gestured to one of the lines jutting out from *Beyond III*. The other end, with the tangled cables of the detached harpoons, resembled a collapsed spider's web, stuck to the *Interloper.*

"I think expedience is key."

"You're expecting retribution?" David tapped the top of the breach kit with his gloved finger.

"Maybe. We can't wait around for them to fire again."

David sighed loudly. "Fine. Are you certain you can make it?"

Lennon was calm. She'd experienced over two hundred dives. Completed forty-one successful missions for the Dark Leader. This was nothing. She still swallowed a lump in her throat before answering. "I'm sure."

"Clear out. Lennon, attach the cable, and we'll send the kit over on a lanyard with Zasha. Start on cutting the hatch opening, and the rest will come when it's completed. Understood?" David waited for them to nod or agree. "Get to it, people!"

Zasha arrived with the weapons, distributing them to the rest of the crew while Lennon strapped herself to the tether coupling inside the airlock. She accepted a custom-designed high caliber handgun. The interior door sealed, leaving her with Zasha in the airlock.

"*Depressurizing now,*" Carter said through the room's speakers.

The air hissed, and she closed her eyes. A few minutes later, the hatch beeped and opened. Lennon had the one side of the cable attached to their ship. It would take extreme force to tear it off, and she didn't expect any issues on that front.

She flung the hatch open, half-expecting to be tossed from *Beyond.* Instead she remained stable, garnering a better view of the *Interloper* without the door impeding. The hull eclipsed the rest of space. It was gigantic. Carter's concerns about missing it seemed comical now.

Lennon went slowly, using the handholds on the ceiling to move closer. It was spectacular. A white light burst in the center of the nearest cluster of green, and then it all vanished, returning to black. They had no knowledge of the interior, so one location seemed as good as the next to cut a hole for the portable hatch. Earlier, Lennon had asked the others for advice, and they'd agreed that the ideal landing spot was the middle.

She pictured herself as a dart, trying to make a bulls-eye. Lennon double-checked the line was secure, and clasped the far end to her suit's belt. The metal pulled tight, and she returned her attention to the *Interloper.*

Lennon peered backwards, finding all three crew members staring through the airlock porthole. When she was done, the airlock would seal again, and they would proceed on an individual basis.

"You going to help?" Lennon asked Zasha.

The Russian woman was blinking quickly, locked on the alien hull. "I can't do this."

"Of course you can." Lennon had seen countless recruits with the same expression early in her career. Once she'd joined Team Dark, she'd been surrounded with competent team members. Professional soldiers like her.

"They're going to kill us," Zasha said.

Lennon sighed as she bounded into the airlock, landing near the other woman. She stood so close, their helmets touched. "This is the easy part. We're going to sail over with our gear and break into the ship. The people of Earth need us, Miss Petrov." At the sound of her last name, Zasha recovered. She undid the strapping, and joined Lennon at the edge of *Beyond*.

"I'm going to make the jump." Lennon held the rungs, and pulled herself to the edge of their own ship. The boots pressed to the outer surface, and she smiled when she turned her head. This was life. Or death. And Lennon would accept any eventuality.

She kicked off and floated from *Beyond* toward the hull, drifting through empty space. One hundred and sixty feet came quicker than she'd expected, and before she banged into the matte finish, she aimed the object in her grasp. The harpoon tip held an explosive charge, and the moment it contacted the hull, a series of spikes emerged, slicing into the alien vessel. It stuck there like an arrow, holding her in place.

"Nice work, Baxter." David's words of encouragement fell flat. This was only the beginning.

"Securing it." Lennon slid a second clip onto the cable and cinched it tight. It paid to be extra cautious. Lennon attached the tether's end to the *Interloper,* and they were connected.

She stared at their crumpled rocket, shaking her head gently. It was a crumbling mess: melted like a candle in areas, and squished in others. She noted the fact she was the very first human to touch an alien craft, and laughed.

"Something amusing, Baxter?" David asked through her helmet's speaker.

"No, sir. Zasha, I'm ready for you."

The woman clasped a second rope and carabiner to her suit and the harpooned length. Zasha slowly approached Lennon, pulling the breach kit attached behind her. Lennon counted the seconds in her mind, and when Zasha arrived it was almost five minutes later.

Plenty of time for the occupants to react to the invaders. But the *Interloper* remained silent.

They used a sonar camera to determine the location of a sealed room nearby. Lennon felt the tug of the straps on her suit's belt, and realized that if this line broke, she'd be gone forever. Floating in space until her oxygen tank was depleted. It was a horrible thought, but even in mission-mode she couldn't help but consider the possibility.

Lennon and Zasha spent the next hour securing the portable hatch to the alien hull, and when it flashed yellow on the control panel, she tested the technology.

"The atmosphere will be sucked out on the other side. We'll know immediately if the entire ship will be affected, or if that room is safely depressurized on its own," Carter told them from the safety of *Beyond*. He was watching from a live camera feed in Lennon's helmet.

"Here goes nothing," Zasha said, tapping the button. Air vented out from the center of the round hatch in a misting white stream.

"That's water vapor," Liu said over their comms. "Water could mean there's life on board."

"There'd better be," Carter added. "I didn't come all this way to say hi to a computer."

Lennon expected complications, but four minutes later, the hatch stopped venting air. "It worked?" She was excited to enter the *Interloper*. What kind of technology would they discover? Where had these beings come from? Were they hostile? A thousand questions rolled through her mind, but she tried to ignore them.

"All clear, Commander," Zasha said.

"Well done, team. We're on the way."

Lennon touched the airlock hatch, and Zasha tugged on her arm. "Where do you think you're going?"

"Inside."

"Not until the commander gets here. His orders."

Lennon almost shoved her off, but she stopped herself. "Fine."

The crew traveled in single form along the cable, each carrying supplies. Carter came last, bringing a container of spare oxygen tanks with him.

It was crowded at the hatch, and the commander unclasped his carabiner, clipping it to change places with Zasha. "Lennon, want to go first?"

She smiled. "Yes, sir."

"You've earned it."

Lennon opened the door and unclipped from the harpoon cable as she climbed through the three-foot rounded entrance. It was pitch black inside, but her helmet lamps flicked on automatically, giving her sight. She left her gun at her suit's hip and scanned the room. It was empty. "All clear."

The rest entered, and Carter pushed the spare oxygen tanks through one at a time. Once the hatch was closed and powered on, Lennon fired small jets in her suit to move to the far wall, searching for an exit. She placed her helmet against the bulkhead, hoping to hear something, but there were no sounds carrying from within the ship. She saw the gleam of a strange but familiar pattern on the surface. "Over here." She felt for the door handle, which wasn't a variation of the knobs or levers they were used to. It had three indentations.

Lennon froze, thinking of the tattoo on her right arm. Three dots in a triangle. It couldn't be a coincidence. How was this possible?

"Baxter, you look like you've seen a ghost," Carter whispered.

She pressed three fingers into the indents. They were deep enough to obtain a grip. She turned her hand left, and a circular panel moved. Then she twisted right. Something unlatched, and the door slid open. Air blasted into the room, pushing her back and slamming her into the opposite wall.

A moment later, they drifted to the floor, with gravity taking hold. She felt subtle vibrations in her boots upon landing.

"Cool," Carter mumbled.

"How...?" Zasha marveled. "Is this artificial gravity?"

"Maybe," David said.

"It's lighter than Earth," Carter added.

"That should make it easy to get around," Lennon said.

They went to the open door, and found themselves in a corridor with a curved ceiling, everything black.

Liu produced a scanner from his belt and began waving it. "The air pressure is point seven atmospheres. Sixty-two percent nitrogen, twenty-nine percent oxygen, six percent argon, nearly three percent water vapor, and trace amounts of other gases," Liu said. "External temperature is five point three degrees centigrade."

"Chilly," Carter said.

"Almost Earth's atmosphere," Zasha said. "Could we breathe?"

"Maybe, but I wouldn't risk it," Liu replied. "We don't know what possible toxins are present."

"Is this rock?" Commander David Bryce rapped his knuckles on the wall, and his eyes went wide. "What is this?"

The corridor was lit by soft green lights, embedded into the floor and ceiling. Lennon followed the curve to where it led into a larger space. Everything was the same. Rock. "It's like the lava tubes in Hawaii," Liu said. "Remarkable."

Lennon touched the material with her glove, seeing thousands of tiny holes. Her heart raced at the sight.

"What the hell..." Carter pulled his finger off the wall, a sticky substance stretching off it.

"Don't move." Liu stalked over. He set a pack down and unzipped it, retrieving a sample jar. He scooped the slime into the container with a sampling spoon.

"Shouldn't we be going?" Zasha's eyes darted nervously down the corridor.

"Everyone has their Holos?" Lennon asked.

They all nodded.

"Utilize the mapping program. It'll track our paths. Pin this location so we can return to it," she said. David took the lead, not contradicting her, and she appreciated the gesture. This would be a lot smoother with one person in charge. And she was more qualified.

"What about the tanks?" Carter gestured to the room they'd entered the *Interloper* on.

"Leave them. It'll slow us down." Lennon started her Holo and dropped a marker. She'd have to separate from the rest of the crew, to return to *Beyond* for the explosives. It would be tricky, but with the air tanks as an excuse, it might work at some later point. She could volunteer to return for them. A successful mission had options and multiple escape routes. That's what she needed here.

"That only gives us sixteen hours," Carter whinged.

"Check again." David tapped the control panel on his left wrist. "Fourteen and change."

"If we're on board for longer than that, we're never leaving," Lennon said, and they all stared at her. She could tell they were waiting for her to go first. She turned from them, and felt good despite the dire circumstances. Regardless of the fact they were waltzing onto a gigantic alien ship with nothing but handguns, she was in control again.

Lennon proceeded with caution, rounding a bend in the rock corridor. There were more blotches of slime on the walls, and Liu slowed to capture high-res images via his in-helmet camera.

"Stay with us," Lennon told him, and he jogged to catch up.

David was eerily quiet, his eyes wide as they strode forward. A combination of their headlamps and the ship's own lights guided their path. Lennon checked her map, seeing the curving red line appearing on the blank rectangle.

"This is natural," David whispered.

"What?" Zasha asked.

"As Liu said, this entire section is a natural rock formation," David replied.

"That's impossible. It's a starship," Carter said.

"Maybe..." Lennon heard the hint of a sound carrying from farther down the tube. She stopped, lifting a palm to silence the others. There it was again. A scraping noise. "Did you catch that?"

"No. What are you talking about?" Zasha asked.

Lennon kept her arm raised, but it was gone. "Never mind. Let's keep moving."

The corridor ended after growing taller, and they filed into an enormous cavern. The lights on the walls were more muted in such a large space, and the ceiling seemed infinite. It was unnerving.

"This reminds me of the caves near my hometown," Carter remarked. "We used to go spelunking when we were younger. Almost got stuck once. My friend's brother was lost for a day. We all thought he was dead, but when they found him, he was asleep with a pack of smokes and an empty whiskey bottle beside him…"

"Would you shut up?" Zasha barked.

"Sorry. I get chatty when I'm nervous," he apologized with a smirk.

Lennon slowly walked to the center of the space. She spun around, scanning the room for signs of life. She stared upwards, thinking she heard shuffling. A blob of slime landed directly on her visor, dripping over her face shield. Lennon wiped it away and sidestepped. "Let's go. I don't like this. Liu, what is that stuff?"

"Good question," he said. "We don't have the means to analyze it."

"We should return to *Beyond* and find out…" Carter's voice was small.

"No," David said.

"Which way?" Zasha gestured at the dozen or so options dimly radiating from the cavernous space.

Lennon guessed this was a hub, and the connecting tubes would lead to various sections of the ship. She thought that perhaps the central ducts would be the smartest options. Two were situated closely, and she went in that direction, stopping in between the exits. Her left hand ached from an old injury, and that made her mind up. Maybe it was a sign; the universe aiding her decision. She stepped into the left tunnel first, and Carter collided with her from behind. "Would you watch where you're going?"

"Hey, what's this?" He stared at a flat panel on the wall with raised dots on it.

He hovered a finger near one of the circles. "Don't do that!" She tried to stop him, but it was too late. The button depressed and a door slammed shut, separating them from the rest of the crew.

"You idiot!" She shoved Carter, his helmet striking the rock.

"I didn't know it would do anything!" he exclaimed.

"We'll be fine." Lennon took a deep breath. She guessed both the panel and the buttons were made of stone.

"Try it again."

Lennon fought the urge to punch Carter.

"*Are you okay?*" It was David on the comms.

"Yes," she responded.

"*Can you... et... out?*" His voice broke up.

"That door must be pretty thick," Carter muttered. "Commander, do you read me?"

This time David's reply was completely garbled.

Lennon hit the same button Carter had, but nothing happened. Then once more, with the same result. She tested the other two, but the door stayed shut. They were trapped.

TWENTY

The Interloper

"D AMN IT! CARTER, COME in!" David yelled over the comms while Zasha used a cutting torch from her belt on the door.

Static hissed in his ear.

"It's not even making a dent," Zasha said after a few more seconds. "The melting point must be incredibly high."

Liu was busy tracing the hidden edges of the door that had divided them. It was black, but smooth and clearly artificial. It reminded David of the outer hull. Probably the same material.

"Keep trying," he told Zasha. "If we weaken a section, we should be able to break through this barrier."

Zasha continued blasting it with the blue-white flame of the torch for several minutes. Eventually, she cursed in Russian and stepped away. "It's not working."

"It's not metal," Liu concluded after scanning the surface with one of his instruments. "But it's not rock, either. Perhaps some type of carbon composite?"

"Then why is it blocking our comms signals?" David asked.

Liu shook his head and shrugged. David nodded to Zasha. "Do we have anything better than that torch?"

"The equipment in the hatch used a combination of plasma beams and physical blades," Zasha said, clipping the tool to her belt. "But those were integrated into the breach kit."

"We don't have a spare?" David asked.

"Back on the *Beyond*," Zasha said.

David slammed the door with his palm and placed his helmet against the surface, listening for a reciprocal slap on the other side.

He tried again, and this time he heard a muffled bang. "They're okay," he said, hitting it once more and receiving a duplicate *bang* in response. "Hello?" he asked using the external speakers in his helmet.

"Commander?" Lennon said, her voice muted by the barrier between them.

"Thank God," he breathed, and upped the volume on his suit's external audio pickups. "We've been unable to break through. We'll return to *Beyond* for the spare breach kit."

"Don't," Lennon said.

"What?"

"It would be faster to find a way around," Lennon explained.

"That's risky," David said.

"This whole mission's a risk. Besides, we have fourteen hours of air. Even if I'm wrong, there'll be plenty of time to get back here."

"I don't like the idea of splitting up, Baxter."

"We came here to explore, didn't we? We'll cover more ground with two teams instead of one. Should be easier with half the effort."

David ground his teeth as he warred with himself over the decision. "Okay, but if you get into any trouble, or you don't find a way to the *Beyond* in the next six hours, I want you back here. I'll have the breach kit ready and waiting to go."

"Copy that," Lennon said.

"Set a timer on your holo. Six hours and counting."

"Done. Good luck, Commander."

"Likewise," he said, pulling away from the door to set his own clock.

Zasha let out a frustrated breath.

"S... ess... on?" Liu asked.

"What?" Static roared in David's ears, chopping off in an electronic squeal that made him wince. He deactivated his comms and indicated the speakers and audio pick-ups in the chin of his helmet. "Switch to external audio. Something's jamming us."

"I guess that explains how a fancy plastic door was blocking our signals. It wasn't," Zasha concluded. "But they are. I hate to be the bearer of bad news, but comms jamming is another hostile move."

"Let's not jump to any conclusions just yet," David said.

"We press on?" Liu tried again.

"Yes," David confirmed. "These corridors probably link up again at some point, and the tracker app on our Holos should make it easy to map out a route."

"That doesn't mean we'll cross paths with Lennon and Carter. This ship is big enough that we could wander around for days and still not bump into each other."

"Which is why we're set to rendezvous here or at the *Beyond* in six hours."

"Doesn't leave much time for exploring," Zasha said.

"Then we'd better start," David replied, and entered the tunnel adjacent to where Lennon and Carter had gone.

The pale green glow from the walls and ceiling grew brighter from the close confines, and their headlamps cast flickering shadows in every alcove and corner. Some of the adjoining tunnels were much smaller, no bigger around than David's gloved fist.

"I wonder what those are for?" he asked as he crouched to shine his lamps inside.

"A type of air duct," Liu suggested.

A scuttling sound registered in David's ears, and his heart seized in his chest as he noticed movement within the tunnel.

"Did you see that?" he whispered to Liu.

"I did indeed..."

"Something is definitely alive in here," David said, reaching for his gun, but he stopped short of drawing the weapon.

"Commander..." Zasha whispered.

He registered the alarm in her voice and turned to face her. "What is it, Petrov?"

Her eyes were wide and staring behind her helmet. "Don't move," she mouthed.

A faint disturbance reached his ears through the external audio pickups. The black ovoid of a spider the size of his palm crawled around from his back to his chest. It had a spiked carapace that reminded him of the outside of the ship, and too many legs to count. Its limbs were slim and snake-like. As he watched, dozens of hair-thin black hairs rose from the creature, waving in the air above it, as if sensing something. He couldn't see any hint of eyes, and it wasn't reacting to the light shining from his headlamps.

"Incredible," Liu muttered, leaning closer to the being.

It made a sharp whistling noise, retreating before rotating its body to face him. The creature raised eight of its jointless legs toward Liu in what resembled a defensive gesture.

"I wonder if..." Liu continued, reaching toward it.

It sprang off David's chest, and Liu managed to duck just before it could land on his visor. He spun away and watched as the spider tucked its legs and vanished into one of the narrow tunnels.

"You scared it off," David whispered. He realized from his burning lungs that he'd been holding his breath.

Zasha was watching the walls and ceiling warily with her gun in grip. "I *hate* spiders," she muttered.

"I don't believe they are a danger to us," Liu said.

"How can you possibly know that?" she countered.

"Because I didn't spot any teeth, and its legs are soft and unarmored, unlike its shell. It wouldn't be able to pierce our suits."

"Let's keep going," David said, and continued through the winding corridor. It branched up ahead, and he chose the left fork because it was closer to where they'd lost track of Lennon and Carter.

"I wonder if those creatures built this ship," Zasha said.

"I doubt it. They're too small," David replied.

"Maybe that's the real crew's offspring."

"Anything is conceivable at this point," Liu said.

Silence thickened the air as the corridor widened. It quickly expanded into another cavernous chamber. The ground was covered in rock formations that appeared vaguely like stalagmites. David led the way to the nearest one and dropped to his haunches to examine it. Liu joined him there.

The rock was glistening, coated in a thick layer of the sticky slime they'd found on the walls earlier.

A hint of movement within the sludge caught David's eye. Tiny versions of the spider they'd encountered were wading through the viscous substance, ducking in and out of the holes in the porous rock beneath it.

"Are those..." Zasha trailed off as she joined them, crouching in front of the rocks.

"Babies," Liu confirmed, smiling behind his helmet. "These must be eggs. Or incubators of some kind."

"Why are you so happy?" Zasha demanded.

"It's life, Miss Petrov. Alien life. And for all we know, it could even be sentient."

A pulse of green light shot through the room, sending them reeling. They drew their weapons and stood. David blinked away the glare from his eyes, wondering where that flash had come from.

"We should go," Zasha said.

"Wait," Liu said. The chamber was gradually increasing in brightness. Then the rounded rocks on the floor pulsed brightly from within, and this time David caught a glimpse of the interior of the rocky eggs. They were teeming with baby spiders.

"Maybe we *should* go," David agreed. "This way. We'll circumvent them." He gave the hatching zone a wide berth. Another two flashes of light chased them into a room with a gleaming, glassy floor that stretched on into darkness. Big ripples raced along it, swishing on the rocky shore.

A massive version of the insectoid alien crawled out.

Zasha's sidearm snapped up.

"Don't shoot!" Liu cried.

The beast screamed, a horrible sound that froze David in his tracks.

"Run!" David shouted.

They turned to leave, only to find the cavern floor churning toward them like a living carpet. Millions of scampering legs rose to a rumbling roar, and the walls began to writhe as hordes of multi-legged creatures came flowing down. They were trapped between a giant spider and thousands of its offspring.

Zasha screamed as the insectoids ambushed her, quickly coating her suit from head to toe. A gunshot rang out from her weapon, followed by another.

The massive alien screeched again, and then came a blinding blast of green light. David stumbled forward. "Don't shoot, Zasha!" He swept the spiders off her visor, which left trails of sticky slime in their wake, but he still couldn't see her face. In its place was a writhing mass of legs. They'd somehow burrowed themselves inside her helmet. Blood sprayed it from the inside, and Zasha sank to her knees, falling to the floor. The creatures swarmed her body. David lingered, staring in shock. Hands pulled him away, slapping stray insects from his arms and torso.

"Into the water," Liu cried, as if it might offer some protection. But the largest threat had originated from that direction. So far, it hadn't moved, however, and anything was better than suffering Zasha's fate.

David wheeled dizzily to the water, stumbling after Liu. They waded in, splashing noisily. The spider queen faced them and shrieked again.

The wave of babies that had killed Zasha surged for the water.

"Below the surface! Quickly!" Liu said.

He dove in and David went after him, their headlamps illuminating the murky depths. He risked a peek behind him as they swam. No sign of the creatures giving chase, but he saw the water stirring violently around the big one's legs.

David swam as fast as he could. Liu was swimming into the black depths of the pool, with no end in sight.

David risked a final glance behind him, and his headlamps reflected off the dull black carapace of the monster. It was wading in casually, as if it knew they were trapped.

David tried the comms to warn Liu, but the electronic squeal of jamming returned, and he swiftly cut the connection.

After a few more seconds of desperately clawing through the water, a fuzzy green ambiance appeared. Then the glow resolved to the oval rim of a narrow tunnel. It looked wide enough for them to enter, but too narrow for the predator chasing them. Liu gestured at it, and they swam harder, aiming for the mouth of the tunnel.

Liu proceeded first, and wormed his way through the corridor. For a moment David feared Liu was stuck, and he checked for signs of pursuit.

The dark mass was roiling behind them, stirring up sediment.

When David glanced up, Liu was gone. He swam inside and clawed the walls to pull himself through. The tunnel curved up sharply, making it difficult to angle his body in the proper direction. Liu was slimmer, giving him the advantage. David's breathing grew shallow, and his heart rate sped up. Something grabbed onto his ankle, wrapping around it like a snake. He kicked it with his other foot and searched for handholds to tug himself up.

His fingers tucked into a hole, and he heaved just as the pursuer's limbs caught his ankle. He stomped at them repeatedly.

His suit dragged against the rock, and he maneuvered into the vertical section of the tunnel. A bright light shone from above. It quickly resolved into two as he rocketed to the top of the tube. Liu's headlamps.

Liu helped him up, grunting as he lifted David's dead weight. He rolled onto the floor of a new cavern and lay there, gasping and shaking from spent adrenaline. A buzzing sound rang in his ears. Zasha's loss washed over him, filling him with despair. He let out an anguished cry and sat up, glaring at Liu. "You said they weren't a threat."

Liu's face crumpled with that rebuke, and David immediately regretted his outburst. "I'm sorry. You couldn't have known."

Liu nodded. "But my assumption cost Zasha her life."

"No. We were trapped. Even if we had been more careful... there's nothing we could have done differently." David found himself staring at his ankle and listening to the humming in his ears. His skin was tingling where that giant spider had grabbed him. And it felt...

Wet.

He inspected the wound. His suit was torn all the way to his boot, and puncture marks radiated around the tough material. He noticed the flashing alert on the HUD inside his helmet that indicated his suit had lost pressure. An emergency seal had automatically cinched off the leak below his knee, so he wouldn't run out of air anytime soon, but that still left concerns about alien venom, blood loss, or even anaphylaxis from an allergic reaction to that spider's saliva.

"Take off the boot," Liu said as he shrugged out of the pack he wore beside his air tank and produced a med kit from the bag.

David winced as he undid the clasps and cautiously slid it off. His ankle was ringed with dark, bloody puncture wounds above the joint, and his sock was already soaked crimson. Liu hastily collected blood samples, disinfected the wounds, and bound it with a bandage to stop the bleeding.

"That should do it, Commander, but tell me the minute you have any symptoms."

"A tingling."

"Is it spreading?"

"No."

"It may be a local analgesic. To prevent their prey from feeling pain."

Liu stored the blood sample in his bag, and David put his boot on. It wasn't much comfort, but maybe Zasha hadn't suffered in her final moments. Even so, it was a gruesome way to go—punctured in a hundred different places by alien spiders until one of them struck a vital artery and she bled out.

Both Zasha and Lennon had insisted that the aliens were hostile, and he hadn't listened. If anyone was to blame for this, it was him, and he was going to have to live with that for the rest of his life. However short it might be.

Pushing off the ground, he tested his weight on his ankle, and found that he could walk. "Let's keep going.

We have to get to *Beyond*." He drew his gun, and kept it at the ready.

Liu nodded as he slung on his pack and did the same.

The dull, throbbing ache in David's ankle was a grim reminder of his mistake. He just hoped that Lennon and Carter would escape before they suffered the same fate as Zasha.

TWENTY-ONE

Da Nang, Vietnam

ATLAS GAPED AT THE ceaseless waves of the East Vietnam Sea. Their boat bobbed repeatedly, but Atlas had enough experience on the water to have capable sea legs. The crew were all salty locals, and he was surprised to find two younger women on the staff. They worked hard with the best of them, anchoring the vessel in the murky waters.

"Hurry," Hung said in choppy English. He tapped his wrist like he was wearing a watch. The sun was beginning its descent, and Atlas assumed everyone was eager to return home. Or, by the looks of them, at least to the local dock bar.

"How deep is it?" Atlas asked.

"Here? Continental shelf... about a hundred meters." Hung pointed to the deck.

The wind gusted, and Atlas glanced up to see a pair of birds circling high above. He felt like prey lately. Was this general watching him from a satellite or a drone at this very moment?

"This should be simple, then," Atlas told him. But the chances were high that someone else had already combed this segment extensively in the last twenty years. There had been an influx of collectors for war antiquities, and Vietnam era were among the most sought after.

But the ocean was a vast place, and Atlas clung to the hope his prize had yet to be claimed.

He watched as two of the men utilized a ten-foot-tall crane that clutched the Sea Diver 9000, an old model of underwater exploratory drones. He'd operated a similar version years before, and this one looked like it had gone through the paces. The red painted numbers were nearly worn off, the light lenses caked in grime.

"Does it work?" he asked Hung.

"Yes." Hung cleared his throat and spat on the boat deck.

Atlas stepped aside to the railing, holding tight as the Diver was lowered into the waves. The claw released it, and he joined Hung and a woman in the captain's cabin. It stank of sweat and sea, a combination sure to make anyone queasy.

"Anh will show you." Hung went to a cabinet and poured himself a drink. He offered a glass to Atlas, but given the torn label and dirty cup, he thought better.

"No, thank you." Atlas turned his attention to the screen on the desk.

"We take it lower." Anh used the controls, spinning the joystick lever, and she pressed a series of buttons, activating the lights.

A fish swam by, darting in shock from the sudden ambiance.

Sweat dripped down Atlas' side. He was nervous. This might be it. What if he found the relic he'd been searching for? Was there really an alien ship here?

"Come on," he muttered to himself.

Anh glanced up and continued, descending the drone deeper into the sea. The Sea Diver sent bubbles out, blocking the view as it released air. The water cleared the lower it went, and Atlas held his breath as he saw the first hint of the ocean floor.

Seaweed littered the sand, stunted at this depth. *Where is it?* He double checked the coordinates, and saw they were at precisely the right location. Then why wasn't the vessel nearby? He wondered how he'd explain it to these people, should they encounter a ship from another world. He hadn't thought this far ahead, not after being in such a rush.

It wasn't as if he had a lot of money to bribe them with.

The drone hovered a few yards above the silt, and Atlas stared at the screen as the camera showed the image slowly spinning in a full three-sixty. There was nothing here.

"Son of a…" He caught himself when he noticed a depression in the seaweed. "What is that?"

Anh spoke in Vietnamese, and moved the drone closer.

"Hung, any ideas?" Atlas gestured at the bare spot. It was relatively deep, sunken five feet below the otherwise flat sea bottom. Almost like an old impact crater that had been filled in over the years.

"I no see anything," Hung said.

Atlas frowned. It wasn't much, but this could be where the crashed vessel had lain. If it was, someone had beaten him to it.

"Take it up. We're done here." Atlas went outside, wiping a sheen of sweat off his face. All this way and effort just to find an empty crater.

He stood on the edge of the boat as they returned to the shore, and an hour later, they were docking as the rain began. Atlas let the drops saturate him, not caring if he was soaked. This was the end of the line.

"Thank you," he told Hung, providing the rest of the promised payment.

Hung grunted, and Anh waved at him from the deck while he walked under the awning of the nearest building.

His Holo rang, startling him. Who could be calling? He saw his brother's name, and almost ignored it. But he was too depressed to be alone.

"Hello," he flipped the table.

His brother filled the screen. "Atlas, where the hell are you?"

"Vietnam," he said.

"I'll never understand what you're doing," Hayden said.

Atlas heard the kids playing in the background, and little Paige sat at the table with a coloring book. "How is everyone?"

"The usual... school's in full force. Lisa's working overtime at the hospital, so I'm on daddy duty most nights. What about you? Living the bachelor's dream?" Hayden laughed, and Atlas suddenly wondered what he was doing here.

"I'm coming home," he whispered.

"Are you okay?"

"Sure."

"You have bags under your eyes, and you're soaked. Seriously... what's going on?" Hayden insisted.

He had to fight the urge to tell his older brother the truth. "It's nothing. Do you mind if I visit?"

"We'd love to see you. You'll have to sleep in Wyatt's bed, but..."

"That's perfect."

Hayden scratched his stubble. "When are you landing?"

"Soon. I'll try for a flight tomorrow. Give me a couple of days."

"Great. You sure you're okay? You need anything? Money?"

Atlas found that amusing, but kept it inside. "No. I appreciate the gesture, though."

The call ended, and he caught a glimpse of Anh entering a nearby bar. She paused at the entrance and held it open, as if inviting Atlas in. That was a bad idea, but his curiosity got the better of him.

The rain pelted against the overhang, dripping in a big pool on the slotted wooden walkway, and he deftly avoided stepping in it. "Hello," he greeted her.

"Hi. Care for a drink?" she asked with a backward glance as she went inside.

He shrugged. The joint was half full, and he spotted a few of the crew he'd just shared a boat with. One of them glanced up at the newcomers, but quickly returned his attention to the beer in front of him.

Anh walked to the bar and lifted two fingers, sitting at the end. A dark wooden stool creaked as Atlas sat on it, and the bartender, a young man with a black t-shirt and a white apron on, passed two pints of a pale yellow lager to them.

"I know what you were after." Anh took a long drink, smacking her lips.

"You do?" Atlas cocked an eyebrow as he tested the bitter beer.

"My uncle used to work for a man. They collected planes and boats. Sunken. They might be able to help you."

"Oh?" Atlas's interest was piqued, but he contained his enthusiasm. "Where is he? Your uncle?"

"Passed away."

"Ah. Sorry to hear it." Atlas grimaced and sipped his beer. Another dead end.

"Where are you from?" she asked.

"The States. You?"

"Here. Born a mile away. On the water," she laughed.

"It shows. You like what you do?"

Anh took another drink. "It's okay."

"What do you think I was after?"

"A rock."

Atlas titled his chin and stared at her. "A *rock*?"

"Maybe he's still around," Anh suggested.

"The man your uncle worked for?" Atlas ventured.

She nodded.

"What was the company name? Do you recall?"

"Not a company. A boat." Anh rose, walking to the far corner of the bar. Atlas followed, taking his beer. The wall was covered in a series of photos, old pictures ranging from black and white Polaroids from before the Vietnam War, to modern fishing ships with bright crew uniforms and cheerful faces.

She strode up and down the line, pausing in the middle. She yanked one off the wall, the pin tearing through the photo. Anh grinned, and tapped the image of her uncle. "Chi was a kind man."

Atlas looked at the guy, then the name of the boat. He didn't recognize the specific script. "What does that mean?" He pointed to the characters scrawled on the vessel, barely visible behind her uncle's legs.

"*Chim*. Small bird."

Atlas reached for the photo. "Do you mind?"

She shook her head.

He brought it to the bar, pulling his Holo out. With a quick search, he managed to match the characters and found a few references to the vessel. "Have you seen it in these waters, Anh?"

"No. Not in years."

Atlas eventually discovered the company it was registered under had gone bankrupt. "Just my luck."

He was about to give up when he noticed a hit five spaces below. It had the owner's last name. He typed it in, using the word *Chim*, and got a result. Pham Hoang Phu. The man operated a business two hours down the coastline.

Atlas gazed at Anh, who seemed eager for his company. "You're leaving now?"

He left a bill for the beers. "I don't have much time. Thank you." Anh acted disappointed, but nodded in reply.

Atlas rushed out into the rain, towards his rental car in the parking lot. Without hesitation, he plugged the address into the GPS and started driving.

There was no time for sleep. He was close to a break-through. He could feel it.

TWENTY-TWO

The Interloper

"**D**ID YOU HEAR THAT?" Carter stared at the ceiling. She had. Muffled screams through the comms. "Don't worry about it." She checked the teams' locations on the tracker, finding them stationary. The dense rock was messing with all systems, not just the comms.

"Come in, Commander," Carter said. "What is your status?" He smacked his helmet with a palm, as if it might solve their communication issue. "This is the worst."

"I thought you wanted to explore?" Lennon pressed on, walking through the ever-rising tunnel. It bent, and she followed the path to another opening. "It's so big."

"I will investigate the ship, but not like this. We should try to meet up with Bryce and the others."

If there are any others. Lennon should have been with the crew to protect them, but none of it was going to matter if she blew up the *Interloper*. And that meant returning to *Beyond* to retrieve the explosives. Dark Leader was counting on her, but could she even do it? Push the detonator and watch it all explode?

"Lennon?" Carter trudged forward, stopping at the round doorway.

She joined him, peering at their two options. "Last time we went left, and you remember what happened. Let's go right." She stepped into the next corridor, and the green lights dimmed at their approach. Her suit lamps brightened in contrast.

"Please tell me I'm not the only one scared out of my mind," Carter muttered.

"It's unsettling," she agreed. But she was calm. This was no worse than running into an active war zone. The danger was almost exhilarating.

"Unsettling? This is downright terrifying. So where are they?"

"Who?"

"The aliens! We've only seen some slime... and this rock. Are we inside an asteroid?" Carter jabbed at the wall.

"That's it..."

"What's it?" Carter gave her a perplexed look.

"The *Interloper*... it was built around an asteroid."

"With tunnels throughout?" Carter eyed the three indentations of another door handle, and she slapped his arm away.

"Don't touch anything," she ordered. "And yes, maybe they burrowed through the rock."

"What could do that? Zasha's torch wouldn't even make a dent."

He was right. "The doors are a different material, similar to the hull, but it would take a high-tech tool to sculpt these tunnels," she whispered.

"We should find them," Carter urged.

"The aliens?"

"We're here, aren't we? It's why we came."

"I thought you were afraid."

"I am, but we can't die before we complete the mission." Carter went first.

Lennon shrugged and joined him, her footsteps light in the low gravity. She checked the Holo, seeing the line of red indicating their progress. She rotated the view, noticing the rise in their trajectory, and guessed they were nearing the top of the ship.

A few minutes later, they reached another black door, this one closed. "No exit," she said.

"Dammit. A dead end?" Carter placed his finger in one of the holes, and it clicked as he turned it. "No way." He rotated it the opposite direction, and the door slid up with a hiss of air.

"Stay back," Lennon ordered, placing a finger on his chest. She unstrapped the gun, and held it up as she stepped into the new hall. The other side of the corridor was made from artificial material. "We're exiting the asteroid section." The lights seemed brighter here, and her suit dimmed.

Carter's jaw dropped. "We're close."

She didn't respond, just checked both directions for any signs of threats. There was nothing but silence.

Lennon tested the comms. "David, Zasha, Liu, come in."

Static.

"Commander, what is your position?" Carter bellowed, and she shushed him.

"Easy, Carter. You trying to wake them up?" Lennon noted that the space they occupied was designed to match the rocky tunnels. The molded material curved at the ceiling, and they'd even added in the miniscule holes.

"No answer. I thought maybe once we left the asteroid, the comms might connect again," he said, checking his Holo.

Lennon saw movement on her right, and swung the gun in a loop.

"What's the problem?"

"I saw something."

"Shit." Carter fumbled with his gun, and it fell to the floor.

Lennon ignored him, stepping at the shadows. She crouched, touching a drop of the slime. "We're not alone."

"I knew I should have stayed on Earth. My brother opened an auto repair shop. He's made enough to buy a lake house. Can you believe it? And here I am..."

"Would you please shut up?" Lennon murmured.

"Sorry. Like I said..."

Lennon heard it again, a scraping noise in the distance. The ceiling rose twelve feet, and the hall was half that wide. The light grew darker, and she sensed a shape was blocking the green glow from farther down. That meant it was big.

"Go."

"Where? We have..."

She shoved him, and he ran. Lennon peered over her shoulder as she pounded after him, seeing the monstrous creature silhouetted against the green light. It had numerous legs, allowing it to run very quickly. She didn't spy anything resembling a face on the thing's torso, but one target was as good as another. Lennon tapped the trigger, striking it in the central carapace. It slowed momentarily, then renewed its pursuit.

"What the hell is that?!" Carter's arms pumped as he ran, leaping in the low gravity with each long step.

"Keep moving!" Lennon's heart raced as they neared a corner in the hall. "Inside!" The doorway was open, and Carter spun as he entered, twisting his fingers into the handle. She circled around, kicking off, and slid on her back end, aiming at the spider's core as it tore through the hall, angrily thrashing its appendages. It screeched, revealing its mouth. That's where she aimed. One. Two. Three taps, and the door closed between them. The enemy crashed into the panel, denting it in the middle.

Lennon heard it collapse to the floor.

"Is it...?"

She waited a beat, listening for sounds of movement. Not hearing any, she nodded, hoping she was right. "It's dead."

"That was messed up," Carter panted.

Lennon jumped to her feet and peered around the room. "This is different." A shiny black table centered the space, and when she walked to it, a light emanated from the middle. A projection appeared, and Lennon saw what it was. The *Interloper*.

"It's a 3D render," Carter whispered. He put a hand through the hologram, and it dissipated for a moment before returning. A yellow icon blinked near the top of the ship.

"That's where we are," Lennon guessed, trying to gather her bearings and breath.

"And we smashed *Beyond III* into her hull, here." He pointed at the far end of the *Interloper.*

Lennon hunted for a solution, and found a trail leading to their rocket if she stayed on the outer levels and avoided the asteroid tunnels. The trip would be much easier, but would those creatures be out there, searching for her?

She had ten hours of air remaining. Her muscles were growing tired. She checked her timer. Two more hours to go before the rendezvous with David. Could they return in time? Lennon wasn't sure how she'd be able to retrieve the explosives without being seen. She didn't want to run into Zasha, since she'd gone to get the spare breach kit out of storage.

"What's this place?" Carter gestured to the bow of the *Interloper*, which didn't reveal itself on the map. "It's blank. Hollow, maybe?"

"No idea." She couldn't worry about that now. The explosives were priority.

"Why would they have a map, and leave part of it empty?" Carter's visor lit up with the glow of the projection, and he blinked before looking at her.

"Carter..." The far door opened, and Lennon cursed herself for not noticing a second entrance. She positioned herself between it and Carter, clutching her gun.

The being ducked to fit inside, dozens of legs folding then spreading as it stalked them.

"We come in peace," Carter said, shoving his Holo out. A strange noise emitted from the device.

"What the hell are you doing?" Lennon asked.

"It's the sound a tarantula makes when it confronts another spider. I translated..."

"You're trying to *talk* to it?"

"Why not?"

The creature seemed to pause. She noticed wriggling hairs on the thing's torso as a drop of ooze dripped from its underside. Its body was as big as a black bear's, but with all those legs it looked a lot larger.

"We're not here to harm you," Carter said, his hands raised, and the Holo spat out a chittering sound.

Lennon saw the thing's mouth open and close, and it screamed, a piercing noise that made her cringe. She didn't hesitate. Lennon fired repeatedly, until she was out of bullets. The monster rushed them, knocking Carter's Holo to the floor. It stepped on the device, cracking the screen, and he fell back. His gun was on the ground next to him, and Lennon dove, rolling to her feet with the weapon in her grip.

Carter screamed as she blasted the alien from behind. After a few seconds, it ceased flailing and fell onto her crewmate. Luckily the bulk of it missed him, or he'd have been crushed, even in this gravity.

Lennon tugged on his arm, and he slid from beneath the pile of twitching legs.

"Are you okay?" she asked.

"I think... I rolled my ankle." He sat up, wheezing his breaths. He was clutching his ankle and wincing.

"Damn it," she muttered, staring at the huge carcass. She tried to think of a solution. "I'll find help."

"You can't leave me here!"

Lennon grabbed a spare magazine, slamming it in place, and passed the gun to him, handle first. "Stay put."

"How would I go anywhere?"

"I'll close the door behind me."

"Lennon, please..." he pleaded.

"I'll go to *Beyond* and bring a spare oxygen tank for you. Our six hours are almost up. David and the others will be waiting. I'll bring help." Lennon stayed near him on the floor, smiling. "You'll be okay. How many of these giant abominations can there be?"

"Judging by the size of this ship... a lot!"

"Stay quiet. If something comes in, hide under this corpse. And don't try to make nice," she said.

"Be fast," he whispered, giving in.

She laid a palm on his thigh. "I will."

Lennon hopped up, feeling a renewed sense of energy. Carter was hurt, but this was the perfect opportunity. Now she could operate freely.

Dark Three exited the room without hesitation, and sealed the door by twisting the strange three-circle handle. Were these the aliens they were supposed to meet? She tried to imagine that hideous beast creating such an intricate structure. The 3D projections. It didn't come across as overly intelligent, but she realized that was being closed-minded. She was thinking like someone from Earth.

But they *were* deadly, and that was enough to keep Lennon on edge as she returned to *Beyond*. She stalked down the replicated corridors with renewed purpose.

The mission always came first.

TWENTY-THREE

The Interloper

D AVID SIPPED WATER FROM the straw inside his suit and took a moment to gather himself before pushing off the deck. He winced as he put weight on his injured ankle, and Liu stepped over to help.

"I'm okay," David said, waving him off.

"What now?" Liu asked, glancing to the top of the flooded tunnel they'd found to escape from their enemies. His helmet's lamps flashed off the surface, then at David.

He checked the timer he'd set on the heads-up display in his helmet. "We're two hours from the rendezvous with Lennon and Carter."

"I won't go back..." Liu said.

"No. We can't," David agreed, remembering the spiders that had mercilessly killed Zasha. He peered down the narrow rock tunnel. It was much taller than it was wide, giving the impression that they were at the bottom of a deep crevasse. Faint green lights pulsed steadily, reminding him of the ominous flashes that had erupted from the giant spider. Could the glow be coming from the small versions?

He suppressed a shiver and reached for his sidearm. Unclasping it from the holster, he drew the weapon and held it in a two-handed grip. "Stay close," he whispered to Liu. The other man merely nodded.

The darkness fled before their headlamps as they proceeded along the tunnel. Each new bend had them slowing with the threat of what could be lurking beyond, but so far there was no sign of the creatures.

The shaft widened and led to a sealed door. It was flat and black, and made of the same material as the one that had cut them off from Lennon and Carter.

"Now what?" Liu breathed. "Should we try a different path?"

David had lost track of how many times the corridors had split or branched off, but he'd yet to find the original path. He checked the mapping app on his Holo via his HUD and saw the route they'd taken through the ship.

The point where they'd left Carter and Lennon was marked with a red X. They were almost a full kilometer away, and the *Interloper* was only two and a half klicks from stem to stern. Having boarded near the midpoint that meant they had to be getting close to the aft end.

"It looks like we're almost at the aft end," he said to Liu. "If we keep going, the corridors should wrap around and take us back."

Liu nodded to the door. "But this passage is blocked."

David stared at the barrier with a frown. He began running his hands around the edge of it, feeling for a seam or a control surface.

Almost by accident his fingertips brushed a series of three holes arranged in a triangle. He fitted his fingers to them. While searching for buttons inside those indentations, he accidentally twisted his wrist, and a circular section rotated.

"What was that?" Liu asked.

"It's a locking mechanism," David realized, twisting the controls one way, then the other. He turned it a few more times, but the door stayed shut. "It seems like a combination lock," he realized.

"The only problem is we don't know the code."

David stared at the rotary inset, trying to identify notches or symbols that might indicate different positions. There was nothing that he could see, so it had to be simpler than he was thinking. He tried spinning it counter clockwise, then clockwise.

The slab remained sealed.

Then he reversed it: clockwise, counter clockwise.

The door swished open, and David grinned.

"You did it!" Liu said. "Now we won't have to cut through to reach Lennon and Carter."

"Maybe not, but we still have to locate them. Come on." They came upon a very different kind of space. It was made of a porous black material, but the walls were no longer rough and uneven. Straight surfaces finished in sweeping curves along the ceiling and floor. Dim green lights glowed above them at regular intervals, as well as limning a series of doors on both sides of the corridor.

David hesitated before taking another step and flexed his hands on the grip of his weapon. These rooms wouldn't be occupied by vaguely intelligent alien spiders. A suspicion curled in David's gut. They were entering the part of the *Interloper* used by the creators of the ship.

"You don't think these rooms are inhabited?" Liu whispered.

Before he could reply, a door swished open, revealing a sleek black creature. Tall and willowy, it walked on four slender legs, with two extending above, and two below its round dark body. It strolled on both the deck and the ceiling simultaneously.

David aimed his weapon at the alien, but he held his fire when it began to leave. Somehow, it hadn't noticed their headlamps shining on it.

The door it had emerged from gently shut.

"Commander," Liu whispered urgently.

The creature froze at the sound of his voice.

Liu made a strangled sound and took a quick step back. David spared a hand from his gun to grab Liu's arm. He squeezed hard to get the point across, but it was too late. The being shrieked and spun around, revealing a horrendous, glistening white maw ringed with concentric circles of crystalline teeth. David couldn't see any sign of eyes or a nose, but the body was covered in the same worm-like hairs as the spiders.

"Run!" Liu cried, tearing his arm free.

The four-legged thing became a blur as it launched itself down the tunnel, its jaws gaping wide for the kill.

David pulled the trigger, aiming for the creature's gullet. The weapon went off with a deafening *bang*, and the monster recoiled as the bullet struck its body. The shot glanced off with a high-pitched, quasi-metallic *plink*.

The alien landed at David's feet, but swiftly rose on lean legs until its mouth was at eye-level with his head. Its upper set of limbs clutched his shoulders, and he felt sharp spikes sinking through his suit.

Stifling a scream, he fired continuously as its horrible mouth surged for his helmet.

At point-blank range it was impossible to miss. The bullets sank into flesh with meaty *thwups*, making the monster scream as it retreated into darkness.

Another emerged from a door farther down.

"Get out of there!" Liu called. David frantically returned to the rocky labyrinth. Finding the circular panel in the wall, he reversed the sequence he'd used to open the door, and it slammed closed, catching a willowy black limb. Translucent liquid sprayed out, and a muffled shriek sounded from the other side. A severed piece of the appendage fell to the ground at their feet. Like the spiders, this appendage seemed to have no joints. It wriggled violently, as if still seeking its prey.

Were these the aliens they'd come to meet? If so, that door wouldn't stay shut for long. "Let's go," he said.

But Liu had shrugged out of his sample bag and was crouching beside the severed alien limb.

"What are you doing?"

"One moment please, Commander."

"We have to go! They could open that door at any moment!"

"They why haven't they?" Liu challenged.

David blinked and frowned, taking a moment to still his racing heart with a few calming breaths. David watched as Liu withdrew a large plastic container and used a scalpel to cut a piece of the alien leg. He dropped it inside, screwed the lid on tight, and returned it to his bag. "Now we can go," he said, straightening and spinning in a slow circle. "Where to?"

David nodded sideways to indicate the rocky fissure they'd come from. "We're going back to try another tunnel," he said, echoing Liu's earlier suggestion.

David led them to the first junction, this time taking a different fork. Minutes raced by, the rocky walls blurring as they rounded bend after bend. Every so often, scuttling sounds echoed deep within the walls, and occasionally they saw a fleeting shadow. It felt like they were being watched from the myriad holes in the walls, but that was wrong. The aliens had no eyes, so they definitely weren't *watching*.

David decided to risk taking a break. Upon seeing a relatively straight stretch of tunnel with good sightlines on both ends, David lifted his arm, making Liu stop.

"Liu." David sipped water from a straw near his mouth.

"Yes, Commander?" Liu whispered.

"Have you noticed that none of the beings we've met so far have had any eyes?"

"I did observe that, yes."

"And what do you make of it?"

"I believe they must utilize other senses. Hearing and touch. Possibly smell."

"That's my thinking, too," David agreed. "So if we run into them again, we might be able to slip by undetected if we're careful not to cause any disturbances."

Liu nodded, adding nothing more to their new policy. David smiled tightly and continued on. It wasn't long before they came to a dead end. This time David hesitated before using the controls. If they stumbled into another corridor full of spiders or pods, they might not be lucky enough to escape.

But they didn't have much choice. There were less than two hours until their rendezvous with Lennon.

David fastened his grip on the door handle.

"Wait," Liu said, and reached for the UWB scanner on his belt. It used a combination of radio waves and sound waves to map the inside of semi-solid objects. "Let me check what's through there first." He placed the circular dish at the tip of the wand-shaped scanner against the door. A moment later they'd both connected to the device, and 3D imagery from the other side appeared on his Holo.

It was a vast cavern with a cluster of giant ovoid boulders seated on skinny black pillars in the center of the floor, which was perfectly flat and smooth, unlike the rocky surface of the tunnel where they stood.

"It's another nest," Liu whispered sharply, his eyes widening with terror behind his visor.

"I don't know..." David trailed off.

The eggs they'd found with Zasha had been much smaller, and they'd had a shape like stalagmites, while these were seated precariously on an artificial deck. And they were too regularly spaced to have been chosen at random by a rudimentary alien intelligence to lay their eggs. The formation felt more artificial to David's eye.

"We have to continue. If we do run into something, at least we're prepared. Don't make a sound."

Liu blew out a breath and withdrew the scanner. "I hope you know what you're doing."

Me too, David thought as he operated the handle. The thick metal slab opened, revealing the vast chamber. A perfectly flat deck led to a cluster of massive elliptical boulders seated on thin dark columns. Pulsing green light washed through the room in waves, almost like the sweep of an ambulance's siren. Giant circular shadows cast by the boulders elongated through the room with each pulse of the light.

Liu hefted his UWB scanner and aimed at the nearest boulder. His intent was clear. He wanted to scan the rocks and make sure they weren't secretly hollow and teeming with swarms of spiders.

They approached cautiously. David's eyes were everywhere, checking for darting shadows, but there wasn't anything, and they reached the first of the massive rocks in less than a minute.

Liu placed the scanner against the underside of the rock, which sat at about shoulder height. Status lights on the device flashed as the scan initiated.

In the same instant, a roar erupted from somewhere high above. David looked up sharply, just in time to find a sweep of the emerald lights illuminating a writhing carpet of shadows scurrying from holes in the rocky ceiling.

Spiders.

A distant shriek pierced the silence in the cavernous compartment. Liu hurriedly flicked off the scanner, but it was too late. They should have known better. The UWB used both radio waves and low-frequency *sound* to image inside of objects. Those aliens had sensed the vibrations and emerged from their hiding spots.

TWENTY-FOUR

The Interloper

"**D**ON'T MOVE," DAVID WHISPERED to Liu. The medical officer obeyed. Insects poured from the top of the cavern and across the deck, flooding the entire area.

Liu broke and tried to run as the wave of aliens drew near, but David's arm snapped out to stop him. Together they held their ground against the advancing swarm. The mass enveloped their boots before proceeding upward.

Liu's eyes flew wide as one of them crawled up his torso, but to his credit, he stood frozen like a statue. Maybe he'd locked up with fear, or he understood *why* David had told him to stay still. Vibrations. If they took so much as a single step, the blind alien would recognize that something was alive inside these suits, and they would succumb to the same fate as Zasha.

The seconds dragged by. David watched the spiders at his feet. They had more legs than arachnids from Earth, but it was the closest analog to his experience.

One of them climbed up his body, then jumped off when it reached his navel. It was working. The crawlers couldn't tell the difference between them and inanimate objects.

But the spider on Liu's torso hadn't jumped off yet, and it was probing around with its dozens of wormlike legs.

Shorter versions of those appendages sprouted from its ovoid body as if sensing something in the air. Liu's chest rose and fell steadily with his breath. The spider was detecting that movement.

Liu seemed to recognize the problem, and he held his breath. Moments later the spider sprang off to join its friends on the floor. Finally, the mass of aliens went on, darting up the walls, and then vanishing into the darkness.

David waited a few seconds more before finally cracking out of his frozen posture. His muscles and joints ached as he rolled them out. Holding perfectly still for several minutes wasn't easy, but they'd succeeded.

Rather than speak audibly, David simply gestured to the far end of the cavernous space. They had to keep pushing. The timer on his HUD indicated an hour and a half before the rendezvous, but there was a full kilometer of corridors to traverse before they returned there.

David led the way to the shadowy recesses of the echoing space. As he continued between the round stones, he realized that something about them was off. Roughly egg-shaped and black like the rest of the rock inside the ship, but perfectly smooth—unlike the walls of the tunnels, which were riddled with different-sized holes. They reminded David of giant river rocks, but that wasn't what made them so remarkable. Each was nearly identical to the last.

Nothing they'd come across seemed smart enough to have built this vessel. Those beings hadn't worn any clothes or armor, nor had they borne any weapons. And simply locking a door had stymied them.

So where were the *Interloper*'s proper owners?

David used another handle, and readied himself for what lay beyond.

The hall was lined with nondescript doors. According to the tracker app, this was the right way. David faced Liu and held a finger up to his lips. Liu nodded.

They drew their sidearms before entering. David left the door open, not wanting to create noise or vibrations. Maybe they'd stumble upon more pod creatures, but that might be the lesser evil after witnessing a swarm of several thousand spiders.

They hurried towards a sealed exit at the end. To his amazement, the compartment beyond had furniture and equipment. The deck was covered with pedestals that reminded him of tree trunks. Arrayed around those were circular blue-green lights. David probed the nearest with his foot, and it yielded. It was a cushion with a lamp inside. David surveyed the area, realizing what they were looking at.

"This is a mess hall," David whispered. The 'trunks' were tables, the cushions seats.

Liu bobbed his head. "But for who?"

David thought he spied a food prep area or a galley along the far end. On the other side was a vast, curving black wall with pinpricks of light shining from it. David's brain caught up a split-second later. Those pinpricks were stars. It was a massive floor-to-ceiling viewport. And yet, it couldn't be. They'd spent months on their approach studying the exterior of the *Interloper* through the *Beyond*'s telescopic cameras.

It didn't have any windows, unless this had been hidden on the far edge of the *Interloper*. It was conceivable, David supposed. But if you're going to put windows on a ship, why only one, and why in the mess hall? More likely it was some type of digital display. And that was the biggest indication, besides the ship itself, of any advanced technology on board.

David and Liu crossed the deck to the viewport. He placed a hand on the surface. It was smooth and extremely high resolution, but didn't respond to his touch. It was indistinguishable from an actual window, except perhaps that it was cleaner, with no signs of smudges from alien creatures placing their hands or faces against the glass.

"Remarkable," Liu said.

David nodded. "Let's keep exploring. If these are the living quarters for the actual crew, we could run into them soon."

David continued to the far end of the chamber, eventually coming to an exit. Before leaving, he studied the mess hall once more.

"What is it?" Liu asked.

"If the size and the number of tables and seats are anything to go by, this place could feed about a hundred beings at any given time."

"Yes. I believe so," Liu agreed.

"So how many crew did they set out with? Maybe two or three hundred, if they were assigned to different eating schedules. Double that if they have another mess hall somewhere else."

"There could be even more than two," Liu said.

"If I had to guess, I'd say they have less than a thousand crew, but they have thousands of spiders on board, and an unknown number of those four-legged pod-things."

"Correct."

"Then who was this ship built for? So far we've seen more space devoted to the animals than anything else."

Liu smiled behind his helmet. "You're suggesting that the function of this vessel is to support its non-sentient inhabitants."

"Exactly." David glanced at Liu. "But what sense would that make? We don't build spaceships for wildlife exhibits or nature preserves. Who would go to that much trouble to move a population of animals from one planet to another?"

"Perhaps we're looking at it the wrong way."

"What do you mean?" David asked.

"It's an entire ecosystem. The tunnels. The beings. The water. Their nests. Somehow the *Interloper* has been sustaining them for hundreds or even thousands of years. But why? The crew would need a food source."

David made a face. "Spiders for breakfast, lunch, and dinner?"

"Not all diets are as diverse as ours. Felines are pure carnivores."

"What other purpose?" David asked, not sure that theory made perfect sense.

"They could be distant relatives. Another gender or caste, but not intelligent like them. Maybe the giant alien is their leader. And you saw the similarities between the arachnids and the four-legged ones. They could be variations of the same species."

David studied the size of the cushions around the tree-stump tables and shook his head. "No, this compartment wasn't designed for giant aliens. Neither were the door handles."

"True," Liu replied. "Or else..."

David stared at Liu, waiting for him to go on.

"The spiders and pod-creatures could be an alien army."

A chill rolled through David's spine. *An army.* Somehow, that explanation fit. A bloody memory tore through his mind's eye—insectoids swarming over Zasha, eating through her suit and slicing her open in a thousand different places. He shuddered to think what they could do on Earth if they were to infest the planet.

"Let's keep going," David whispered.

Atlas

Quang Nam Province, Vietnam

Atlas cruised down the roads, but slowed as he rounded the corner. Water seeped from both ditches, covering the way. There were no streetlights, and it was pitch black in this remote region. His windshield wipers were on full, sloshing water over the glass. The rain was relentless.

An hour or so after leaving the city limits, he'd become aware of the headlights behind him. Now as he slowed, so did they. Atlas glanced at the bag beside him, nervous he'd been found.

He couldn't tell how deep the overflow went, and wasn't sure he should risk submerging his car. It was a dilemma. With a huff, he climbed from the car, leaving it running, and walked to the gushing river of run-off, rolling from higher ground on the left. He grabbed a broken stick fallen off a nearby tree, and poked it, seeing the water was a foot deep. It might be safe to drive past.

The lights from the car remained on, and Atlas peered up at a strange noise. Helicopter rotors echoed through the stormy air, and he waited with rain pouring, trying to determine the direction it was heading.

The sound drifted away, carrying to the south, and Atlas returned to the car, no longer seeing the vehicle that had been trailing him.

"It's just your imagination," he whispered, and threw the car in gear. It rolled silently into the water, and in a minute, he was past it, with nothing but mud to show for the delay.

The rest of the trip was uneventful, and he drove on to a modest village. The rain had tapered off this far out, and a few people were walking near the edge of the road. Atlas had forgotten what day of the week it was, but guessed it was Wednesday or Thursday. Most of the town was already asleep.

He continued past the handful of buildings and signaled, heading toward the coast. His destination was on the right, and he pulled up to a chain-link gate. Atlas got out and checked the latch, finding it secured with a padlock.

There wasn't a listed phone number, and Atlas had no means of contacting the owner. "Here goes nothing." He took his bag and wiped the bottoms of his shoes, clearing the mud off. Atlas had climbed a few fences in his day, and this one was easier than most. He landed on the other side unscathed, and glanced around, searching for a guard dog. When he was greeted with silence, he was grateful.

The closest building appeared to be an office. No light shone in any of the grimy windows. Behind it was a large warehouse, and a truck sat parked between the two locations. The vehicle was old, and in the poor lighting, Atlas couldn't tell if it was black or blue.

"Hello!" he called as he neared the offices. The lights came on in a back room. "Hello! I'm here to speak with Hoang Phu."

He stared at the front door, willing someone to walk through.

The sounds of a helicopter in the sky drifted to his ear, but this time he couldn't see anything.

"What do you want?" The door opened wide, a bell chiming as the proprietor stepped outside. He wore white boxers and a matching stained tank top, but the most noticeable thing about him was the rifle in his grip, aimed directly at Atlas.

Atlas tried to maintain his cool. "Are you Pham Hoang Phu?"

"Who's asking?" His English was excellent.

"Atlas Donovan. Rare artifact hunter." He offered his hand, and Hoang Phu just glared at it.

"It's after midnight."

"You live here?"

"Don't judge me." The barrel lowered slightly, and Atlas saw his opening.

"I can pay you," he offered.

The man grimaced, settling the rifle's tip on the ground. "Come in."

Atlas clutched the bag in his arms, and entered after the business owner. The interior was tidy, with a front desk and two chairs facing it. But he noted that it had last year's calendar on the wall, the boxes unmarked. An empty coffee cup sat near the door, and the contents were thick and green. "Been a slow week?" He'd wanted to say *year*, but thought better.

"You're not kidding. My father had a dream to be the biggest war memorabilia seller in the country, and he sank every red cent into this hellhole," Hoang Phu said.

"You have an American accent," Atlas told him.

"My mother was from Delaware. Her parents immigrated there when she was young. She came back and married Pops after college. Taught me how to speak, and I thought it would help me find buyers overseas. But it's been too many years. Not enough people are interested in our little nation any longer." He motioned to a seat in the compact kitchen off the front office. Atlas saw a bathroom connected, and a commercial coffee carafe near the sink.

"Your father..."

"He died years ago and I took over." He gazed around the room. "I should have burned it to the ground."

Atlas saw desperation, which usually meant opportunity. "Do you have any records of your father's collection?"

"What are you looking for? Another of those guys hoping to find a UH-1E Huey? I hate to burst your bubble, but I don't have one." He poured a glass of water from a noisy tap, and offered it to Atlas. Black dots floated to the surface.

Atlas shook his head. "Nothing like that."

"Pops didn't keep proper files. He used to, but his mind wandered for a few years. I have a couple of books, though."

Atlas felt his chances slipping away. He thought about what Anh said. "What about a rock?"

"Rock?" the man stared blankly. "What the hell do you …" Something changed, and he smiled. "I might have what you're seeking."

"How much do you want?" Atlas hoped he wasn't going to be paying for nothing.

"Two million," the guy said, and Atlas almost forgot he was asking for Vietnamese dongs. The conversion on their currency equalled about a hundred US bucks.

"For the piece?"

"No. To access the warehouse."

So he was a negotiator. "Fine." Atlas slipped the bills from his pocket, and passed them to Huong Phu. The money disappeared in a blink.

"Let me get dressed." The guy vanished to the other room, and Atlas peered through the window, observing the warehouse. Could it be so simple? Was the prize he'd been hunting for within those four walls?

Huong Phu returned in a ratty bathrobe with a set of keys. He rattled them, and shuffled outside.

Atlas listened for signs of that helicopter in the air; this time he only heard the cicadas buzzing. They slowly walked to the bay doors, and Atlas prayed his search had finally come to an end.

TWENTY-FIVE

The Interloper

T HE GREEN LIGHTS DIMMED a few seconds after she passed them in the corridor. Lennon didn't want to cross paths with the crew, so she slowed, checking on the Holo's map. She sipped from the water straw, trying to conserve the suit's liquid. Which way to go? She knew the exit would be straight down the hall, but that might put her face to face with David. From what she could tell, this was the same level where they'd set the airlock.

The markings on the wall were consistent. She'd seen the floor above, and a different symbol had adorned the space between the doorways. It either denoted another deck or purpose. Lennon assumed that on a human ship, this might say Science Station, or Medical Bay. But she wasn't about to explore each room, not when there were explosives on *Beyond III* waiting to be placed on the *Interloper*.

Something hissed behind her, and she flattened against the wall. The creature that emerged was horrific. It took a moment to comprehend what she was seeing. For a second she thought it was walking on the ceiling, but then saw the dark legs on the floor as well. Knobby knees bent from both ends of the alien, and she fought the urge to vomit. It was so inhuman, her nerves were on fire. Tiny wiggling appendages waved on its torso, and she couldn't spot a face on the thing. It reminded her of the giant spider, but only in the way that a bat was like a bird.

It paused, turning in a full circle. Was it sensing her, since it had no sight? Lennon spotted the grate in the bulkhead, and she pried it open. It was big enough for a person to crawl into, and she did just that, trying to secure the metal grate back. It fell with a clang, and she instantly heard movement as the creature dashed toward her.

Lennon was in a utility shaft, and she let go, falling an entire deck. She shoved her arms out, slowing her landing, and her spine jarred as her feet hit the floor. With a quick glance above, she saw the thing hadn't followed her.

Lennon checked her timer, aware the deadline to meet with David was almost upon her. Another forty minutes. She needed to hurry.

She'd seen enough evidence of alien life on board the *Interloper*. These beings were hostile. Dark Leader's voice echoed in her head. *Destroy them, Lennon. You wanted to die. Here's your chance to go out in the blaze of glory. Think about Rutger.*

She closed her eyes, picturing his face as she slammed the door shut between them, sealing his fate. She deserved this. Not the glory of defending Earth, but of finally conceding her life.

Lennon found the exit, removed the grate, and went into another corridor. This one had fewer lights, and the walls dripped with moisture. She suspected she was near the bottom of the ship. Pipes ran overhead in intricate patterns, seemingly random, and she ran in the direction of *Beyond III*.

The passageway turned on a few occasions, but Lennon persisted, confident she was near the exit. For a brief moment she wondered if Carter was okay. But in the end, it wasn't going to matter. They'd all be dead within the hour.

Lennon examined her Holo, finding the original red line pinpointing directly above her position. The room with the airlock was directly above. She searched for another utility shaft, finding one twenty meters from her position.

"Here goes nothing," she whispered, her energy suddenly renewed with the thoughts of completing the mission. Her final mission.

What if it's the wrong decision? She heard Rutger's voice in her mind, the subtle German accent.

Lennon felt tears streaming down her cheeks, but in the suit, she couldn't wipe them. "Not now!" she screamed.

He told you to leave me behind. Do you remember? What if you hadn't listened to him? We could be on a beach together, oblivious to any of this. Lennon Baxter, are you a soldier or a human first? Think about the others. David. Carter. Zasha and Liu. You can still find a way out of this.

Rutger's voice subsided, and she sat on the floor, clutching her knees to her chest. "You're dead."

It had been like this for the first couple of years. But he'd gone eventually, receding into her subconscious. She knew he wasn't really there, but that didn't prevent him from materializing at the most inopportune moments.

Think about it. Make your own choices.

"You have no idea what it's like! We can't let these things get to Earth!" Lennon realized she was yelling at a ghost, and got to her feet. When Rutger didn't respond, she shoved her fear deeper and shuffled into the shaft, peering up the narrow tube.

She gripped her boots to the sides, and used her upper body and legs to shimmy up the vent. Lennon emerged in the room and saw the spare tanks near the exit. The hatch she and Zasha had attached was sealed shut, and Lennon took a deep breath. This needed finesse.

Before leaving, she double checked to ensure the *Interloper* was sealed on the other side of the space, and finally, she flipped the lever on the portable airlock, letting the vacuum suck the air from the room. Lennon stood there, buffeted in the lashing wind, wondering if this was her best choice. Maybe her subconscious was right. Find David and the rest of the crew, come clean and tell them everything. Maybe they could work together to get home.

But where was home? She couldn't return to Three Points, Arizona, to a crappy trailer park in the middle of nowhere.

"Finish the job," she muttered, opening the airlock. *Beyond III* blocked her view from a short distance away, the harpoon tethers still pulled taut, connecting the human vessel to the alien ship.

Lennon secured her suit to the rope and rotated her grip, sliding toward her redemption. As she approached *Beyond*'s damaged hull, she glanced at the terrible blackness of the *Interloper* and cringed. It needed to be destroyed.

Before she headed to the storage compartment, she proceeded to her quarters. It was so strange being alone on board. Lennon tried to picture Akira's smile as she mimed singing her favorite song, and felt the familiar rush of dread.

When she grabbed the private Holo, she saw a message waiting from Dark Leader.

Lennon pressed the screen open and read the missive. *Await further orders. Things have changed.*

Atlas

Quang Nam Province, Vietnam

Huong Phu remained outside, and Atlas toured the warehouse, glancing at the old metal junk scattered throughout. The ancient sodium lamps flickered and took a full five minutes before stabilizing. The lighting was still dull, and Atlas wandered the aisles, seeing dozens of broken US military vehicles. He walked through the Vietnam variety of trucks, planes, and weapons, all well past their prime.

Atlas stopped near an M113. The clunky APC was in pieces, the treads worn off the wheels. Everything was coated in a layer of rust, either from being submerged or from being stuck in a damp jungle for decades before retrieval.

The warehouse was big, but crammed full of useless war machines. No one would spend money on these, and Atlas assumed that's why they were gathering dust.

He scoured every row, touching the rotor of a beat-up helicopter, the sagging frame of a truck. An old jet turbine. An hour later, he sat down, rubbing his temples. Where was it? Had he wasted all this time?

Atlas thought about the effort it had taken to get here. His mother's face flashed in front of his eyes, but he only saw her as a blurry specter. It had been too many years since her death. He couldn't recall the details of her face, but he knew her scent, her voice telling him he could do anything. Even on her deathbed, she'd praised him, vowing that the world was his oyster. He only needed to believe it.

Things had never been the same after that. His relationship with his father grew distant, his own brother ashamed of him for dropping out of college. It was easy to separate from the toxic cloud they spewed at him, but now, inside this dirty warehouse, he wondered if they hadn't been right all along.

His gaze drifted across the mess, and he noticed a tarp at the back, tucked in behind a UH-1 Iroquois helicopter.

Atlas hopped to his feet and jogged to the dirt-brown cover. It was heavy, made from cloth long before cheap plastic versions became readily available. He tested it, finding it secured at the edges. He slipped a pocketknife from his pants, flicking the blade out. The rope was dry and frayed, making this job easy. A minute later, he had it free. The tarp slid off, dropping to the ground.

Atlas didn't know whether to laugh or cry. It was a rock.

He kicked it, angry at himself for being such a fool.

But instead of the solid thump he'd expected, he heard subtle reverberations.

"It can't be," Atlas whispered.

He knocked on it with his knuckles, but it was impossible to tell if the thing was hollow. He ran outside, finding Huong Pho near the office.

"Do you have records of this stuff?"

"Some of it. Might be able to scrounge it up. "

"The rock. What's the weight?"

The man puffed on a cigarette. "You're asking me how much a rock weighs?"

"Can you find out?"

"Sure." He tossed the butt and went inside.

Atlas could only pace as he waited. He tried to calculate it himself, using the rudimentary system he'd learned from his first-year geology elective in college.

Huong emerged with a journal and slid a finger down the page. "20,000 pounds."

"That's far too light," Atlas mumbled. "Do you have a truck that can transport it?"

"You want to take it?"

"Yes." Atlas stared at the other man, who just shrugged.

"What the hell. It's yours. But the truck will cost you."

Atlas didn't care. He'd do anything to keep it in his possession. A meteor had landed in the water off Vietnam, and all these years later, he'd found the actual rock, miraculously still in one piece. This was no ordinary meteor. "How much?"

"What do you have?"

They haggled, and Atlas ultimately agreed to an exorbitant sum, paid via a combination of crypto currencies and the remainder of his cash, for the purchase of an ancient truck. He used the flatbed's picker to lift the prize onto the back of the vehicle. The suspension groaned under the weight, but it seemed to be holding. He sent the man a hefty sum, far more than the vehicle was worth, through his Holo and climbed into the cab as the happy proprietor opened the gate for him.

The interior of the truck smelled like stale coffee and ashes, and the gear stick jammed from first to second, forcing him to stomp on the clutch, but he drove off, carrying what he suspected was an actual alien ship.

Now, all Atlas needed to do was open it.

TWENTY-SIX

Beyond III

"**N**o." SHE STARED AT the message in disbelief. Why would Dark Leader change her orders at the last minute? It didn't make sense.

She carefully typed a response. *Negative. Proceeding as planned. Hostiles on board. One crewmate dead, another wounded.* She had no clue if there had been more casualties than Akira, considering she'd been out of communication since soon after they'd stepped onto the *Interloper*.

Lennon couldn't afford to wait for his response. She took the second Holo, shoving it into her suit's baggy pocket, and bounded through the ship. Clinging to handholds, she dashed down the rungs, floating into the storage compartment. The explosives were where she'd left them, and she moved to the detonator, linking the blue spheres to the device. All in, the bombs were extremely compact, and they filled a blue cloth satchel. In zero gravity, they weighed next to nothing, and she carefully brought them to the airlock.

Before exiting *Beyond* she took one final glance at the Dark Leader's Holo. It had been well past the time to receive a return message, but none waited for her on the screen.

"Fine." She felt betrayed by his silence. Here she was, sent to do a mission, and he changed the orders. Probably from the comfort of a penthouse apartment with a stiff drink. No. It was her call. Whatever the *Interloper* held, it was not meant for Earth. If those spiders breached the surface, or the four-legged freaks... she shuddered at the thought. The two atmospheres were very similar. Odds were they'd infest the planet quite easily.

Yet she was curious. Could either of those creatures have built such an elaborate piece of machinery? She doubted it. There was still a vast section of the *Interloper* left unexplored. Perhaps they had yet to meet the real threat. And that rankled her mind.

With the press of the hatch, she entered the airlock, once again staring at the bulk of the *Interloper*. The green lights had dimmed to dark, and it looked dead in space.

"David, come in," she tried. "Carter. Zasha. Liu."

She heard a faint crackle of a reply, then nothing.

"Come in!" she called, but this time she was only greeted with silence. Good. It was better this way.

Lennon clasped the bombs to the same tether that linked the pair of airlock hatches. Their own ship had no fuel, and after the collision it was far beyond repair. With no rescue in sight, the crew was as good as dead regardless of what Lennon did. The knowledge that they would die whether she destroyed the *Interloper* or not made it easier to carry out the mission.

Lennon tried not to worry about the crew's fate. They wouldn't realize it was her fault, and that comforted her. Because she'd grown to appreciate each of them.

Zasha was like a sister, protective and wary. Liu was intelligent and kind. Carter, despite his constant kidding around, was on the verge of some major breakthroughs with his translation technologies, and now he'd never have the chance to complete his life's work.

Then there was David Bryce. The all-American square-jawed paragon she'd clashed with, but that assessment hadn't been fair. He was flawed, like all of them. She was pretty sure the man even had a virtual game of chess going with his son. He was a good father, and probably a solid husband.

And here she was, about to end their existence. Lennon peered past the hull, lower so she could see the blackness of space beyond the giant alien craft. Where had the *Interloper* come from? It was almost a shame to destroy her, when the details of the people that built it would be obliterated with her.

Lennon ground her teeth, and started to cross the tether. The bombs slid over the cable on their own carabiner, and Lennon grunted as she finally reached the modified hatch again. She opened it, gently pushing the satchel into the *Interloper.*

She recalled the Dark Leader suggesting the engineering section was in the rear third, so instead of going to the heart of the ship, she turned right, toward the stern.

The glowing green lights flickered on with her movement, reminding her that this was virtually a ghost ship. From what she could tell, it was running on reserve power. Whoever had built it wasn't on board, or else they were sleeping. Goosebumps rose on her skin beneath the space suit and thin layer of undergarments. Were they here? Was she being watched from a secure control center?

It was almost time for the meet-up with David, Zasha, and Liu, but if the commander made it to the rendezvous point, he wouldn't find her. He'd probably assume she'd been killed by the ship's strange inhabitants. She decided that was for the best.

This section of the craft was quiet, and Lennon made it a quarter of a kilometer without finding anything out of place. When she checked the Holo, she saw she was likely nearing the last third of the vessel, and she stopped, hefting the pack to a more suitable position on her shoulder.

Lennon heard the door open before she saw it. Long black legs snaked in. Writhing, fleshy organic fingers coated its body... She stopped.

Her fingers rested on the holstered gun, and she didn't breathe as it stepped tentatively closer. The top legs lifted off the ceiling, joints cracking as it bent over. Lennon saw that it did have a face. A round, puckered mouth swiveled up from beneath its round form, revealing a sucking maw full of teeth. Adding to the horror, the creature's upper set of legs lowered toward her, and the soles of its feet each had a hole within them. She couldn't tell what their function was.

The openings were the size of her fists. Lennon stayed frozen as both of the upper feet dropped nearer.

The organism was straight from a nightmare, a monster made by the imagination, not nature. But here it was, coming from another planet, on a starship headed for the sun. Two more arrived, and Lennon feared she'd be overwhelmed should they attack. She only had a single gun. Her left wrist ached as she slipped it inside the satchel, wrapping her fingers around a blue explosive. She had one chance to escape.

Lennon needed to inhale. Her lungs were quivering, and she guessed it had been two full minutes without so much as a single intake of air.

Before she could stop herself, the air flowed through her mouth, and the being in front of her stiffened suddenly. It let out a bellow from an unseen orifice. The others screeched as well, rushing her. Lennon armed the bomb with the touch of a button, yanked on the monster's upper leg, and shoved the blinking sphere into the gaping hole. It flew back, bashing into the wall in agitation, and Lennon tossed the bag, sliding it across the floor as she dove past the creature.

When she was on her feet again, she grabbed the satchel and ran. Legs pumping, she used the detonation device, tapping it once. The hall erupted as the single bomb discharged, sending pieces of the three aliens onto the walls, ceiling, and floor. Lennon stole a short glance and kept running. If these things were pressure, vibration, or movement sensitive, there were going to be a lot more of them arriving to investigate. She wasn't planning on being around when they did.

Atlas

Quang Ngai, Vietnam

He drove for an hour, stopping at the northern outskirts of Quang Ngai. It was still dark outside, and he pulled the truck over, finding a secluded road leading deeper inland. There were no people in sight. He knew that just a mile or two down the street, the city began, but leading up to it was pure jungle. He continued driving for longer than he'd wanted, until he encountered an old Buddhist temple. The building was crumbling, the grounds overgrown. The perfect location to investigate the rock on the flatbed of the recently purchased truck.

Atlas parked near an overhanging tree, and quickly scanned the low-lying branches for snakes. The entire area was quiet, except for the constant buzzing of insects.

Before he got out, his Holo beeped, and the glow of the screen almost blinded him as he opened the file.

Bill, his contact with the US Army, had sent him a message. *I found him. Man's name is Allan Booth.*

A picture filled his screen: a man in his forties, with a scar on the right side of his face. *Photo is dated, but this is the mysterious general. Booth is bad news. There are hundreds of confidential files on him, but I can't access any of them. I asked my supervisor, and he threatened my job if I ever poked around this again. Whatever it is you're doing, Atlas, I suggest you stop. Now.*

Atlas grimaced. That didn't change anything. This was the man that had sent Dark Nine, aka Bethany, to spy on him, and he was confident he'd ordered Atlas dead in northern China. He listened for any sounds of pursuit, and when it seemed safe, he exited the truck. His feet splashed on the damp ground as he jogged to the rear.

"What are you?" he asked the rock. Before he dove any deeper, he grabbed his bag from the cab, containing the pair of artifacts. The material wasn't the same as the boulder he'd secured. Maybe it was just a hunk of stone.

Atlas unfolded the cloth from the first piece his father had salvaged from Malaysia. The section was cold to the touch, with its Braille-like surface. Perfectly round, but not quite the same as the second object, stolen from Mattia's home in Lake Como. Atlas rotated that one, seeing a series of depressions on the opposite side of the three dots.

"The hell?" Atlas dropped the cloth and hefted the pair of artifacts in his hands. For the first time, he appraised them as if they might not be from different ships. He'd always assumed they were related, but not one piece, mostly because of the vast distance between Croatia and Malaysia.

If the vessel had entered our atmosphere and burned up, it could have broken apart, spreading the pieces far and wide. What if...

He set the second piece onto the first, and something clicked. The sound was audible, and he attempted to pull them apart, but couldn't. They were sealed together.

Atlas laughed and touched the top section. The part with the three depressed dots rotated freely now. He spun it one direction, then the other, but nothing happened. "How do you work?" Atlas sat on the edge of the flatbed, attempting to understand what he held in his possession. Part of it had broken off.

He made several attempts, and when he spun the rotary dial to the far left, it stuck.

The air filled with static, causing his hair to stand on end. Atlas dropped the alien device and fell out of the truck, landing on the dirt. Fiery light blazed from the rock beneath the tarp, and he cut it free, releasing it. An orange rectangle shone on the thing's surface, and he climbed up again as the static dissipated. He anticipated it to be hot to the touch, but he only got a mild shock from the cool surface. The orange light pulsed three times, and the glowing section protruded from it. It was a doorway.

Atlas' heart raced in his chest as rain began to fall from the dark sky. Above roared the sound of a helicopter, and before he had a chance to investigate the interior, a bright searchlight struck his location.

"Freeze! We have you in our sights. If you take another step, we will open fire," an amplified voice demanded.

The general had found him.

TWENTY-SEVEN

The Interloper

D AVID AND LIU WANDERED through the crew compartments for what seemed like forever. One corridor blurred into the next. They'd noted a few rooms that could be sleeping quarters, but the 'beds' were shaped like burrows, and the furniture had been sparse and incomprehensible.

Several larger areas had deep pools of water in them. Bath houses? Restrooms? Passages between levels? Maybe all three. David hadn't lingered in those spaces.

He glanced at the timer inside his helmet. Five minutes left. They weren't going to make it to the rendezvous with Lennon and Carter. Hopefully they'd wait for him and Liu. Or better yet, they were already aboard the *Beyond.*

They arrived at another sealed door. Liu stood ready with his sidearm.

They stepped into a cavernous space, domed with stars reflecting off the glossy dark floor. He and Liu gawked at the view as they toured the echoing chamber. There was an odd, shoulder-height pedestal in the center. Green and blue lights pulsed slowly from multiple surfaces. At the top of the platform was a hovering black sphere, outlined in a dim emerald glow. But it was too far out of reach. He might manage to brush it with his fingertips if he stood on his toes.

"What is that?" Liu whispered.

"Let's find out," David said as they approached the alien obelisk.

"Are you sure about this?"

"It could be the control system and our ticket home."

Liu nodded, doing him the courtesy of not stating the obvious. Even if it was as David suggested, that didn't mean they'd be able to operate it.

David reached the pedestal, and his gaze slid to the panels. Some had radiant symbols scrawled beneath.

"It's a written language," Liu muttered. "But the lettering is smooth."

David arched an eyebrow at him. "So?"

"None of the aliens we've encountered have eyes. They wouldn't be capable of reading this." Liu ran a finger over a string of illuminated markings.

"I wonder what that one does?" David pointed to a big yellow button in the center of the control cluster, at shoulder height, directly below the floating sphere.

"I wonder what any of them do," Liu replied. "It's a pity Carter isn't here. He might intuit something from these keys."

"Maybe," David agreed. "But he's not, so we're going to have to figure it out."

"Impossible. There's no common frame of reference."

"Perhaps not, but a big button in the center of a control panel seems universal to me." David hovered his palm over it.

"Are you sure about this?"

"What do we have to lose?"

"Well..."

David stabbed the button.

Nothing happened.

"Well, that's anti-climatic," Liu said.

David frowned and smacked the button repeatedly.

The third time, a tweeting chime sounded, and the entire console powered to life. The black sphere became luminous and blue. A bright spotlight shone over the deck, surrounding them. Then came a groan of ancient machinery. Panels slid open beneath David's feet, and a strange, curving piece of furniture emerged directly below him. He let out a startled cry and rode it up, clinging to the top.

"Commander!" Liu cautioned.

"It's okay," he said. "It's a chair."

"Is it?"

David understood his confusion. It was padded with glowing cushions of various shapes and sizes, reminiscent of what they'd seen around the tables in the mess hall. The seat hadn't been made for anything resembling human anatomy. It was almost built like a massage chair, with multiple pads for knees or elbows and chest, and it was far too large for him to sit or rest upon comfortably. But now the luminous blue ball at the top of the console was well within his reach.

David balanced precariously with both feet on one of the lower cushions and stretched for the sphere with both hands. But before he could even touch it, he heard a distant rumble from deep within the ship. David peered at Liu, who was casting about wildly with his gun, scanning for targets. The door they'd entered by was now closed, making it easier to imagine deadly swarms of alien creatures waiting behind it.

A thunderous *boom* sounded, sending shivers up the chair.

"Maybe we should go," Liu said.

The room spun around David. His arms flew out to seize the top of the chair and steady himself. The room really was rotating. Stars pinwheeled around them as the ship turned.

"We're changing course," David whispered.

***

Lennon

The Interloper

Lennon was drenched in sweat. At some point her climate control had deactivated, and she didn't know if she'd damaged it running from the four-legged freaks, or earlier, falling down the chute. Drops of perspiration fell from her brow, and she blinked, trying to keep it from her eyes.

This was it. She was on the lowest deck at the access hatch. If Dark Leader's assumptions were accurate, engineering was close. Whatever powered the *Interloper* was nearby, meaning this handful of explosives should be enough to incapacitate, if not destroy, the enemy craft.

Because that's what this enormous vessel was. The enemy.

Lennon climbed the rungs with ease in the light gravity, and she hesitated, listening for sounds of the spiders or four-leggers beyond the grate. When there was no indication of them, she pressed the panel, catching the grate before it clanged to the floor.

She climbed out, and her breath caught in her chest.

This was phenomenal.

Three floating orbs of light drifted within a central tube, the glow from them reflected off the walls, creating strange patterns.

The floor vibrated gently as she stepped into the cavernous space. She peered up, finding that it went on for the entire height of the *Interloper*. Lennon was at a loss for words. The energy balls were ten feet in diameter, ever-so-slightly bouncing off each other.

They pulsed, and Lennon noticed a shift. Her knees ached, and her hand spasmed.

She'd been so distracted by the unusual sight that she hadn't observed the screen on the walls. Stars and space scrolled by steadily. They were moving.

"Shit," she muttered.

Lennon had to be quick. She stooped at the tube holding the giant spheres, assuming they were the source of power for the *Interloper*. She placed five of the explosives at the base, and left another at the engineering room's exit.

Before leaving, she spied something across the engineering compartment. The computer console was huge, and curiosity overwhelmed her common sense. Lennon strolled to it, seeing a bizarre keypad. Ten circles were inset into the panel, each with three depressions. Lennon inserted the fingers of her right hand into one, and considered spinning it. Her Dark team was somehow connected to the *Interloper.* Their tattoos matched these controls. But why? And how? Was it coincidence or fate that Lennon would be the soldier to finish this task?

She scanned the room a final time, in awe at the alien technology. This was so far removed from anything they knew on Earth. Maybe that's why Dark Leader had asked her to hold off. Perhaps he'd been bought, and a corporation at home wanted the knowledge.

But Lennon couldn't let these things reach Earth. She pictured the arachnids dropping from the sky, landing like ballooning spiders from the fields near her hometown every spring. Except these wouldn't be a minor nuisance. They'd infest. Take control. And slaughter thousands.

"Complete the mission," she told herself, and returned to the lower-level corridor.

Lennon rushed to the exit to *Beyond*, wondering if she'd encounter David or the rest of the crew when she crossed the gap in space. Could she look them in the eye and detonate the devices? She imagined she could, but her stomach churned at the thought of it.

Lennon dropped the remaining bombs sequentially. She figured spreading them out was a safer course of action.

Eventually she slowed near the dead monsters, and didn't find their allies investigating. She shuddered, and returned to the airlock on the upper level. Her grip slipped on the top rung when her old injury flared, and she held tight, banging against the wall. Instead of panicking, she pulled herself up. She couldn't see any sign of David, Liu, Zasha, or Carter–not that she expected the British linguist to have gone far with his sprained ankle.

"David?" She tested the comms, but there was no reply.

Beyond floated alongside the *Interloper,* the tethers tugging tight as the trajectory of the giant ship changed, and she stared at the cable she'd connected to the hull. Would it hold? She could detonate the bombs from here just as easily as she could on *Beyond III*, but something held her back.

That damned message from Dark Leader replayed in her mind. *Await further orders. Things have changed.* Despite believing her plan to stick to the original mission was the right one, she felt compelled to check if he'd sent another communication.

Curiosity was a trap. The ship was moving. But what if David was at the helm? She tried to picture that circumstance, and couldn't. There was no way the crew was behind this. They were probably dead.

"Here goes nothing," she muttered, and secured the cable. She clasped her carabiner onto it, and tugged on the loop connecting to her suit.

Lennon's limbs were like jello after this arduous day, but she tapped into her reserves of energy to slide herself across the tether, suspended weightlessly in a shining black sea of stars. Hearing her breath echo within her helmet, she focused on her destination. Just a bit farther. The rocket they'd used to make it here was in shambles, squished and torn apart like a recycled beer can in her mother's old trailer.

Lennon saw a flash of light, and the thrusters on the *Interloper* emitted a bright green color, causing the ship to spin clockwise. The rope broke free of *Beyond's* hull, and she knew this was it.

Lennon grabbed for the detonator, but it slipped from her grip, gliding away. She gasped, seeing her destiny slip out of reach.

But she still had a shot. There were more detonator tablets in the storage compartment. She'd only taken one.

Lennon floated between the two spacecraft, and looked each direction before choosing. Using the maneuvering jets in her suit, she spun slowly, and pushed them both at the same moment. *Beyond* drifted away from her, shifting gently from the momentum of the *Interloper's* movements. She timed it, hoping her judgment was accurate.

If she was wrong, she'd miss the target and float on endlessly, dying from a lack of oxygen in a few short hours.

Lennon cried out when she realized she'd aimed too high, and kicked her leg toward the airlock, latching under an overhang. It held. With every inch of her body thrumming with anxiety, she bent her knee and clasped the hatch, desperate for breath.

A moment later, she was inside the relative safety of their ship, and felt the rocket being dragged along as the *Interloper's* thrusters eased off.

From her new position, she could see the front end of the alien vessel, and she stared through the porthole, her helmet knocking against the barrier.

The rounded point of the *Interloper* began to shift, panels sliding and retreating, revealing something bright and dangerous in the bow.

"Is that a weapon?" Lennon saw the giant barrel, the flashing green spikes protecting the central section.

Before she could investigate it more, the alien craft's thrusters fired on. It was done changing direction, and now they were heading for their new destination. She'd spent enough time on *Beyond* over the last couple of months to know exactly where that was.

Earth lay in a straight line from the *Interloper*'s nose.

The remaining tethers strained, throwing her against the wall as the *Beyond* moved toward the alien hull. They were on a collision course. Again.

She rushed into the ship, diving down the rungs, and discovered the secondary detonators where she'd left them, half hidden in the storage area.

"Come on," she said out loud. The impact knocked the tablet from her hands, and it floated free as *Beyond*'s emergency lights turned off. Backup security bulbs blinked on, but she had to rely on her helmet's headlamps to find the detonator.

She tried to link them, her fingers shaking inside the suit's gloves. "Work!" She fumbled with it, hoping the bombs weren't out of range. Lennon watched in horror as an illuminated circle slowly rotated, searching for the explosives.

Lennon grinned when they connected.

Beyond battered the hull once more, and she slammed into the ceiling. She needed to secure it somehow, or there might be nothing left of their rocket.

Lennon bypassed the interior sections and reached her quarters.

She checked for a message from Dark Leader, but the screen was blank.

He'd abandoned her.

Lennon took the detonator to the bridge, and watched through the viewscreen, seeing a tiny blue dot in the distance.

Her fingers waited impatiently over the tablet.

It was time.

TWENTY-EIGHT

The Interloper

"Is THAT WHAT I think it is?" Liu asked.

David squinted out into space, seeing a familiar blue planet that now lay dead center of the dome-shaped alien displays. "They're headed for Earth," he realized.

"Why now?"

David glanced back to the control console. When he'd touched that yellow button, somehow, he'd activated the guidance system, and the *Interloper* had redirected itself for Earth.

"This isn't good," Liu muttered, glancing around the big, echoing chamber where they stood.

David jumped from the alien seat, triggering a spasm in his injured ankle. He guessed you'd have to be nine feet tall to fit in such a chair. And the occupant wouldn't stand on two legs, or at least not the way humans did. Had they met the real inhabitants of this ship? Were they even more deadly than those encountered so far? Regardless, it would be a disaster for those giant spiders and four-legged pods to make it to Earth.

"We have to locate the others and then get to the *Beyond*. Mission control needs to know what's coming," David said.

"But what can they do?" Liu asked. "Shoot the *Interloper* with nuclear missiles? And what exactly is coming?

They're headed for our home, but we don't know their intentions. We don't know anything yet."

"At this point, their motives aren't up for debate. They attacked us and killed Zasha."

"Is a lion guilty for killing a gazelle?" Liu countered.

David shot him an angry glare. "She was our crew mate. And our friend."

"I meant no offense, Commander. I'm suggesting that the spiders didn't kill her because of some overarching alien agenda. Maybe they did it because she was intruding on their territory, or a threat to their eggs. The creatures we've met so far don't appear to be sentient, or capable of notions such as wars and invasions."

"Aren't you the one who proposed the insectoids could be an army? Now you're saying they attacked us because they were hungry?"

"I'm trying to keep all possibilities on the table. The two ideas might not be as divergent as you think. The Britons used dogs to fight against the Romans, and war elephants were common in India. Employing animals in battle isn't a foreign concept to us. But we shouldn't assume anything quite yet."

"So, we shouldn't raise the alarm?"

"I'm afraid if we do, we could provoke an overreaction, and inadvertently start a war."

"It's not really up to us," David pointed out. "Our job is to report what we've discovered. The rest is up to the governments who sent us. And even if this ship were less of a threat than it seems—maybe some type of alien menagerie designed to plant the seeds of life on other worlds—it still has the potential to harm a lot of people."

"Duty first," Liu sighed. "Very well. How do we find the others? The time for the rendezvous is past, and by now Lennon and Carter might be lost, or worse..."

"Let's stay positive. They could be waiting for us. If not, then the logical place to search for them is either in the airlock we entered by, or aboard the *Beyond*."

Liu nodded in agreement, and David pulled out his Holo to study the mapping app.

"Look at this," David said, and turned the screen so Liu could see. "We're here." He indicated a blinking dot near the top of the *Interloper*'s hull, almost directly above the spot where they'd boarded the *Interloper*. "We've been winding up this entire time. If I had to guess, I'd say we've risen ten or fifteen levels."

"We came in just above the bottom half," Liu said, tracing the outline of the *Interloper* with his finger.

"Exactly. So all we need to do is find some type of elevator or access chute." David turned and strode for the exit.

"Oh, is that all?" Liu quipped, hurrying to keep up.

David frowned, then gestured to the scanner on Liu's belt. "The UWB might be able to help us with that. It can look through the walls and identify a shaft."

"That is a good idea," Liu replied, retrieving the scanner.

"Maybe draw your gun, too," David suggested before fitting his fingers to the handle. "Is there anything I should be aware of?"

Liu aimed both his weapon and the tool at the door. David connected wirelessly to the device and saw the results on the HUD inside his helmet. The corridor beyond was empty.

For now.

David minimized the display and hurried into another dark corridor, made of smooth but porous black material. David led them back the direction they'd come, keeping to a measured pace to give Liu time to scan the walls.

"Found something!"

"Already?" David asked, blinking in surprise.

Liu placed his instruments on the floor and reached for the wall, running his fingers along it like a mime trying to find his way out of a box.

A luminous outline of the structures behind the bulkhead appeared. There was an elaborate system of ducts beside the corridor.

"Got it!" Liu cried, as a large square panel of the wall popped free and swung out on a concealed hinge. Liu peered in, using his helmet lamps to illuminate the darkened space. It was big enough for them to traverse if they hunched over.

"What do you think it is?" Liu asked.

"I don't know, but we don't have time to figure it out. There's a vertical section dead ahead. I assume that will take us lower." David climbed in and activated his helmet lamps. He crept slowly, crouching low and holding his gun in a two-handed grip. Upon reaching the vertical shaft, he peered over the edge into a fathomless abyss.

"It's a straight drop," Liu said.

"We could use friction to slow our fall," David suggested, not ready to give up.

A pulse of light flashed out from below and raced up the shaft, making David flinch and stumble away from the opening. An invisible force had physically *pushed* him.

"Hang on..." He stepped to the edge and waited.

"What is it?" Liu breathed.

The pulse came again. This time David was prepared, and he braced himself, but it wasn't enough; he was forced back once more. Beside him, Liu fell over and sat blinking in shock.

David grinned and helped him up. "I think this is some type of elevator shaft."

"Possibly," Liu agreed.

"Only one way to find out."

"Wait—"

David stepped over the edge.

His stomach leapt into his throat as he plunged. The wave of emerald color enveloped him, and he suddenly became light as a feather. "Come on!" He called up to Liu. "You can't fall very far."

Liu's cries were muffled as he jumped into the shaft.

David holstered his gun and put the mapping app on his HUD to watch his progress. He and Liu went through multiple cycles of falling and floating between levels. Each occasion was somehow synchronized so that they drifted slowly past the opening of a horizontal section of the tunnels.

They were finally coming into line with the level of the rendezvous point, and he lunged for the exit, dropping to his knees. Spinning around, he turned to find Liu at eye-level with him, and he reached for the man with a grunt of effort.

"You all right?" he asked.

"I think I'm going to be sick," Liu replied, teetering near the edge.

David knew what he meant. That ride had made him feel like a human yo-yo.

"Deep breaths. You don't want to do that inside your suit."

Liu nodded and they continued on, meeting the entrance to the familiar stretch of rocky warrens.

"Back to the spiders' lair," Liu muttered quietly.

"That's where we came in," David whispered as he crawled out and checked for signs of trouble. Thick slime oozed from the walls. So far, no sign of the deadly insects, but David wasn't planning to stick around and wait for them. He studied the mapping app, choosing his route.

They crept along, emerging in a vast cavern full of branching corridors. He recognized the space and recalled that two of the tunnels had been right beside each other, but now one was sealed with a slab of rock that was almost indistinguishable from the walls.

"We were separated here. Lennon, Carter, come in," David tried over his comms.

An eerie rustle of static whistled in response.

Frowning, David examined the door, searching for a handle. No such luck. If there was one, it was incredibly well hidden.

"We should get a breach kit," Liu suggested, glancing around nervously. "We're close to the *Beyond,* aren't we?"

A faint, scampering sound pricked David's ears, and both of them froze, sweeping their headlamps around to check for signs of approaching enemies.

The noise came again, but farther away. His heart hammering, David focused on the barrier. On a whim, he crouched down.

And there it was. A flat control panel near the bottom of the wall, with four raised off-color gray and black stone circles that resembled buttons. The design of the panel was so primitive that it might have been constructed for an equally primitive being to use.

"Look at that," David marveled quietly. "It was here all along." He tried one of the buttons, and some type of mechanism rumbled. *A lock?* he wondered. He tested another, and this time the door ground aside. A crew member lay sprawled behind it.

David rushed through and glimpsed the faceplate of their helmet. It was Carter, but his eyes were closed. Fearing the worst, David dropped to his knees and shook him.

"Hmmm?" Carter's eyelids fluttered and he sat up. "Commander?" He was wide awake now. "I guess I must've passed out," Carter finished with a wince.

"Where's Lennon?" David asked. "What happened?"

"Ran into the locals," Carter said, nodding to indicate the darkened depths of the tunnel. "Dragged myself here. Wasn't easy..." He trailed off, gritting his teeth.

"You're hurt," David realized.

"My ankle. Damn thing fell on me and I think I sprained it."

"And Lennon?" David asked.

Carter's eyes glazed over.

"Snap out of it!" David hissed, shaking him.

"Hmmm?"

Liu unslung the sample bag from his shoulders and searched for a syringe and a needle. He fitted it to a port on the arm of Carter's suit and injected a painkiller laced with a stimulant.

Carter's eyes flew wide. "Whoa. What was that?"

"Caffeine's evil twin," Liu said.

"Carter. Focus. Lennon."

"Oh she... she's not with you?" he asked.

"No."

"Lennon was heading to the *Beyond.* Where's Zasha?"

"She didn't make it."

Carter's face fell dramatically. "She was supposed to get married."

David drew in a deep breath. "Yeah. I know. We'd better join Lennon," he said, nodding to Liu. "Help me with Carter."

Liu draped one arm across his shoulders, and David took the other. They rose, and Carter stifled a cry as the movement disturbed his ankle.

"This way." David continued on their path through the *Interloper*. Soon they were making steady, limping progress toward the compartment they'd first entered.

"What's that?" Carter asked, staring at a shiny blue sphere in the wall.

David peeled away to examine it. "Is it a grenade?"

"Definitely an explosive device," Liu agreed. "Where did it come from? That wasn't here before."

"No," David said. The bomb was covered in a thick layer of translucent slime. "It has markings on it." He rotated the sphere so Liu could read it.

"M99," the other man said, examining the markings.

"That's one of ours," Carter realized. "Our alphabet. Our numerals."

"Lennon's doing?" Liu asked.

"Who else?" David replied. He carefully returned the sphere. "Come on. We'll have to ask her about it when we catch up aboard *Beyond III*."

The muffled roar of an explosion came shuddering to their ears, and they went flying into the opposite wall.

Atlas

Quang Ngai, Vietnam

The light from the helicopter was blinding. Atlas considered his options. He could drive off, hoping to lose the tail, but they were in a chopper, making success unlikely. And Atlas didn't have a gun, so there went the possibility of fighting. If this was the general or his team, they'd be armed to the teeth.

His odds were terrible either way he shook it.

Somehow Atlas had managed to activate this rock, and now he was about to lose everything he'd worked so hard to achieve.

The rotors were loud as they neared, his shirt flapping in the heavy winds.

"Stand down!" the same voice said, and when the copter landed, a man sprang from the open doors with an automatic rifle pointed at Atlas. The red laser sight lingered on his chest.

With the searchlight off him, Atlas recognized the face. "James Wan!" he called.

"Atlas Donovan," James replied. He looked much the same as the pictures in his northern China house, only older, and he wore a black uniform, blending him into the night.

The man peered past Atlas to the square doorway that was gently glowing from inside. "You found it," James whispered.

"I did."

"Get off the truck."

"Are you going to kill me?" Atlas asked.

James seemed to consider this, and held a finger to his earpiece. Atlas assumed someone else was calling the shots.

"Is that the general?"

James motioned him to the ground, and Atlas hopped off the flatbed. "That's not how we know him."

"Okay." Atlas moved away with the pair of relics in his grip. The rock's entrance hissed and ground shut. Interesting. Rain began to spray them with more ferocity, and he heard the rumblings of thunder in the distance.

"What did you do?" James asked.

The alien vessel was sealed once more.

"If you kill me, you won't know how to access it."

"Come with us." James gestured to the helicopter.

"I won't leave it."

"Don't make me ask you twice," James yelled.

Two more soldiers, dressed in dark camo suits, exited the helicopter. James said something to them, then looked up and added, "Atlas, give them the keys."

Atlas cursed under his breath. They were going to take the ship. But he was alive, and now he knew the truth. Aliens had visited Earth during the nineteen sixties. This had to connect to the recent Mars mission. "I want in!"

James turned, holding the earpiece. Atlas saw his lips moving, but couldn't hear him over the rush of the helicopter's rotors. James glanced at him and nodded.

"Dark Leader will meet with you."

Atlas couldn't decide if he should thank the guy or run. "Fine." Atlas took the keys out, tossing them to a tall woman. "The gears are sticky. Go easy between first and second."

She shrugged and shouldered her rifle, heading for the cab.

"Get in." James waited for Atlas to enter the helicopter, and when he did, they lifted off the ground, with James taking the seat across from him.

"Sorry about your house," Atlas said.

James grimaced. "I guess we're glad you survived."

"What was the plan? Steal the artifacts from a burned skeleton?"

"Something like that."

Atlas glanced out the windows, noting they were aimed south, over the sea.

"Where are we going?" he asked.

"Australia."

"I've never been. What'll happen to—"

"They will load it in a military transport. They might even beat us," James said.

"Do you know who they are?"

James didn't flinch as his jaw muscles bunched.

"Come on. If we're on the same team, at least tell me if there are any others," Atlas said.

James met his gaze, his voice low. "Mr. Donovan, if Dark Leader wants to, he'll tell you. Until then, keep your mouth shut, and your eyes on the floor."

Atlas shifted on the bench, and peered out the window as a sliver of sun inched over the horizon.

TWENTY-NINE

The Interloper

D AVID PEELED HIMSELF OFF the deck and helped Carter to his feet.

"What *was* that?" Liu asked.

"Lennon's blowing the ship up with us inside!" Carter decided.

"No," David replied. He pointed to the shiny blue explosive device still nestled into the wall. "If it was her, then why didn't that one go off?"

"She could be detonating them in sequence," Carter argued.

David grimaced and retrieved the explosive. He found the switch to disarm it, then handed it to Liu, who stuffed it in his pack.

"Let's go," David said. He pulled Carter along, and Liu hurried to keep up. They encountered more explosives, and David disarmed them, too. Another muffled roar came thundering through the *Interloper,* and they slammed into the wall, almost collapsing in a tangled heap from the force of the impact.

"Again?" Carter muttered. "This place is falling apart!"

"We have to keep moving," David insisted. They stumbled on for several more minutes before a third and then a fourth explosion sent them sprawling.

Carter was right. The *Interloper* had to be cracking in half by now...

Lennon

Beyond III

It didn't work. All this effort to send Lennon to stop the *Interloper*, and the damned detonator wasn't doing its job. Lennon tried to determine what the issue was, but from here, a kilometer from the bombs, nothing appeared to be malfunctioning. The link showed strong. Each of the explosives was connected to the device. She'd spent five minutes disarming and re-connecting them, but the act of pressing the button to detonate was anti-climactic.

Instead of feeling the guilt that came with the action, she was furious. Mad that she was here, burdened with this decision.

The *Interloper* sped along, dragging *Beyond*, which was still grinding the hull of the larger ship as it battered against the tethers.

Lennon wished she could talk with David, to learn what the hell was going on. Was anyone else alive on the alien craft?

The only way she could ensure the explosives went off was to do it personally. Hardwire the detonator to the units. Or use the manual option, which would be a nasty way to go, but so was letting this craft full of deadly aliens invade Earth. She'd make the ultimate sacrifice for a world that had never accepted her in the first place.

There was only one place that ever made her feel part of something bigger than her own small existence. And Dark Leader had stopped communicating with her. But that wasn't entirely true. The crew of *Beyond* had given her a place among their ranks, despite her precarious replacement of their beloved Jess.

Lennon bounded to the storage compartment, grabbing the last two harpoon tips, and connected them to another tether, wrapping it around until it was only a few meters long. She yanked on either end, knowing there was nothing that could tear this rope apart.

Beyond was drifting toward the *Interloper* again, and she needed to hurry if she wanted to get inside the alien vessel before the two collided once more.

The gigantic hull, spiked with black appendages and twinkling lights, approached swiftly, and Lennon pulled her own tether tight. It was now or never. She climbed out of the airlock, trying to forget that she could be squished by the impact if she didn't time this properly.

She counted off, and activated the harpoon tips, facing their ends in opposite directions. With a thrust of her palm, she returned to *Beyond*'s airlock as the lower section contacted the *Interloper*'s side. The shock wasn't as strong as the first three impacts, and she moved safely as the harpoon's tips exploded and dug into each ship's hull. Instead of *Beyond* swinging away, it clung to the *Interloper*.

Lennon grimaced as she floated beside the hatch she and Zasha had placed on the *Interloper.*

She rushed in, anxious to complete her mission. It wasn't easy having to return to a hot zone. She'd done this twice in her career. The first time was at a camp ten miles from Kandahar. Lennon could still feel the heat, the burn of sand against her cheeks while they stormed the house, sent back an hour later when they realized they'd missed the intended target. Luckily for them, only local reinforcements had been there. Lennon, Rutger, and James had made quick work of the job. Five confirmed dead. The strike hadn't made any news. Just the way they preferred it.

The second occasion was something she wouldn't let herself recall.

As she shoved down the access hatch, heading for the ship's lowest level, she wondered where James was. He'd been there her final day on the job, and she'd never forget the hatred in his eyes after they'd been evacuated.

"Get it together, Baxter," she told herself. "This isn't the time for memory lane."

She slowed, gasping for air as she ran.

"What the hell?" The explosive she'd left wasn't there. Lennon crouched, poking a blob of slime. Had one of those... things... taken it? No wonder the detonator had failed.

Lennon checked farther down the corridor, finding the same results. All her bombs were missing.

She bounded for engineering, her steps lighter in the low gravity, and shut her headlamps off as she heard something inside. Lennon held her breath, and walked to the doorway, gun raised.

The creature turned and sniffed the air. Three fingered hands. Wide shoulders and bared teeth.

Lennon screamed as she fired.

David

The Interloper

Finally, they reached their starting point. David shut the entryway behind them, and stood peering up at the glowing yellow status light around the circular hatch of their breach kit. The rungs of a ladder were extended below it, but David couldn't recall deploying it earlier. Lennon must have done that when she came this way.

"How do we get up there with Carter?" Liu wondered aloud.

"I can manage, hopping on one leg," he said.

"Is your suit still pressurized?" David asked.

He nodded. "Yes."

"Good."

"And yours?" Liu countered, staring openly at David's ankle.

"The emergency seals are holding. Let's go." He led the way up to the hatch. "Everyone grab onto something," he said, glancing at Liu and Carter.

They grabbed the ladder, and David triggered the hatch open, not bothering to depressurize first. If the ship was disintegrating around them, they didn't have any time to waste.

The breach kit sprang wide and the air roared out into space in a condensing white stream of vapor that buffeted David with hurricane force.

Utter silence rang in the wake of that storm, and a clear view of the *Beyond* materialized. It was much closer than it should be, and clouds of debris were scattered between the two vessels.

"What do you see?" Liu asked, his voice crackling over the comms.

"Those weren't explosions we heard earlier," David realized. "It was the *Beyond* colliding with the *Interloper*. It appears to be stuck to the hull now."

"But those *were* explosives that we found," Carter insisted.

"Yes," David agreed. "They were."

"And she had to have planted them, because it wasn't any of us."

"We'll ask her about it. Come on. I think we can access the rear airlock from here. It's time to find out why Lennon was really assigned to this mission."

"To kill us, apparently," Carter muttered.

"Don't flatter yourself," Liu said. "We're not that important."

No, maybe we're not, David realized. But a hostile alien spacecraft? That would be worth sending a secret agent on a suicide mission. Even if it meant that five astronauts would become collateral damage.

Heroes, they'll affectionately call us.

David scowled as he carefully climbed out onto the hull of the *Interloper,* using an attached harpoon cable to steady himself. Lennon had a lot of explaining to do.

David snatched the tether from his suit and clipped it to the one fastened to the *Interloper*'s hull. Adjusting his position, he reached down to help Carter. Once he was free from the artificial gravity aboard the *Interloper,* he had a much easier time dealing with his broken leg. Liu clung to the railing around the breach hatch.

"Ready?" David asked.

Both men nodded.

He scanned the length of the tether and mentally measured the gap to the *Beyond.* The ruined aft end of *Beyond* had lodged itself in the side of the alien hull, but the amidships airlock of the *Beyond* was still a good fifteen or twenty feet away. Nowhere near as much as they'd had to traverse on the trip over. David clutched the cable and crossed the distance, putting one hand in front of the other. Liu and Carter were both doing the same, with their suits tethered to the line behind him. David tried the comms repeatedly to see if he could obtain a response from Lennon now that they were leaving the alien vessel's jamming field.

They reached the *Beyond*'s airlock, and David cycled it to let them in. They waited for the compartment to fill with air, but kept their suits on—just in case the repeated collisions had depressurized other sections of the ship.

As soon as the inner doors parted, David tried his comms again. "Lennon?"

Nothing but static hissed in his ear.

Pushing through the airlock, they drifted into the *Beyond* to find it in complete disarray. Cargo sailed freely, pushed up from the storage sections below.

"Check the upper decks," David said.

"She would have replied over the comms if she were on board," Liu replied, looking worried.

"Not if she's busy carrying out someone else's agenda," David said.

"Perhaps," Liu agreed.

"Keep that gun handy," Carter added.

David bypassed the floating debris to the storage area, hoping to find more of the strange, spherical explosives they'd discovered aboard the *Interloper.*

Breaking into it was a chore, as he had to override the hatch that sealed it off from the rest of the ship. That done, he rode a jet of escaping air into the compartment. He waded through a sea of food, bottled water, and spare parts to reach where they'd stored their weapons, thinking that the explosives might have been there all along and he'd simply missed them. If so, that would absolve Lennon of a more sinister covert plot.

But the compartment was a twisted ruin. Depressurized, and almost completely impassable. Short of finding Lennon and hearing answers directly from her, he wouldn't figure this out.

As David was climbing the rungs of the ladder to the upper decks, he met Liu.

"Any sign of her?" David asked.

"None. *Beyond* is empty," Liu replied. He climbed down the last few rungs to the deck, and held himself in place with one hand.

"Then she's on the *Interloper*," David realized.

"Perhaps no longer among the living..."

"We're going back."

"Surely, you're not being serious," Liu replied.

"I am—Carter?"

"He's resting in his quarters," Liu answered for him.

Carter poked his head out. "Beauty sleep can wait. What do you need, Commander?"

"Use the comms. Contact mission control and give them an update. We have to find Lennon, if anything's still operational." Judging by the state of their ship, it might be a stretch, but they had to try.

"Understood."

"We could use more weapons," Liu said.

"Storage is wrecked," David said. "But you have those explosives, right?" He nodded to the pack Liu was carrying.

Liu frowned. "But no detonator."

"The switch had a manual setting. We could use them like grenades in a bind."

"We're not soldiers," Liu replied.

"We are now. Let's go."

David shoved off the ladder, drifting to the airlock again. He cycled it, and soon they were crossing back to the *Interloper*. David tested the comms once more, but still no reply from Lennon.

The breach hatch remained open, so they simply climbed in and sealed it behind them.

"How are we even going to find her?" Liu asked once they were both standing on the deck again.

"She must have tried to detonate them. I'm guessing she's returned to the scene of the crime."

"And if she's dead?" Liu insisted. "We could be risking our lives for a corpse."

"I have to see a body before I believe that." The room re-pressurized before they exited it, and David checked the mapping app on his HUD to gather his bearings.

They continued to the lower level, moving quietly down the slope of the tunnels in case company awaited them, but the bowels of the ship were silent.

The HUD chimed, and David saw it. A green dot to one side of the pair that represented him and Liu.

"She's right there!" David crowed.

"Where?" Liu asked.

A gunshot cracked in the distance, and they spun toward the sound. It was coming from the same direction as Lennon's marker on the map.

"This way!" David tore down the corridor. Another gunshot rang out as they approached a big open chamber full of strangely-configured technology.

Lennon was on the far end of the compartment with her back to the wall and a monstrous thing approaching her on four skinny legs that seemed to project from the same hip joints. It reached for her with willowy black arms and long, skinny fingers. A bald, spiky black head extended from a thick neck, making the creature nine or ten feet tall. Lennon screamed and fired again.

The bullet plinked off its shoulder.

It had to have some type of armor, or at least an exoskeleton. Its arms encircled Lennon's body, hoisting her high into the air. David sprinted across the room as Lennon kicked and struggled, firing again and again to no effect, her bullets bouncing off.

Judging his moment, David stopped and launched himself onto the alien's back, wrapping his arm around its neck. He squeezed as hard as he could, but it was wasted effort, as the creature's exoskeleton was as unyielding as a metal pipe.

But even so, the being unleashed a chittering roar, and bucked like a bronco, trying to throw him off. When that failed, the alien dropped Lennon, scrabbling for him instead. He felt an iron grip on his left calf, and it tugged with terrifying force. David's muscles stretched to their breaking point.

"Liu! Pass me an explosive!" David cried.

But Lennon was faster. She already had one in hand. She raced in and sprang off the alien's knee, launching herself above it. The thing shrieked, and David caught a glimpse of a mouth full of thin, dagger-long translucent teeth, gnashing angrily around a blinking blue sphere. Two pairs of beady black eyes winked at him in alternating sets to either side of the snapping jaws. A single black nostril dilated where a human's forehead would be. It shuddered and snorted.

"Let go!" Lennon screamed as she leaped clear.

David slid off its back, but it still had hold of his leg, and he fell face-first at its feet.

The explosive went off with a gut-punching *boom* and a blinding flash.

THIRTY

The Interloper

L ENNON EXPECTED TO BE dead. It had all come to this. Somehow, against appalling odds, Commander David Bryce had arrived with Liu, right when she was about to be killed by this monstrosity. What kind of skin could withstand a bullet?

Its grip had been so tight, so debilitating, but Lennon wasn't the type to throw in the towel. And seeing David diving for the huge beast was almost as shocking as discovering they were still alive.

But it had been for nothing.

The explosion was fierce, and she felt shrapnel sticking into her suit as she slammed against the central tube and fell to the floor.

"Commander!" It was Liu, his voice strained and desperate.

Lennon saw images flash before her eyes. Her mother, a glow over her face as they strode to the park when she was just a little girl, before the drugs had taken her life. Graduation day from flight training, the flutter in her chest as she was welcomed into the Air Force with distinction. Rutger showing her ten ways to kill a man, using a hospital-grade CPR mannequin.

"Lennon! Are you okay?" Liu stopped at her side, despite the fact David was a crumpled heap on the floor.

She stared blankly, a ringing in her ears drowning out his voice. "I'm fine," she lied, and closed her eyes. But maybe it was true. This bastard had tried to kill her, and she was alive. All those years of wishing she wasn't suddenly felt like a waste. Lennon climbed to her knees, and crawled to David's unmoving form.

Lennon tried to find the black spiked demon, but it was nowhere in sight. "Liu, be careful. It might come back."

He looked at her like she was delusional, and gestured to the walls and ceiling. "Lennon. He's paint."

She understood what he meant, and steeled herself. She'd witnessed worse. Endured gruesome missions. But a hulking alien's guts and brains all over your commander was almost enough to put her over the edge. She rolled David onto his back and wiped his helmet. It streaked, and she kept at it until she could see his face. "David!"

Liu no longer cared about the suit being sealed. They were all screwed if that mattered. Lennon's was torn in a few sections, and pieces flapped with each movement.

"He's alive," Liu whispered.

"How? He was in the monster's grip when it detonated."

"I think it has an exoskeleton. The force of the explosion was blocked by its armor, since the bomb was inside the creature's mouth. It's the only reason he's alive. If you'd have flung it under him, we'd all be dead."

Lennon glanced at the three stacked colored spheres and groaned. "Maybe that would have caused enough damage to stop it." The tube had the slightest of cracks where she'd barreled into it, but it seemed to be holding.

David coughed, and Liu unclasped the helmet, removing it. His brow was covered in sweat. Suddenly Lennon was claustrophobic, and she tossed her helmet aside. There would be no returning to *Beyond,* not with their suits in this condition.

"David," Liu muttered. "Can you breathe?"

David tested the theory, and let out a gasp. He coughed and tried again, lifting his arm to give a thumbs up. "The wind was knocked out of me." David appeared to finally notice Lennon, and she wiped a sweaty strand of hair behind her ear. "You," he croaked. "What have you done?"

"Well, sir," she seethed. "I just saved your life."

"After I saved yours," he reminded her, and she laughed. The sound escaped her lips, and it was like it came from a stranger. Once she started, she couldn't stop.

Lennon bent over, and she wiped her mouth before seeing Liu and David watching her silently. "If you're not laughing, you're not living," she muttered, repeating something Dark Seven used to say. Sarcastically, of course. James was a tough man to read.

"Who are you?" David sat up, leaning against the wall.

"I'm Lennon Baxter," she answered.

"No. Who do you work for?"

"The same people you do. ORB."

David gave her an angry scowl. "Lennon…" He coughed, a drop of blood landing on the floor between them.

"Commander, the commotion might have triggered something. You're injured. We have to…"

David slapped the man's hand away. "Liu, for the love of God, let me talk to Lennon."

"What the hell," she said. "We're all dead anyway. I'm not lying about my name. I was in the Air Force, for a short spell. Took the preliminary Space Force training, back when I didn't know better. Then I got recruited by a secret organization. My codename is Dark Three. Dark Leader sent me here…"

"Dark Leader?"

"A man. Former six-star…"

"Six-star? I thought Washington was the only…"

"You just haven't heard of them. Who do you think cleans up all the messes?" Lennon asked. "If the public knew half the shit we've dealt with, people would be flocking to churches and keeping their kids at home."

David stared at her. "What were you told to do?"

"I was to integrate into the crew. Make friends. Get on board the *Interloper*." She shrugged. "And destroy it."

"With us on board."

"I saw those... things. One of them nearly killed Carter. I suspect he's dead," she told him.

"No. We found him. He's safe on the *Beyond*. Safe as he can be, anyway."

For some reason, relief flooded Lennon, and she felt absolved of guilt she didn't realize she'd been clinging to.

"What happened?"

"I tried to set them off, but the link didn't work." She looked at Liu. "I guess it's because you manually deactivated them."

"Not long ago. They were coated in slime. I don't know how we didn't cross paths."

"I took a circuitous route to avoid these monsters," she whispered. "You think their saliva somehow blocked the signal from the detonator?"

From the tunnel, she heard the opening of a door in the distance.

"We have to leave," David said, struggling to his feet.

"Not without destroying this." Lennon pointed to the tube.

"Lennon, you still want to blow us up?" David barked.

"This thing is heading for Earth, or did you not notice?" Lennon was the first to the exit, and she craned her neck into the hall, searching for signs of adversaries. When she didn't see any, she offered her hand. "Give them to me."

David nodded at Liu, and the man passed her two explosives. She tried to flick the manual override, but the goop had eaten into the button. The same happened on the other one. "They're useless. Where are the rest?"

"We left them near the hatch," David admitted.

Lennon set one near the tube, and waved the men from the room. "Here goes nothing."

"Wait!" David shouted.

Lennon's finger hovered beside the gun's trigger as she aimed for the bomb. "What?"

"My family. I didn't get to say goodbye," David whispered.

"None of us did."

"What if we find another way to stop the ship?" Liu asked. "Its new course could be part of an automatic response, seeking the nearest habitable world, for example."

"After all we've been through, you still think the ship is running itself?" Lennon nodded to the splatter across the room. "Must I remind you about that guy?"

"But we still don't know if they plan to invade Earth," Liu offered.

"I don't care. You didn't see the weapon on the bow of the *Interloper,* did you?" Lennon asked, her gloved fingers touching the door frame. The subtlest of vibrations reached her, growing in intensity.

"What weapon?" David spoke, but the words barely registered.

"Something's coming."

Lennon witnessed the mass of black specks rushing down the corridor, and she shoved the others farther into the hall.

"Don't move," David hissed, and Lennon went rigid.

The carpet of tiny insectoids hurried over the ceiling, walls, and floor, arriving at engineering. They paid the three humans no mind as they blanketed the room.

She stood in awe as they scattered over the area. They moved as one, a swarm of like-minded beings, cleaning away the mess. The spiked alien's remains were cleared in seconds, and the dent in the tube was fixed soon after.

"How are they doing that?" Liu whispered.

"We can't stay here. Once they're done, we're next." David's lips hardly moved as he spoke.

"Okay." Lennon double-checked that the bomb's manual override was destroyed, and wiped it clean. The detonator was in her pocket, and she pulled it free, finding the screen cracked in two places. It was still linked. "This better work."

She stepped back, and whispered for them to run. As soon as they were clear, she rolled the explosive toward the entrance, and darted away, tapping the button. Before it exploded, thousands of the miniscule insects rushed the bomb, enveloping it. The detonation was subdued under the weight of the creatures.

Lennon sprinted after David and Liu, but when she risked a glance, it looked like the bomb had only blasted a hole in the floor and torn half the doorway off. The reactor tube was undoubtedly intact. Without another thought, they dashed from the swarm. Lennon's mind raced as they fled through the shadowy tunnels.

She had no idea what came next. They were running out of options.

THIRTY-ONE

Kalumburu, Australia

"WHY HERE?" ATLAS ASKED James as they began their descent to the barren location.

"You can see why," James said.

There was nothing around for miles. Atlas kept quiet as they landed within a fenced yard. It was midmorning and the sun was sweltering. The carrier James mentioned earlier was the only vehicle in sight, and it appeared Atlas' rock had indeed beaten them to Australia. He glanced to the coast, and saw a boat rushing into the east.

The rotors slowed, and eventually it was silent. After a few hours in the air, and a couple refills of fuel, his ears had acclimated to the noise.

"This way," James muttered, leading Atlas across the grounds. The only building in the vicinity was a barn-like metallic structure.

"That's the general's quarters?" Atlas joked.

James ignored his question, and the doors buzzed loudly at their approach.

Atlas glanced up at the five cameras facing them, mounted high above. He moved his arm, and they all followed.

Atlas wasn't sure what he expected to see inside, but when the doors opened, he was shocked to find it empty. "Kind of anticlimactic," he said.

The floor groaned and spread apart in the center of the barn, revealing a set of stairs.

"That's our intention." James walked ahead, and Atlas followed slowly. He had a moment of worry that if he descended into this facility, he'd never see the light of day again.

James must have noticed his hesitancy, and he stopped halfway down. "If he wanted you dead, you'd be buried in Vietnam right now."

Atlas guessed he was being truthful and continued.

The wall lights were dim, casting a yellow shine on the stone stairs, and he counted three stories as they turned twice before ending at a stainless double door. James pressed his thumb to a screen, opening the barricade.

A woman greeted them, her expression blank. "Dark Seven."

"Dark Thirteen," he responded.

"You guys are really into these nicknames, aren't you?" Atlas asked, and quickly regretted it. They both shot daggers at him with their eyes.

"This way." Dark Thirteen led him, and James remained where he was.

The ceilings were low in the foyer, a desk with a single chair. A TV which, no doubt, displayed the camera feeds from the structure above.

What were they hiding down here?

Atlas considered asking, but knew this woman wouldn't be any more talkative than her counterpart.

When they came to another door, she stayed behind Atlas. "He's ready to see you." She walked off, her footsteps muted in the dense stone hall.

Someone faced him as the entrance slid to the left. "Mr. Donovan." He was probably in his sixties, obviously the same guy from that photo with James Wan, but he looked like he'd lived a hundred lifetimes since. It was in the way his eyes cautiously glanced over Atlas, his back and shoulders tense. This was a man who'd seen too much. Atlas tried not to stare at the scar covering the right side of his face.

"What do I call you?"

"Dark Leader," he said, his voice thick like a baritone.

"Why doesn't that surprise me?" Atlas peered past him, and noticed how different this room was from the rest of the hidden base. "Quite the operation you have. I expected… more staff."

"It's best to keep the liabilities at a minimum. There are only three operatives posted." He turned his back to Atlas, clearly not feeling in danger.

"I met a couple of them. Lovely people." He thought back to Bethany, who'd been killed in Lawrence's condo.

"Yes. Dark Nine. That loss hurt," he said. "But perhaps it was beneficial to keep you alive."

"I'd like to think so," Atlas grumbled.

Dark Leader wore a navy suit with a black tie. His shoes were polished, cufflinks sparkling. This was a man who paid close attention to even the most precise details. Atlas appraised himself, seeing his own clothing covered in mud. There was dirt under his fingernails, his hair greasy. "Would you care for a drink?"

Atlas shook his head, but Dark Leader waved him to a side table nonetheless. He poured two stiff servings into opulent crystal glasses, and handed one to Atlas. "You'll appreciate this, trust me."

Atlas accepted it, and looked around. A plethora of screens were mounted on the walls, a single chair facing them, with an automatic rifle leaning against it. He glanced to the ceiling, and counted ten vents.

"What is this place?"

"This is Ground Zero." Dark Leader gulped his drink, draining it within seconds. The glass tottered on the table, and settled while he stalked away. "Mr. Donovan, do you believe in aliens?"

"I think you know the answer to that."

"But seriously. You were chasing a dream when you searched for those pieces. Did you take the time to contemplate what they belonged to? Where they might have hailed from? Or why they were here?"

Atlas was about to answer with a definitive 'yes,' but the truth was, he rarely considered it. He'd been so focused on the search that he'd failed to ask the bigger questions. "Sometimes."

"And what did you assume occurred?"

Atlas took a sip, feeling the Scotch warm his throat. He licked his lips, and set the glass onto the table. "I suppose I assumed they were just visiting and burned up in the atmosphere."

Dark Leader smirked. "If only it were so simple."

"Enlighten me." Atlas was sick of the suspense. "If you have all the answers, let's hear them."

"It was March 17th, 1966. Three flashes of light erupted over Asia, but back then we didn't have the technology to capture the events as we do today."

"Three?"

"That's right. Three."

It made sense. One ship torn apart and spread over the eastern hemisphere; the second intact, hidden in the Vietnam Sea until a salvage crew discovered what they thought to be a rock. But that didn't explain the third.

"Who are they?"

"That, I'd rather show than tell." Dark Leader's shoes clipped across the shiny black floor and after a retinal scan, another door opened.

A tank sat in the middle of the room, and at first, Atlas thought it was empty. It went from the floor to the ceiling, ten feet in diameter, clear for the middle section. Lights glowed from the top and bottom, and the area hummed from an unseen power source.

"What are we looking at?" Atlas inched closer and froze. The hair on his arms stood on end, and white dots blurred his vision. The being was suspended inside the liquid, unmoving and dreadful.

The first thing Atlas noticed was the hand with three fingers. It made him recall the disk he'd carried around since he was a child. Stubby black spikes jutted from its body. Four thin legs, drooping to a point, with a broad chest and shoulders, complete with lengthy arms.

But it was the face that scared him the most. He thought the eyes were closed, but realized they were open, black orbs to match the rest of it. Two sets, making a total of four eyes. The brow curved up, and Atlas thought the slot above was a nostril. He couldn't see a mouth, but assumed it was shut, maybe in the location one might expect.

"It's got to be eight feet tall," he finally whispered.

"Nine feet, three inches," the general replied.

"Is it…?"

"No. It's dead."

Atlas felt a sense of relief, followed by disappointment. "Good."

"Maybe." Dark Leader strode up to the tube. "But there were more."

"More?" The wall lifted behind the tube, and Atlas couldn't believe his eyes. He rubbed them, and steadied himself.

"This is everything we have from the Stalkers." Dark Leader motioned to the collection.

There were several pieces of a ship, each placed together on a metal frame. The vessel was easily ten times the size of the rock he'd obtained, and barely half of the hull had been recreated. The rest sat empty. "We scoured the globe to find these, but we were missing crucial components." He indicated a spot near the bow of the vessel, and Atlas saw it was the exact shape of his first artifact.

Dark Leader picked up a satchel, the very same one the woman in Vietnam had taken from Atlas, and unwrapped the objects. They had remained connected, and he set them on the frame. "Perfect fit."

Atlas laughed now. His years of searching, and he was standing at the actual ship his father's relic had come from. "I don't understand."

"Which part?" Dark Leader asked.

"The rock. It looks different," Atlas mustered.

"Precisely. And you're wondering how this opened it?"

Atlas nodded, and the man smiled. "There's something else I have to show you."

The space was high-tech, the walls lined with glass cases, each section dark, but one by one the lights turned on, showcasing the displayed items secured within. Weapons. Armor. All large enough to be utilized by these giant Stalkers. "You found all this?"

"Yes."

"Where?" Atlas imagined the guns in the wrong hands. "Is there..."

"That's what I need your help with," Dark Leader said.

"What can I do?"

"You found one of their ships," he told Atlas.

"So?" He realized what the general was implying. "*One* of them? There's more?"

"Come. The helicopter is waiting." Dark Leader exited the room, and Atlas stayed, eyeballing a black suit of armor.

"Where are we going?" Atlas stirred to life, recuperating from his shock, and chased Dark Leader up the stairs.

"To see the opposing side of this mess."

Atlas had more questions than answers as they departed the building, returning to the helicopter where James Wan waited for them.

THIRTY-TWO

The Interloper

D AVID RAN AS FAST as his legs would carry him, but his wounded ankle forced him to limp. Liu and Lennon's footsteps echoed after his. They wound through the rocky tunnels, fleeing the swarm. David clung to his sidearm as if it were a lifeline, even though their enemies were bullet-proof.

At least Lennon's explosives had been enough to kill the one they'd encountered, but what if they ran into more of them?

And that wasn't even their biggest problem. The explosion they'd triggered had ripped their suits open with shrapnel. There was no way they were getting to the *Beyond* now, not unless Carter crawled over with three spare suits. And with his bad leg...

"We have to grab the rest of the bombs from where we came in..." Lennon said, her breath ragged with exhaustion.

"Understood." David led them up the shaft, his movements slowing as the exertion of the day's events took their toll on him.

The airlock was as they'd left it, and David knew Carter was only a few meters away, on board *Beyond*.

David tried the comms, to see if the jamming field was still active. "Carter. Come in."

A squeal of static made him wince. Not even a hint of Carter's reply. They were on their own.

"Put them in here," Liu said, opening his sample bag.

Lennon glanced at the contents. "Got anything to give us a boost?"

"I should have thought of that," Liu said, retrieving a vial and three needles. He stuck her first, dropping the used device on the floor. David was next, and he gritted his teeth as the point entered his shoulder.

"What is it?" David asked.

"A stimulant to keep us awake, at least for a couple of hours," Liu said.

"Okay." He wasn't sure if it was the administered drug, or the placebo effect of knowing he'd been injected, but David already felt better: his mind less muddled, his muscles regaining some of their former strength.

Lennon used her detonator, linking the last five bombs, and she wiped them clean. "I think they'll work. The controls weren't as caked as the others."

"We need to move." David went ahead, with Liu shouldering his bag. David noticed Lennon kept one of the bombs in her hand.

Eventually, David slowed as he approached a bend in the corridor, and he leaned around it to check that the way was clear. Muted green lights extended into shadows as the tunnel snaked up to a higher level, but there was no sign of spiders, or the sinister creatures with four eyes.

Lennon slowed alongside him, and she let out a ragged breath. "Where is this leading?"

David produced his Holo from a mag-sealed pocket on his hip. Thankfully it hadn't been too damaged in the blast. The mapping app gave him some notion. They'd distanced themselves from the splattered guts of the alien crewman, and were headed to an unexplored region in the bow of the ship.

"We don't know what's in there," Lennon said.

"Or who," Liu added in a dark whisper.

"Maybe not, but we can't go back," David stated. "Besides, if we're lucky we might find some type of escape pod we can sneak into."

"And also be fortunate enough to figure out how to operate it?" Lennon asked.

"Do you have a better idea?"

"We need to stop them before they arrive."

"You tried that."

"So we try again. We have more explosives."

"The swarm is there," David argued. "No."

Not waiting for further argument, David crept forward, keeping his sidearm at the ready. The tunnel twisted higher, and all three of them were laboring for breath. Eventually they came to a dead end as David touched the door handle.

"Wait," Liu said, and assessed it with his scanner. They'd left their helmets behind, forcing them to crowd around the small holographic display at the back of the device. "Clear," David whispered, before opening the barrier into a more artificial corridor. About a hundred meters later, they found a vast chamber full of glowing aisles with illuminated tanks stacked atop each other. They were filled with the same lanky monsters they'd encountered down in the engineering section.

Lennon gasped and cursed under her breath.

David rocked on his heels as a dull wave of shock rolled over him. It was exactly as they'd predicted. Some type of cryo room or suspended animation chamber. In a daze, he drifted toward the nearest tank for a better look.

Two sets of eyes to either side of a vertical, slitted mouth. They were shut with semi-translucent lids that made the creature appear blind. A spiked black carapace, lengthy limbs and three-fingered hands. Four legs that extended from two bony hip joints that trailed to a point near the bottom of the tank. The being was suspended in the liquid, connected to multiple tubes and clear, hair-like cables that faded behind its skull. A single black orifice at the top of its curved forehead was puckered shut.

"There must be thousands of them..." Liu whispered, his gaze scanning the room.

"We should leave."

Liu gawked at the tank. "Look." His hand came up and brushed a blinking panel set into the tube.

Something clicked and whirred. The lights flashed from green and blue to solid yellow, and the tank rose several inches above the floor. The fluid inside the tank began to swirl.

"What did you do?" Lennon hissed.

"I didn't..." Liu staggered away, shaking his head.

David leveled his weapon at the tank, watching as the contents steadily drained. The alien stirred to life. Translucent lids fluttered, the eyes roving behind them.

"It's waking up! We need to leave!" Lennon said.

Its palms slapped the glass as the fluid no longer held it in stasis. "Come on!" Lennon pleaded, tugging at his arm.

David nodded, breaking his stare.

The alien stared right at him. It let out a muffled roar, and he froze. Lips receded from interlocking sets of translucent six-inch teeth that vaguely reminded David of a Venetian flytrap. It hit the inside of the tank with a fist, and it sprang open. The thing stepped out, fumbling with the tubes connected to its chest before yanking on the bundle of hair-thin wires attached to its skull.

BANG.

A bullet plinked off its head, barely missing one of its eyes. The alien shrieked and snapped its jaws. It lunged for David, but he ducked the blow. Lennon came to his aid, firing relentlessly, but her aim was off target.

"Run!" Liu cried, even as he let off a hasty shot of his own.

David joined their assault. The alien staggered and let out a sibilant hiss as one bullet hit the mark and its upper right eye exploded in a fountain of clear, viscous blood that splattered David's face. The creature sagged to one knee, clutching its ruined eye.

A thunderous clunking and groaning sound erupted, and all of the glowing tanks simultaneously rose off the deck, fluid swirling as pumps emptied their liquid contents.

"They're waking up!" Lennon said. "We have to go now!"

David didn't hesitate. He turned and tore after Lennon, sprinting through the exit.

THIRTY-THREE

Off the Australian Coast

T HE IMAGE OF THE alien suspended in that tank stuck in
Atlas' mind. He tried to focus on the conversation to
distract himself from the maelstrom of questions churning through his thoughts.

"Dark Seven has been with me for years." The general
indicated James Wan. "One of the originals."

"What are you guys?" Atlas asked.

"Merely a covert operation. We deal with global issues
that require discretion," he said.

"So you're mercenaries." Atlas glanced out the window,
seeing the choppy waves below them.

Dark Leader laughed, the noise booming even with
the sound of the rotors. "Mr. Donovan, you are still in
denial. Without us, the world would have already ended.
I promise you that."

Atlas identified a black dot in the water, and assumed
it was their destination. A minute later, he saw it was an
aircraft carrier, only there were no jets parked on the
runway. The smaller boat he'd seen near the coast was
floating nearby.

He noted it was unmarked as they set down on the
helicopter pad. "Tell me about the Mars operation."

"Mars, or the *Beyond III*'s mission?"

"Are they different?"

"Vastly. *Beyond* was sent to intercept..."

"An alien ship," Atlas finished. "I heard something about the change of trajectory."

"Is that so?" Dark Leader lifted an eyebrow. "It seems you're more astute than I gave you credit for."

"Who are they?"

The general stepped out of the helicopter, and Atlas followed. Another armed man greeted them. He wore the same uniform as James Wan, and looked to be eastern European.

"Dark One," the general said. "Thank you for meeting us."

"Anything you need, sir." The man had a slight German accent, but spoke English fluently.

James remained on the platform, and Atlas went with the others to the nearest set of stairs.

Atlas was exhausted, but adrenaline kept him going. Eventually he slowed, struggling to keep up with the pair of operatives. He longed for a shower and something to eat, but the notion of learning more about these Stalkers fueled his movements.

They emerged in an echoing aircraft hangar below the flight deck. The rock was here, somehow already moved from the coast to the carrier. Atlas was astounded with how fast these people operated. Dark Leader held the pair of relics Atlas had once possessed, and walked toward the oval vessel. "Now we learn the truth," the man said.

"What are you hoping to find?"

"My intel suggests a pair of these landed on Earth. One holds a signal."

"For what?"

"We're unsure. My information isn't very reliable. But we fear serious consequences if the Stalkers find it."

Atlas marched closer to the rock and set a palm on its exterior. "There's another ship like this?"

"That's correct."

Dark Leader retrieved his Holo from inside his suit jacket, and passed it to Atlas. The drawing was detailed, created with a digital pen. Green lights shone from a circular stone. "What is it?"

"That's the signal's source," he responded.

Dark Leader stared at his counterpart, who held his automatic rifle to his chest, prepared to use it if necessary. Atlas didn't think it was intended for himself.

"If we're right, the signal might be emanating from within the hull of this craft."

"And if that's the case? Then what?"

"We destroy it," he whispered.

Atlas had a terrible feeling in the pit of his stomach, and was beginning to see the bigger picture. "They're coming here, aren't they? The Stalkers."

"I've sent someone to deal with the *Interloper.*"

Atlas mouthed the word silently.

"Sir, has Dark Three responded yet?" the German asked.

"Wait. You dispatched one of your operatives with the Mars mission?" Atlas asked.

"Yes. She's been ordered to destroy the Stalkers' ship. But I fear something's gone wrong." He took his Holo back, and typed on the screen. "I've lost contact. The last message she received was when I asked her to await further orders."

"Why did you tell her that? Aren't they a threat?"

"Because I needed to see what happened when we activated this." He gestured to the dormant hunk of rock. "But her final response bodes well. *I will place them. We have landed. Hostiles on board. One dead so far.*" Dark Leader read the communication.

"So she *is* going to destroy it?"

"That's the plan."

"But why?" Atlas could think of a million reasons why, but he would have expected Dark Leader would want to study a giant alien spacecraft full of advanced technology.

"Atlas, what happens every time a native population is visited by outsiders?"

"They're conquered."

"Or they bring pestilence and disease. No matter what we think, they will devastate our planet," Dark Leader said. He had the relics in his grip, and he passed them to Atlas. "How did they work?"

Atlas hefted the object, and stuck his three fingers into the depressions. He spun them as he had in the rain before dawn, and he immediately felt vibrations pulsing through the deck. The rock clicked and hummed as the square of light flashed before the doorway opened.

"Dark One, investigate it."

"Sir, yes, sir." He poked his gun inside, and soon he vanished within the vessel, crouching to fit into the opening.

Atlas waited nervously, resisting the urge to fidget. A minute later, the German agent returned. "It's in there."

"It?" Atlas asked. "The signal stone?"

"No. One of them."

Atlas rushed to the craft, peering into the opening. A being was seated in a metal chair, strapped in around the chest. It wore considerable armor, but no helmet, and its shiny black head had lolled to the side, two sets of large eyes staring blankly. It smelled like sour milk. "Why didn't it decay?"

"This ship was sealed up tight. Nothing in or out." Dark Leader brushed past Atlas, searching the small cockpit. "The signal isn't here." He exited, pounding a palm against the hull. "That means it's out there somewhere. And we've already activated it."

By the expression on the man's face, this was distressing. But how did he know? He seemed to know what he was looking for, despite not having found it yet. That made Atlas wonder about his source.

"What do we do?" he asked.

"Prepare for the worst." He faced Dark One. "Contact the Association. Explain our discovery. More will be coming."

Atlas glanced at the skinny alien, seeing that it also had three fingers and four eyes, like the other in the tank. But this one was small and hunching, curled in on itself and somehow shrunken within its glossy armor.

Papery flakes of skin fluttered in a draft from an open doorway, and a vertical slit for a mouth revealed a hint of translucent teeth. But it had only two legs that he could see.

Were these two species related? Their similarities made him wonder. It implied a relationship. Finding out that not one, but two different alien species had visited Earth left his mind spinning with entirely new questions.

Lennon

The Interloper

Walking these corridors was becoming a living nightmare. Lennon found they all looked the same, and she was growing too used to the pale emerald lighting. It was unnerving, and after the series of tense situations they'd experienced, she was seeing monsters within every shadow.

The *Interloper* had an off-putting aroma to it. Now that they were without space suits, the experience had changed. The primary corridors were scentless, the lower decks musky, and the caverns held a tinge of fecal matter and decay.

"You seriously want to return to engineering?" Liu was beginning to lose his composure. "I think we should hide somewhere. Wait them out."

Lennon had heard enough. She shoved the doctor, planting her forearm against his neck as she pinned him to the wall. "Shut up, Liu. Did you see those things? There are thousands of bullet-proof aliens destined for Earth, as well as a giant weapon on the front of this vessel, and we are not prepared to deal with an invasion. Do you understand?"

Liu stared at her, and finally nodded. "Okay."

Lennon appreciated that David kept his nose out of this. He'd obviously resigned himself to her authority on the matter. After seeing those cryo-tubes, and what was in them, how could anyone in their right mind ignore the fact that they needed to destroy the *Interloper?*

"You think it's better to remain here, go for it. Maybe you could draw them out. It'll be a good distraction," Lennon half-kidded. It didn't go over well, considering David's glare.

"No one is staying behind. We're here to support you, Baxter. Let's finish this once and for all," he said, marching past her.

She checked the Holo, finding their destination was only three hundred meters away, and two decks below. "What if we use the shafts?"

"Good idea. They might be guarding engineering," David said. "Liu, can you locate one with the scanner?"

Lennon waited impatiently while he checked the walls. The *Interloper* had been moving quickly, but Lennon had no idea how long it was going to take to reach Earth. Hopefully months. If so, she could tear the vessel apart in the next while, sending the pieces drifting through space. The mission would be a success, and Earth would be safe.

"Here." Liu tapped a hidden panel, and David wretched it loose.

"We have a way in." David stretched toward an explosive from Liu's pack.

Lennon grabbed his arm. "We're planting them. I don't trust the range of this thing." She stared at the detonator. "If it fails, I'll have to override using the manual." Not that she loved the idea of being torn apart by the explosion.

"Fine. But we all go." David climbed in first, and she heard him begin his descent, arms sliding as he pressed them against either side of the shaft.

Lennon let Liu go next, and she glanced behind her, almost expecting to find a hundred of those creatures stalking the corridor to greet her. But it was silent on this deck, half a ship away from the cryo chambers.

She made quick work of the five decks, her arms fatiguing from effort, but she entered engineering, amazed at how pristine it was. There was no evidence of their battle with the spiked black monster.

Lennon sped into the room, setting two of the explosives at the base of the reactor tube. She couldn't believe she was here again. A never-ending circular path on the alien's vessel.

David was at the exit, his hands shaking with the gun in his grip. "They're coming," he whispered.

"Who is? Which ones?" Lennon felt the rumbling under her boots.

"Five, ten–all of them? Does it matter how many?" He stared back, his skin pallid and sweaty.

"Go into the ducts!" she shouted, and David dashed for it. Lennon paused at the opening, watching for the aliens' arrival. The other two were already up the shaft. Lennon meant to take out as many of the beasts as she could.

"Come on, you bastards," she muttered, her finger on the detonator. If this failed, all was lost. The mission would be over.

The moment she saw the spiked carapace enter on four legs, she grinned. Lennon scrambled into the shaft, pressed the detonator, and jumped.

The blazes of Hell raced after her.

THIRTY-FOUR

The Interloper

D AVID RODE THE FIERY heat of the explosion up the shaft, his exposed skin seared by the blast. For a second he thought it might consume them, but then the shock wave faded, leaving them rising on the mysterious pulses of energy flashing by them. He peered between his feet to check on the others.

"Everyone okay?"

"More or less," Lennon grunted. She'd been the last one to jump into the shaft.

David winced at the thought of her being burned beyond recognition. They needed to find a place to dress their wounds with Liu's supplies. A rumble of thunder shivered to his ears, and David felt the tunnel tilt away from the direction of gravity. He slid up the edge of the shaft, his ragged suit squealing against the smooth metal with each pulse of the invisible energy field inside the duct.

The shaft bucked ahead of him, the walls closing in fast. David lunged for the nearest opening to one of the horizontal passages, grabbing the ledge to heave himself in. Sitting on a slope, he spun around and pulled Liu in. He repeated that process with Lennon and saw that his fears had been unfounded. Both crew members were relatively unscathed by the blast.

The three of them sat on the sloping deck inside the duct, breathing heavily as more secondary explosions rocked through the *Interloper*.

"You think that blast finally did it?" Liu asked.

"Maybe," Lennon said, nodding gravely.

A mighty *boom* shook the walls of the access tunnel, sending a painful jolt up David's spine. Rumbling aftershocks rattled through him, setting his teeth on edge.

"It's cracking apart!" Liu cried.

A roar of static erupted from David's pocket. He reached into it and produced his Holo. It was a call from Carter. Having lost their comms with their helmets, Carter had found another way.

"Carter!" David hissed into the audio-pickups of the device.

"You're alive!"

"You sound surprised. What's the situation?"

"Good and bad, depending how you look at it. Whatever you did nearly cracked the *Interloper* in two. It was gushing flames and atmosphere from about a dozen different locations before finally settling. Their engines cut out, and they now have zero measurable acceleration."

"We stopped them?" Lennon asked.

"Not exactly," Carter replied, having heard her.

"Explain," David said.

"The *Interloper* is drifting, but toward Earth."

David felt the blood drain from his face. "How long?"

"One hour."

"One hour before what?" Liu asked, looking dazed.

"Before the *Interloper* carves out a crater on the surface," David clarified.

"How is that even possible?" Lennon asked. "Weren't we several months away from Earth?"

"For us, at the speeds we travel," Carter said. "One minute we were millions of kilometers out; then I went to the head, and when I returned, suddenly we were cruising into a high orbit."

"You mean they used some kind of warp drive?" David asked.

"What else? If it were regular thrust, the kind of acceleration we're talking about would have turned me into a puddle."

They sat with that news for a few seconds before Carter went on. "Anyway, the *Beyond* is still attached at the hip to this thing, so it appears that I'm going to crash with you."

"Not if you use the lifeboat," David said, reminding him that the cockpit had been designed to detach from the rest of the rocket in an emergency.

"But what about you? I can wait for you to get over here," Carter said.

"There's no time. They're going to shoot us down with missiles any minute now," Lennon said.

"You don't know that," Carter said.

"Let's find out. Contact mission control," David said. "Give them an update and let us know what they say."

"Copy that. What are you going to do in the meantime?"

"Find somewhere safe and hunker down."

"You're not even going to try to get here?"

"We can't. Our suits are compromised," David explained.

"Shit."

"Keep us posted, Carter."

"Yes, sir."

"Bryce out."

Lennon set her jaw. "We should stay here. Why even bother searching for shelter? It'll be the same outcome no matter where we are. We're done. But at least we dealt them a crippling blow in the process."

David scowled. "We're not finished until we've stopped breathing. Your mission might be over, but mine isn't. Mine is to get us all to Earth. Alive."

Lennon looked at him like he'd sprouted an extra head. "Have you lost your mind? What are you going to do, find an airlock and skydive without a parachute?"

"No. I'm going to find a lifeboat. Or an escape pod. A ship this size with so many of those creatures sleeping on board should have the ability to evacuate."

Liu looked relieved with the mention of evacuation. "Yes. He's right."

"Let's go," David said, pushing off the floor of the duct. He stuck out a hand to help Lennon up, but she was already climbing to her feet.

"Lead on," she said.

He nodded, and followed the duct to the end. He found a simple push dislodged the panel, and it swung away, exposing a familiar section of the ship.

Behind him, Lennon sucked in a sharp breath. Lying in front of them was a figure in a white pressure suit. "Zasha."

"We should go back," Liu muttered.

"We can't," Lennon whispered. "The ducts don't go any higher."

"Cut the chatter," David whispered. "They're attracted to sound," he said as he exited the tunnel and crept toward Zasha, compelled by morbid curiosity. They hadn't seen what became of her in the end, but he was almost afraid to know now.

There wasn't any sign of the swarming insects, but to their left lay that inky black pool where he and Liu had escaped the queen. To the right was the opening of the cave with the spiders' nest.

David reached Zasha and cringed at the sight of the hollow white skull. Her bones had been picked clean from within her suit, which was flayed open in multiple places and stained red with blood.

"They ate her alive," Liu whispered, crouching near the body.

The silence rang loudly in his ears, begging for a response, but there was nothing he could say to make this better.

A sharp crack and a bright red flash shattered the stillness, followed by a desperate cry from Liu as he fell with flames leaping from his arm.

Lennon spun to face the threat. "Tangos incoming!" she shouted, and returned fire.

David lunged for Liu, catching a glimpse of bright laser beams flashing above his head. David dragged Liu to the opening of the duct, with Lennon falling beside him. Her pistol clicked a few times as she ran out of bullets, and she tossed it with a disgusted grunt.

"Help me get him in!" David said, jerking his chin to the entrance. Liu had patted the flames out, but he looked to be in tremendous pain. Before they could assist him, the hatch swung shut with an ominous *clunk.*

"They locked it!" Lennon cried.

David released Liu and pried desperately at the panel, seeking leverage to force it open again, but it was unyielding.

A familiar roar rumbled through the rocky floor of the cavern. They turned around, staring with horrified anticipation at the opening to the nesting chamber.

"I have explosives," Liu croaked. "Use one. You can seal them off!"

"Where?" Lennon snapped.

"My bag."

She zipped it open and fished a bomb out. She hurled it at the opening. The sphere *thunked* as it hit the floor and rolled along the newfound slope of the deck. Lennon produced the detonator from her belt and paused, watching a glowing circle at the top of the device.

"What are you waiting for?" David screamed.

"That," Lennon said just as a pair of lanky black creatures covered in spikes came stalking into the opening.

Lennon stabbed the switch, and the tunnel erupted in a furious burst of light, briefly silhouetting the two alien predators before the shock wave blinded David and slammed him into the wall.

THIRTY-FIVE

The Interloper

L ENNON HATED IT HERE.
Every breath she took threatened to be her final one. She glanced at her hands, seeing she was out of bombs. A single multi-limbed monster crawled toward her leg, and she used the detonator to swat it away like a baseball bat. The thing smashed against the wall, slumping to the floor.

"We did it," David stuttered through gasping inhales. He looked terrible. Half of his suit had melted off, with cuts and abrasions over his body.

Lennon peered at her own torso, finding herself in a similar state.

"Liu, you good?" The man was barely moving. His arm was burned, and she grabbed Liu's first aid kit. "What do I do?" When he didn't respond, she slapped him across the cheek, and he eventually came to. "Your arm. How do I help?"

"Salve. The pink tube. Then wrap it."

Lennon did so while David examined the caved-in corridor and the remains of the monsters who'd been caught in the blast. She could hear more movement, shrieking, and blasting at the rocky barricade. "At least they're on the opposite side," the commander managed to say.

Lennon's eyes darted around the cavern, wondering if that was true. Their plan to destroy the *Interloper* had failed.

Lennon set the medic bag to the floor. "Carter."

"What about him?" David asked.

"Give me your Holo." When David hesitated, Lennon rushed over and took it. "Carter!"

His voice carried through. "You have to see this."

"Give us a visual!" Lennon barked, and the screen flashed. Carter was holding his Holo up so they could see their imminent crash with Earth. Their home looked gigantic in the Holo, filling most of the display. "We're almost there."

"Carter, can you..." David stopped speaking when the image cut out. "Carter?"

Lennon realized the room across from the rubble was teeming with enemies, and didn't want to remain any longer than necessary.

"Can we change course?" Liu asked.

"How the hell would we do that?" Lennon inquired. "We weren't even able to destroy that reactor tube. It would take a miracle to locate their bridge."

"We were already there," David whispered.

"You were?" Lennon noticed how his gaze averted. "Commander, what aren't you telling me?"

"There was a sphere, and a yellow button..."

"You did this?" Lennon spat.

"Maybe."

"Great. Just perfect. You single-handedly brought the aliens home." Lennon stalked away from the two men.

"We don't know that. It might be circumstantial," Liu suggested. "It's possible something else drew it to Earth." He held his injured arm, cradling it to his chest.

"Guess what, Doctor. I'm sick of your hypotheses. Are you ever right?" Lennon heard something ahead.

"That's not fair," David said, and Lennon lunged at him, shoving a palm over his mouth. He nodded once in understanding.

Lennon glanced above as a shadow streaked down from the ceiling. It was huge.

"Into the water," Liu mumbled.

"What water?" Lennon asked through clenched teeth.

"We used it earlier. After Zasha died," David softly said, and looked to the far end of the cavern.

Lennon risked a glance at the floor, and saw the pool, darkly gleaming in the green glow. "Go."

"How far was it?" Liu asked David as they approached the water's edge.

"I don't know. What does it matter?" David hissed.

"We had air tanks before." Liu gestured to his mouth.

"Damn it all." David's shoulders slumped. "It's our only chance."

The giant creature hopped the last twenty feet, landing a short distance away. Lennon faced it, and heard the other crew members jump in.

She had to delay it. Give them a chance.

Something grabbed at her ankle, and she was about to kick it when she saw it was the commander's hand. He yanked her down with him.

Lennon noticed the monster rushing them, before she was submerged in the cold pool. It was dark, with only the occasional green light to reveal the passage walls.

The next minute was a blur of swimming, then sinking, as they neared the opening of an underwater tunnel. She kicked and twisted behind David. Somewhere along the way, she lost sight of Liu, and thought she saw a series of black appendages thrashing behind her. Lennon couldn't stop to find out what it was; her lungs were about to burst, her eyesight blotching with dark spots.

She thought about skydiving, the rush of wind shooting against her cheeks, the feeling of the ripcord in her grip.

Every time, she'd tugged it. And she wasn't about to give up now.

Lennon saw an actual light at the end of the tunnel, and felt David's hand closing around her arm.

Atlas

Off the Australian Coast

"This is impossible."

For the first time since meeting Dark Leader, his façade of strength and confidence crumbled.

"What's happened?" Atlas asked him.

"The *Interloper.* It's arrived," Dark Leader said.

"The *Interloper*?" Atlas's eyebrows lifted at the unfamiliar name.

"Yes, Mr. Donovan. They're here. Somehow they managed to evade destruction, and they flew to Earth in the span of a couple of hours." His Holo chimed, and the general flipped it around, studying his screen. "Hello, Mr. President."

Atlas watched as President Carver appeared, his usual rugged good looks marred by exhaustion and messy hair. "What the hell is going on, Booth?"

Booth? So his contact had been right.

"Sir, this is beyond my control. I sent the best, but it wasn't good enough."

Atlas noticed how the German soldier crossed his arms. Atlas guessed the man felt slighted that he hadn't been sent instead of that other operative.

"We've sent all we got. Nukes have been deployed, but they're swatting them away like gnats. What can we do, Booth?" Carver asked with a cracking voice.

"I've dispatched Team Dark to the projected crash site." An image flashed on a nearby computer screen, and Atlas hunched over the desk, seeing a red line from the drawing's upper atmosphere to the coast off Boston, Massachusetts. "We've planned for this day, Mr. President. Don't raise alarms. Run the media packets we decided on. It's an unpredicted meteor shower, remember? We can't have them panicking."

Carver nodded. "You're confident we can contain this?"

Atlas noticed the general swallow before answering. He was nervous. "Yes, sir. I believe we can."

"Okay. I'm trusting you." A man wearing a dark suit shifted behind the president, and he whispered into Carver's ear. The president lost all remaining composure. "They're deploying some form of escape pods from the *Interloper*."

Dark Leader huffed a breath, and the German soldier hurried to the computer. Atlas heard him relay a message into his earpiece. "Team Dark, track each of the bogeys. Get a bearing on them. We can't let any escape from our sight."

Carver blanched and stared through the screen. "Booth, you better know what the hell you're doing."

"I do, sir," Dark Leader said, ending the call. "Come, Mr. Donovan. We have a jet to catch."

"A jet?" Atlas dashed up the steps behind him, and when they arrived on the carrier's top level, Atlas spotted the waiting fighter across the runway. He hadn't even heard it landing. "Where are we going?"

"New York," Dark Leader said.

"Wait. Before we leave, just tell me the truth. Who are they?" Atlas stood his ground, feeling the heat of the mid-morning sun on his brow.

"The Stalkers?"

"No. The other ones." Atlas pictured the two-legged slender alien sealed in a rocky tomb just below them on his ship.

"We think the Stalkers followed them to Earth. They have something very important," Booth said.

"What? This signal?"

He nodded. "And I need you to help me find it."

"But they're already here. How can we compete with... those monsters?"

"Wait and see, Mr. Donovan. Are you done with your game of twenty questions?" Dark Leader asked.

"No, but it'll have to do for now." The pilot jumped out of the jet and saluted Dark One, who scaled the fighter, taking over the cockpit. It was a unique model, with seating for three.

"Have you ever flown before?" Dark Leader inquired.

Atlas shook his head. "Not in anything like this."

"One rule. Don't puke on me."

As they settled into the jet, Atlas thought about the crew on board the alien vessel, and wondered what was going through their minds as the *Interloper* careened for Earth.

THIRTY-SIX

The Interloper

"DAMN IT, LIU! WHERE are you?" David muttered.

"I'll find him," Lennon said, stepping to the watery opening of the shaft they'd swum up moments ago. Her foot poised over the surface just as a giant bubble levitated and burst. A split second later, Liu's head emerged, and he coughed, gasping for air.

David and Lennon heaved him out.

"You made it!" David said.

"I almost didn't. I got stuck and that beast grabbed me," he said, rubbing his calf. Bloody puncture marks encircled his tattered suit.

"We have to keep moving," Lennon said. "Can you walk?"

Liu winced as he tried pushing off the deck, but his injured leg wouldn't hold his weight. David helped him up, and draped Liu's arm over his shoulder. "Let's go," he said.

But before they even made it two steps, his Holo began trilling. It was Carter again. David fished the device from his pocket and answered, "Hello?"

"Commander. Mission Control is done crunching numbers. They've pinpointed our impact to somewhere off the coast of Boston. Or maybe right on top of it. They're not totally sure yet."

"That's a heavily-populated city!" David exclaimed.

"Then they're planning to shoot us down?" Lennon asked, crowding in around the device.

"No. They tried. It didn't work."

"What do you mean it didn't *work?*" Lennon asked.

"You remember those lasers they shot us with?" Carter said.

"Oh no..." Liu whispered.

"Well, they intercepted our missiles. About a hundred of them. Just because we took out their thrusters doesn't mean we damaged their defenses."

"Where did they intercept them?" David asked in a hoarse voice.

"Safely, in space."

"Thank God," David breathed.

"I'm not sure how good it is, knowing that we might be responsible for killing millions when we touch down."

"Can't they evacuate?" Liu asked.

"There isn't enough time. We're at ETA twenty-five minutes to impact. All they'd do is incite a panic."

David made a mental note of the time and minimized the call to set the countdown on his Holo from twenty-five minutes.

"Right now, Mission Control is hanging tight," Carter went on. "They're hoping the *Interloper* corrects itself, or that it makes a soft water landing."

"That's the best that any of us can hope for now," David agreed.

"What are you going to do?" Carter asked.

"Locate a secure place to ride this thing down."

"You won't survive. It's impossible."

"So is crossing millions of kilometers in the blink of an eye, and yet somehow the *Interloper* did it."

"That's your plan?" Lennon asked. "You're hoping they have another trick up their sleeve? If they did, don't you think they would have used it by now?"

"Perhaps," David conceded. "Either way—Carter, you need to use the lifeboat."

"Negative, sir. There's a chance I could get to you with spare pressure suits. We can all use the lifeboat together."

"We don't have time, and you know it."

"Maybe if I..." He trailed off.

"Get clear, Carter. That's an order."

"Yes, sir," he replied in a subdued voice.

"Good luck," David added.

"You too, sir. And, uh, see you on the other side, Liu... Lennon."

"You won't see me where I'm going," Lennon quipped.

"Goodbye, Carter," David said, ending the communication. He hobbled on with Liu, bogged down by the man's injuries and even his own.

Lennon trudged ahead, taking point. She produced her own Holo and opened their mapping app. The programs shared data automatically, and with the *Interloper*'s jamming field offline, her app now showed almost half of the ship. Lennon used it to lead the way, navigating the rocky tunnels and winding ever higher through the *Interloper*'s many labyrinthine levels.

"Where are we going?" David asked after a while. He didn't recognize anything, even though he'd come this way with Liu before.

"Somewhere we haven't been yet," Lennon answered, picking another fork in the tunnels, seemingly at random.

"If they have escape pods, we should find them near the outer hull," David added after checking his Holo. It appeared that Lennon was aiming for the very heart of the vessel.

"If they *do* have escape pods, you can bet that their own crew will be flocking there now. The last thing we need is to run into them."

"But if we ride the *Interloper* down to Earth..." Liu began, but left his thought unfinished.

Lennon stopped to face them. "It's big, but its velocity can't be that high. It only ignited the engines recently, so we won't hit with the force of a meteor."

"It would be an extinction level event if we were going faster," David said.

"Yes," Lennon agreed. "But like you said, the *Interloper* could have some form of maneuvering jets or shields to buffer the landing."

"So you're betting we could survive if we're shielded by the bulk of the ship," Liu concluded.

"It's worth a shot, isn't it? What other chance do we have?"

Silence answered her question as they realized that she was right.

"We have to hurry," Lennon said, continuing on.

They came to a door, much like the one before the cryo chamber. Lennon slipped her Holo into her pocket and turned the handle.

The compartment sprang open, and they entered a massive rectangular space that went on as far as their eyes could see. Aisles and stacks of what resembled supply crates ran the length and breadth of the room. It reminded David of a port, with its multi-colored stacks of shipping containers. Except that all of these boxes were gray, black, and silver, and different sizes and shapes.

Lennon produced her Holo again and held it out to measure the range to the far end with a laser. The shimmering red beam vanished into hazy green darkness, making it impossible to tell with the naked eye how far the chamber went.

"This runs fully half the length of the *Interloper*," Lennon whispered in an awed voice. "One point one kilometers. It's perfect."

"Perfect how?" Liu asked. "The cargo will break free and fly around in a crash."

"True, but we're unlikely to become trapped by the collapsing superstructure. It's big and open enough that we could find a way out."

"In the ocean," Liu pointed out.

"Ideally," Lennon said.

"We'll drown."

"Try to stay positive," David replied. "Let's find a sheltered spot. And some means to secure ourselves."

"Copy that," Lennon replied.

They passed aisle after aisle of supply canisters and crates. David checked the timer on his Holo. They had seven minutes, which meant the *Interloper* must have entered the atmosphere already. He tried to pick up the pace, limping along with Liu.

"There!" Lennon veered toward two curving beams along the wall. They created a narrow alcove, and round holes in the supports would make it easy to attach their suits' tethers.

It would have to do.

David helped Liu to the floor beside one of the beams and tied himself to it. Lennon did the same on the other side; then David attached all three tethers.

"Link arms," Lennon suggested as they sat with their backs to the arcing wall.

David noticed the vibrations rumbling through the ship. It reminded him of turbulence, and the force of it was rapidly building.

"How much time do we have?" Lennon asked.

David released Lennon's arm to withdraw his Holo, and balanced it in his lap so the others could see the screen. "Three minutes."

Carter interrupted with a call, and David answered with a voice command.

Carter's face appeared. He looked stricken, and David could have sworn his cheeks were stained with tears, but maybe it was just from the pain of his twisted ankle.

"Hey guys," Carter said. "I'm guessing you're not on any of those pods?"

"What pods?" Liu asked.

"They've been launching for the past ten minutes straight. At least a hundred of them. Still going, in fact."

"So they're abandoning ship."

"The spiders? How could those..." Carter asked, his brow raised.

David slowly shook his head. "We found them."

His eyes widened. "*Them*. As in the crew?"

David nodded.

"Hostile?"

"Very," Lennon replied.

"Shit..."

"Are you safe?" David asked.

"I'm in the lifeboat."

"Good," David said. "Listen. If we don't make it, tell Kate and the kids that..." He trailed off, wondering what Carter could possibly say to ease their grief.

"I'll tell them."

"Thank you," David replies, feeling a knot of tension releasing inside his chest.

"Have we slowed at all?" Lennon asked.

"Uhh..." Carter trailed off, his brow furrowing as he studied something on his end. "Hold up..."

"How fast?" Liu pressed.

"Just under three hundred kilometers per hour. And decelerating."

"Target?" David asked.

"Looks like it'll miss landfall," Carter crowed. "That's good news!"

"It'll generate a massive wave for Boston."

"What about us?" Liu asked.

"Not a lot different," Lennon said. "Water is like cement at this speed."

"But it yields eventually, doesn't it?" Carter said.

"Once we start to sink," Liu muttered.

David winced as the quivering hull reached a crescendo that made it difficult to hear. He counted down the seconds.

"Hang tight, guys," Carter said. "You'll be—"

A deafening roar cut him off, and their locked arms wrenched violently against David's shoulder sockets. He flew out against the slack of their suit tethers, and his head snapped forward, clacking his teeth. David tasted blood. Cargo broke free and thundered around inside the storage room. Massive crates fell like leaves from a tree that had been shaken. The entire compartment reared and heaved as if it were made of paper, and yet, by some miracle, David was still alive and conscious to witness what was happening.

When his eyes focused again, a humungous storage crate was sailing straight for them. "Look out!" David screamed, but he couldn't even hear his own voice.

THIRTY-SEVEN

The Interloper, Atlantic Ocean

D REAMS SATURATED LENNON'S MIND. Foggy memories, and glimpses of futures never developed. They were like old photos raining from the sky, but she could never grab hold of one. She was weightless. And for the first time in her life, she wasn't scared or angry or sad. Or alone.

"Lennon!"

Her eyes opened, and she remembered where she was. But all Lennon wanted to do was sleep.

"Lennon, we have to go!"

Her ears were ringing, and she spat a stream of salty water from her mouth. Everything hurt.

"Where's Liu?" she asked, and saw him floating face-first in the center of the cargo room.

"He didn't make it," David called.

She was about to check on the man when she saw the way his neck was bent. What a shame. All this effort for nothing. He'd survived the battles with the alien freaks, only to die upon their return home.

Water was rushing from all sides of the cargo hold, filling it quickly. Lennon sputtered, and noticed that her ties were undone from the beam. "Thank you," she told David, who kept treading water without a word. "We need to leave."

"What have we done?" he whispered.

"It wasn't our fault," she told him. "We tried."

David nodded, and swiped a wet hand over his soaking head. "I have to get to my family. Protect them."

"You won't do them any good if we don't make it to land." Lennon scoured the space for anything of use. She didn't worry about encountering any of the aliens. There was nothing here to defend themselves with, not out in the open like this. And they didn't have the luxury of time. Another hour exposed in the water, and they'd both be dead from hypothermia.

Something sailed by, and Lennon swam to it, testing its buoyancy. The length of gray plastic floated well enough, and when David lunged on it, his half submerged slightly. "Where's the best exit?" he asked.

Lennon gestured to the biggest rupture, where water was gushing in. "That way."

The cargo hold was three quarters full by the time they kicked their makeshift life raft to the exit, and she paused near the waterfall. "We have to push past it. You ready for this?"

David nodded weakly, mirroring her fatigue.

"You can do this. One more obstacle," she said, realizing that was a lie.

"Ready."

She counted down, loudly, over the surging ocean. And they kicked with all their strength. Lennon frowned as they exited the storage area, and quickly realized there was a powerful current, threatening to drag them under.

After another few minutes of exhausting paddling, they were past it, wandering toward the light. The *Interloper* was trashed. They encountered the outer hull, and she surveyed the wreckage. Pieces burned, flames sputtering into the air.

"Arms to the sky!" someone yelled, as a dozen search-lights hovered above the ruined alien craft.

"I'm Commander David Bryce of *Beyond III*!" David replied.

Lennon almost blacked out, her eyes fluttering. She heard the roar of boat engines, the rotors of nearby helicopters, and something splashed as it fell a short distance away. "Take the rope!"

Lennon felt David's hands on her; then she was hauled from the water, her feet dangling in the air.

She tried to gauge how far they were from the coast, but couldn't tell. She was lowered into a small boat, and saw Carter on deck, a blanket wrapped around him.

"Carter!" She dove across, using the last of her energy to hug the linguist. "You made it."

David arrived, and didn't even attempt to stand. Two women gave him a blanket too, and tossed another to Lennon, who threw it on while her teeth chattered.

"I didn't think I'd ever see you alive," Carter told her. "Thanks for abandoning me."

Lennon shrugged. "I'm an asshole. What can I say?"

A red light flashed on top of the compact boat, and Lennon noticed a team of soldiers approaching the front half of the *Interloper* under a kilometer away. The sun was beginning to set, casting a bright orange glow over the waves. "What are they doing?" Lennon whispered. When no one responded, she grabbed the nearest woman in fatigues. Her name was on the breast. *Collins.* "Tell them this ship is dangerous. There are things aboard that will haunt your nightmares. We have to take them out. Now!"

The woman stared at Lennon like she was certifiable, and spoke into an earpiece. "We have our orders."

The boat started for the coast, and Lennon spotted a helicopter lowering to the crash site. She knew the model well. Team Dark was here.

Lennon pointed toward the Boston city lights. "Was there a tsunami?" she asked the officer.

"Nothing terrible. The ship slowed dramatically before impact," Collins said. She touched her earpiece again. "You three are requested for a meeting."

"With whom?" Carter asked, his British accent thick.

"I think I know," Lennon muttered.

Atlas

Unmarked Building, Long Island, NY

Atlas watched the news on his Holo while they waited for the others to arrive.

"*Scientists are truly baffled by today's meteor storm, Bob. There was no anticipating it, and just as soon as it began, it ended. It's being said that the primary impact is five miles off the coast of Boston, but that's yet to be verified. According to my sources, there's an awful lot of military personnel investigating the scene.*" The woman read the bit from her teleprompter, and the subject changed to another. It was about a shooting in the Midwest. Atlas couldn't believe how quickly the world could move on.

Dark Leader paced the room in clipped strides. "Where are they?"

Atlas turned the Holo off when someone knocked on the door, and in walked Dark One. He passed his boss a device, and Booth turned the screen to face him. "What's the word?"

"It's empty, sir," a voice replied.

"Empty?" Booth asked. "How can that be?"

"We searched every compartment, sir. There are no aliens on board the *Interloper*." Atlas recognized the voice. It was James Wan.

Dark Leader fumed at the news. "Find them! We cannot let these... *things* invade our oceans. It's only a matter of time before they reach land. Then we'll have a real shitstorm with the media!"

The room was dim, and Atlas stood, stretching his back. They'd arrived in New York an hour ago, three hours after impact. At first, he'd expected chaos from the escape pods the aliens had released, but so far, there was no news to spread. It was disconcerting.

"Why aren't we at Boston?" Atlas asked.

"You'll see soon enough." It was all the answer Booth was going to give.

Atlas opened the compact fridge and spied a few locally brewed beers. Since no one had offered him coffee or water, he cracked a bottle's cap off, taking a sip as the doors opened again.

Atlas had never seen three people look so defeated.

David Bryce entered briskly, followed by the British crew member of *Beyond*. At the moment, he didn't remember the guy's name. The third was a woman, and she moved with confidence, despite their circumstances. She had a way about her he appreciated.

Atlas found himself staring at her as her gaze settled on him. Her lip formed a sneer, and she addressed Dark Leader. "We failed..."

Her voice caught when she saw Rutger.

Lennon

It was official. Lennon was broken. She staggered away, her back hitting the door. "This can't be happening," she muttered.

"Dark Three, compose yourself!" Dark Leader's voice was gravelly, and she went rigid.

"Lennon, I'm sorry," Rutger said, but this time, it wasn't in her head like every other occasion.

"You're alive?" She didn't understand. "I saw you die."

"No," he said, managing a smile. "You only thought you did."

Lennon felt the tears soaking her face. The anguish she'd experienced after leaving him on that mission evaporated in a flurry of emotions. She rushed across the room, and drew him into a hug, burrowing her face into his neck. It was him. She could smell it.

"I'm sorry," he mumbled.

Lennon broke free, and let go of him, stepping back. "Not as sorry as me." She swung hard, striking him on the chin. Her knuckles ached sharply and she shook her fist in agony, but it was worth the price. Rutger barely flinched. He was the toughest SOB she'd ever met.

"Now that the soap opera is over, can we get to business?" Dark Leader gestured to the table, where Carter and David were already sitting. They seemed confused.

"Who are you?" David asked.

"I am here to debrief you," Dark Leader said.

"But they just gave me these." Carter snapped the elastic on his borrowed sweatpants. When no one laughed, he sank into his chair.

"Don't mind him. He's harmless," Lennon told them. "David, this is my boss. *Was* my boss."

Dark Leader's eye twitched. "Where are they?"

"Who?" Carter asked.

"What did you encounter? Just the Stalkers?" Dark Leader inquired, his fingers steepled.

Lennon broke it down, relaying the various situations they'd confronted on the *Interloper*. When she was finished, Carter and David added to her notes, and before she knew it, an hour had passed.

"These... spiders are loose in the ocean." Dark Leader glanced at the other man in the room with them.

"Who the hell is this?" Lennon pointed at the stranger.

"Atlas. Atlas Donovan." He offered his hand, but she ignored it.

"Like the Titan? Condemned to hold up the heavens?" Carter inquired.

"Something along those lines," Atlas murmured, dropping his palm to the table. He tore the label on his beer.

"Where did you get the drink?" Lennon asked, and Atlas crossed the room, bringing everyone a bottle.

"I'd say you've earned it," he joked.

"What are we going to do?" David stared at Dark Leader. "Can I go home?"

"No."

David rose, bumping the table. "You can't stop me from seeing my family."

Beyond III is supposed to be on a supply run to Mars. We cannot very well have you witnessed driving your children to school, Commander Bryce. You either, Mr. Robinson," Dark Leader informed them.

That took the wind from David's sails. "I need to see Kate and the kids."

"And you will. I promise."

"What's the plan?" Lennon asked.

"Team Dark has a marker on each of the escape pods, and I'll be sending twenty teams to track the Stalkers. We can't allow them to run around freely," Dark Leader said.

"They won't be easy to stop. Our bullets bounce off their exoskeletons," Lennon told him.

"We have our ways. If you'd care to follow me."

Lennon took her beer and watched Rutger. When the others were gone, she blocked his exit. "I was stuck in Three Points. I wanted to die."

"It was an order. From the top," Rutger said, and it was all she needed to know.

Lennon spun on a heel, walking quickly to catch up to the others. A few months ago, she would have traded her own life to have him returned to this world, but after the ordeal on the *Interloper,* she didn't care any longer.

Dark Leader escorted them to an elevator, and Lennon felt it descending. Carter knocked on the shiny metal wall, and soon the doors opened.

A handful of Dark soldiers were inside, crouching over computer screens and chatting on private comms.

"You asked how we defeat them, Miss Baxter?" Dark Leader pushed his thumb against a sensor near a tall, stainless steel double door. It opened, and he strode in, his polished shoes echoing through the chamber. It was filled with weapons, likely not of this planet. "Welcome to the future."

Lennon touched one of the guns, and a smile snuck onto her face. "I'm in."

EPILOGUE

Boston, Massachusetts

S TARS TWINKLED IN THE clear night sky, and Martinez stared at them, trying to determine where he was. The answer came to him after some searching. Earth. The creature dug its appendage further into the base of Martinez's neck.

Images scattered in his mind, then vanished.

He'd been on the clean-up crew, exploring the crashed alien vessel. The official word was that the *Interloper* was devoid of any living organisms, but a few had remained, latching onto their victims.

Wind blew against his cheeks, and Martinez smiled as the boat docked at the coast. There were still hundreds of soldiers on the water, but his shift had ended.

He pulled his jacket higher on his neck, to shield his miniature hitchhiker.

Martinez had a mission, a calling from his leaders, and it was imperative that he complete the task.

"Hey Martinez, you in for a drink?" Bailey asked.

Martinez shook his head. "I'm going to call it a day. Kind of tired."

Bailey looked disappointed. Martinez remembered they were mates of some kind. "Maybe tomorrow?" he asked, trying to mend the damage.

Bailey brightened at that. "Sounds good."

He strode off the boat, walking along the dock. Instead of heading to the transport, he continued west. An hour later, he spotted two other soldiers catching up to his position, and he slowed, seeing the spiky black bulges beneath their uniforms. They all looked at one another, and separated, marching in opposite directions.

North. South. West.

Martinez plodded along while his guest released its eggs into his bloodstream. He was dimly aware that it should have been unnerving. Instead, he felt gratified, a spreading warmth of fulfillment coursing through him.

His gaze returned to the sky and settled on the glowing moon.

He inhaled, smelling the ocean air.

Earth. It was time to prepare for arrival.

GET THE SEQUEL FOR FREE

The story continues with...

FROM BEYOND: SIGNAL
Get it From Amazon

OR

Get a FREE e-copy if you <u>post an honest review of this book</u> on Amazon and <u>send it to us here:</u> https://files.jaspertscott.com/signalfree.htm

Thank you in advance for your feedback! We read all of our reviews and use them to improve our work.

MORE FROM NATHAN HYSTAD

Keep up to date with his new releases by signing up for his Newsletter at

www.nathanhystad.com

The River Saga
The Survivors Series
The Bridge Sequence
Baldwin's Legacy
Final Days
Space Race
The Resistance
Rise

MORE FROM JASPER T. SCOTT

Keep up to date with his new releases by signing up for his Newsletter at

www.jaspertscott.com

Dark Space Series
New Frontiers
Broken Worlds
Rogue Star
Scott Standalones
Final Days
Ascension Wars
The Cade Korbin Chronicles
The Kyron Invasion
Architects of the Apocalypse

ABOUT THE AUTHORS

NATHAN HYSTAD IS THE best-selling author of The Event. He writes about alien invasion, first contact, colonization, and everything else he devoured growing up. He's had hundreds of thousands of copies sold and read, and loves the fact he's been able to reach so many amazing readers with his stories. Nathan's written over twenty novels, including The Survivors, Baldwin's Legacy, and The Resistance.

Jasper Scott is a USA Today best-selling author of more than 30 sci-fi novels. With over a million books sold, Jasper's work has been translated into various languages and published around the world. Jasper writes fast-paced books with unexpected twists and flawed characters. He was born and raised in Canada by South African parents, with a British heritage on his mother's side and German on his father's. He now lives in an exotic locale with his wife, their two kids, and two Chihuahuas.

Printed in Great Britain
by Amazon